Books by John Marsden and available from Quercus:

Tomorrow, When the War Began
The Dead of the Night
The Third Day, the Frost

Coming soon

Darkness, Be My Friend
Burning for Revenge
The Night Is for Hunting
The Other Side of Dawn

John Marsden

The Tomorrow series

The Third Day, The Frost

Quercus

First published in 1995 by Macmillan Publishers Australia,
1 Market St, Sydney

First published in Great Britain in 1995 by
Macmillan Children's Books, London

This edition published in Great Britain in 2012 by
Quercus
55 Baker Street
7th Floor, South Block
London
W1U 8EW

A CIP catalogue reference for this book is available
from the British Library

ISBN 978 0 85738 875 9

1 3 5 7 9 10 8 6 4 2

Printed and bound in Great Britain by Clays Ltd, St Ives plc.

Acknowledgements

Many thanks for help generously given by Lizzie Farran, Lachlan Dunn, Dallas Wilkinson, Rob Alexander, Peter Stapleton, Heidi Zonneveld, Hayley Reynolds, Anne O'Connor, Rebecca Dunne, Lauren Sundstrom, Robert Rymil and the Bell family.

The first reader of this trilogy was Julia Stiles, and I treasure the memory of her wonderful support and enthusiasm

To my sister and long-time friend,
Rosalind Alexander

'The third day comes a frost, a killing frost . . .'

King Henry VIII, William Shakespeare

Chapter One

Sometimes I think I'd rather be frightened than bored. At least when you're frightened you know you're alive. Energy pumps through your body so hard that it overflows as sweat. Your heart – your heart that does the pumping – bangs away in your chest like an old windmill on a stormy night. There's no room for anything else. You forget that you're tired or cold or hungry. You forget your banged-up knee and your aching tooth. You forget the past, and you forget that there's such a thing as the future.

I'm an expert on fear now. I think I've felt every strong feeling there is: love, hate, jealousy, rage. But fear's the greatest of them all. Nothing reaches inside you and grabs you by the guts the way fear does. Nothing else possesses you like that. It's a kind of illness, a fever, that takes you over.

I've got my tricks for holding fear at bay. We all have, I know. And they work in their own ways, some of the time. One of my tricks is to think of jokes that people have told me over the years. Another's the one Homer taught me. It sounds simple enough. It's to keep saying to yourself: 'I refuse to think fear. I will think strong. I will think brave.'

It helps for mild fear; it's not so good for panic. When true fear sweeps in, when panic knocks down your walls, no defence can keep it out.

The last two weeks I spent in Hell were solid boredom; the kind of time you long for when you're terrified; the kind of time you hate when it's happening. Maybe I was a fear junkie by then, though, because I spent a lot of time lying around thinking of dangerous things we could have done, wild attacks we could have made.

These days I don't know whether I'm murderous, suicidal, addicted to panic, or addicted to boredom.

I wonder what happened to the people who were in the world wars, after the fighting was over? They were mostly men in those wars, but there were plenty of women too. They weren't necessarily soldiers, but you didn't have to be a soldier to be affected by it all. Did they press their 'Off' buttons on the day peace was declared? Can anyone do that? I know I can't do it. I seem to be getting used to the way my life's gone lately, from total frenzy to total nothing. But I often dream of the regularity of my old life. During school terms my days always started the same way: I'd have breakfast, cut my lunch, pack my schoolbag and kiss Mum goodbye. Dad'd usually be out in the paddocks already, but some days I'd get up early to have breakfast with him. Other days when I got up at my normal time he'd still be in the kitchen, toasting his backside against the Aga.

For years – as soon as I was big enough for my feet to reach the pedals of a car – I'd driven myself to the bus. Kids living on properties can get a special licence to drive to school buses, but we never bothered with that. Dad thought it was just another stupid bureaucratic rule. From our house it's about four k's to the gate on Providence Gully Road. It's not our front gate, but it's the only one on the school bus route. Like most people we had a 'paddock basher' – an unregistered bomb – mainly for kids to use, or for stock work. Ours was a Datsun 120Y that Dad bought for eighty bucks at a clearing sale. Usually I took that, but if it wasn't going properly, or if Dad wanted it for something else, I'd take the Land Rover, or a motorbike. Whichever it was, I'd leave it sitting under a tree all day while I was at school and I'd pick it up again when I got off the bus.

School was OK and I enjoyed being with my friends – the social life, the goss, the talking about guys – but, like most rural kids, living on a farm took up as much energy and time and interest as school did. I'm not sure if that's the same for city kids – sometimes I get the feeling that school's more important for them. Oh, it's important for us too, of course, especially nowadays when everyone's so worried that they won't be able to make a living on the land, won't be able to take over their parents' places the way they used to assume they would. Every country kid these days has to think about setting up in some other work.

What am I talking about? For a few minutes there I was back in peacetime when our biggest worry was getting a job. Crazy. Now those dreams of becoming brain surgeons, chefs, hairdressers and barristers have gone up in smoke. Smoke that smells of gunpowder. The dreams now were simply of staying alive. It's what Mr Kassar, our Drama teacher, would call 'a different perspective'.

3

It's nearly six months since our country was invaded. We'd lived in a war zone since January, and now it's July. So short a time, so long a time. They came swarming across the land, like locusts, like mice, like Patterson's Curse. We should have been used to plagues in our country but this was the most swift, sudden and successful plague ever. They were too cunning, too fierce, too well-organised. The more I've learnt about them, the more I can see that they must have been planning it for years. For instance, the way they used different tactics in different places. They didn't bother with isolated communities, or the Outback, or scattered farms, except in places like Wirrawee, my home town. They had to secure Wirrawee because it's on the road from Cobbler's Bay, and they needed Cobbler's Bay because it's such a great deep-water harbour.

But Wirrawee was easy enough for them. They timed the invasion for Commemoration Day, when the whole country's on holiday. In Wirrawee that means Show Day, so all they had to do was grab the Showground and they had ninety per cent of the population. But to take the big towns and cities they needed a bit more imagination. Mostly they used hostages, and for hostages mostly they used children. Their strategy was to make things happen so fast that there was no time for anyone to think straight, no time to consider. At the slightest delay they started blowing things up, killing people. It worked. Those political rats, our leaders, the people who'd spent every day of peacetime telling us how great they were and how we should vote for them, felt the water of the drowning country lapping at their ankles. They took off for Washington, leaving chaos and darkness behind.

4

Yes, it was cunning, it was brutal, it was successful.

And because of them – or because of our own apathy and selfishness – our peacetime ambitions had been vaporised, and we suddenly found ourselves living lives of fear and boredom.

Fear and boredom weren't our only emotions, of course. There were others: even pride came sneaking in occasionally. In mid-autumn, just five of us, Homer, Robyn, Fi, Lee and I, had launched our biggest attack. We'd used gas to blow up a row of houses where a major command post had been based. We'd beaten the odds and caused an explosion that would have registered eleven on the Richter scale. There was no mushroom cloud, but it had everything else. That was spectacular enough, but we didn't fully realise what we'd done till afterwards. We'd struggled back to our mountain hideaway, intending only to detour for some food, and had made the terrible discovery of the body of our friend Chris. We'd brought him with us and buried him in our sanctuary, the wild basin of rock and bush known as Hell. And there we'd stayed for weeks, gradually made aware by the ferocity of the search for us just how far we'd promoted ourselves on the most wanted list. We were scared by the toughness of the search. With no access to news – except for occasional radio bulletins from other countries – we had no way of finding out who we'd killed or what we'd destroyed. But we were obviously in more trouble than a dog in a mosque.

When the search calmed down and the hunting helicopters returned to their lairs we calmed down a bit too. Still, we were in no hurry to do anything rash. We stayed in our bush home for a few more weeks.

With plenty of food – even if there wasn't much variety – we lay around and ate and slept and talked and had bad dreams and shook and cried and jumped up trembling at sudden rustles in the undergrowth. It affected us all in different ways. Lee got a nervous twitch, especially at night, that pulled the right side of his mouth up towards his eye every time he spoke. And when we made love, even though he said he enjoyed it and he'd start off all excited, his body wouldn't do what he wanted it to do.

What I wanted it to do. What we both wanted it to do.

Robyn stopped eating and sleeping. She'd always been nicely plump and round but she starting getting skinny, fast: the kind of ugly skinny that I've always hated in my friends. 'You think you've got problems,' she said to me one day when I lost my temper over a can-opener that wouldn't work. 'I'm a paranoid anorexic insomniac.'

It was one of our few jokes. Only it wasn't very funny.

Homer sank into a silent depression and went for days at a time without a word to anyone. He spent hours sitting on a rock looking up at Tailor's Stitch, and it seemed like the only time he used his voice was to have a tantrum. His temper, which had always been edgy, was now out of control. When it came to arguments I'd always matched Homer yell for yell, but for a few weeks there I joined the others and melted away into the bush when he exploded.

Me, I sort of did a bit of all those things, plus some. My particular specialty was flashbacks that were so lifelike I was sure they were real. I'd smell something and that'd set me off. A bit of plastic on

6

the fire at night and the next thing I was back in Buttercup Lane and the air was full of burning rubber as trucks slid into each other on screaming tyres. My mind couldn't tell what was real and what wasn't. It was like having nightmares, except that I was awake. Sweat ran down my face so fast my eyes would be stinging; then I'd be gasping, and then hyperventilating. Needless to say, I had nightmares when I was asleep too, till I got scared of going to sleep. It's so long since I've had a good night's sleep I can't even imagine any more what it'd be like, but I dream of it – daydreams, that is – and long for it.

The one who handled it best of any of us, at that stage, was Fi. Fi was so lightly built that she looked like a grasshopper. She was all leggy. Maybe that was why I always thought of her as frail, easily broken, needing protection. But she had a strength that I could never quite figure out. I don't know where it came from, or where she stored it. How much heart could she fit inside her little frame? How tough could that balsawood body be? It's not that she had no feelings. Fi had always been mega-sensitive. She seemed strung like a violin: the slightest touch made her vibrate. But the terrible things we'd done didn't eat away inside her like they did the rest of us. She rose above them. One reason, maybe, was that she was so sure we were doing the right thing. She was proud of what we'd done. I felt pride sometimes but, truth to tell, I never knew whether to be proud or ashamed.

For all that, when the call for action came again, we answered it. Maybe we answered like robots, programmed to kill and destroy, but we answered.

Chapter Two

For three weeks there'd been no more aircraft overhead. The wasps and hornets that had prowled up and down the sky, buzzing angrily as they waited for us to break cover, had returned to their nests. Perhaps they thought we'd left the district. They might have suspected that we lived in these mountains, but they couldn't be sure – and even if they were, they couldn't know of our exact whereabouts.

Within a few days of their disappearance we all started to relax a bit, sensing that they had given up.

Lee was the first to say something about us becoming active again. If he hadn't said it, someone else would. I was starting to turn a few ideas over in my mind, feeling a bit guilty about sitting around for so long. There was the fear of doing something and the fear of not doing enough. The fears battled each other all the time. But Lee wanted us to go beyond Wirrawee; all the way to Cobbler's Bay. It was a wildly terrifying idea.

Cobbler's Bay was a wonderful harbour but in peacetime it was too far from the city to be used regularly by big ships. It had been popular with fishing boats, tourist charters and yachts wanting shelter for a night or two. But the enemy had used it a lot since the invasion. So much damage had been done to the major ports that Cobbler's had turned out to be very important to them. Frequent convoys poured down the highway to and from Cobbler's, carrying troops, supplies and weapons.

We'd destroyed the Heron Bridge in Wirrawee, forcing those convoys to make a long detour, and we'd attacked one of the convoys in Buttercup Lane. Now Lee suggested we go to the very source of the convoys.

'But what would we do when we got there?' Fi asked.

'I don't know. Make it up as we go along. That's more or less what we've done everywhere else.'

'We've been so lucky.'

'It's not all luck,' I said, even though I believed in luck myself. Sometimes, anyway. 'Don't forget, we're free agents who can do what we want, when we want. That does give us an advantage. All they can do is guess what we might do, or react after we've done it. It's almost like, I don't know, they go by rules and we don't. They're confined and we aren't. You imagine, if you're playing hockey and one team follows the rules and the other team does whatever they feel like. It's a bit like that. We can pick up the ball and throw it to each other, or we can bash them in the shins with the hockey sticks, and it's not until we've done it that they can react.'

'Yes,' said Homer slowly. 'I'd never thought of it like that. But you're exactly right. If we're going to have a go at Cobbler's we'll have to be as radical as we can be. Totally unpredictable. Make the most of the advantage that Ellie's talking about.'

'So are we going to have a go at Cobbler's?' Robyn asked, in a small voice.

There was a pause; everyone waiting for someone else to commit themselves. Finally I heard my own voice.

'It's a nice place for a holiday.'

I don't know why I talk like a hero sometimes. Blame it on peer pressure. I never never never feel like a hero. But I think we would have all agreed to go take a look at Cobbler's anyway. No one could have stood being cooped up in Hell much longer, and no one had any better ideas.

We left two days later. It was a Sunday morning, as far as I could tell – we all had different theories about the date.

We carried enormous packs. We didn't know how far the district had been colonised while we'd been hiding in Hell. Everything seemed to have been proceeding at such a speed that we had to expect the worst. So we took a lot of stuff. Being winter, most of it was for warmth: jumpers, mitts, balaclavas, woollen socks. We took sleeping bags but not tents – we still didn't have proper tents, since we lost them in the Holloway Valley. We hoped we could find shelter in sheds or caves. But we did carry a heap of food, not knowing what we'd be able to scrounge or steal.

'Steal!' Homer said angrily when I used that word. 'This is our country. Stealing is what they've done; it doesn't apply to us.'

Our main project before leaving was to relocate the chooks. We knocked up a new feeder and filled it to the brim. That would keep them going for many weeks, but the problem was water. Eventually we solved that problem by rebuilding their yard so that the creek now flowed through a corner of it. 'Lateral thinking,' Robyn said proudly. It had been her idea, and she'd done most of the work. The chooks certainly seemed to like it. They clucked around happily, murmuring to each other as they explored their new territory.

It was ten in the morning when we left. The last thing I'd done, just after breakfast, was to make a little bouquet out of leaves and grasses – it was the wrong season for flowers – and take it to Chris' grave. I wasn't surprised to find someone had been there before me, and left a wooden flower, a flower clumsily carved out of wood. It could have been anyone: Homer, Fi, Lee, Robyn, any one of them could have done it.

The weeks of hiding, and the depressions that we'd been through, had taken the edge off our fitness. The heavy packs seemed to have doubled their weight before we reached the first of the giant rock steps that the path threaded around on its way out of Hell. At least the weather was on our side. It was cold but not raining; a moist winter day, when our breaths made us look like chainsmokers. I never tired of blowing the little white clouds and watching them evaporate. Above us was nothing but cloud, the whole sky grey and flat. You knew, just looking at it, that it would be cold all day and there would be no sign of the sun. But it was OK for what we wanted; I had no complaints.

At the top we rested for a while, annoyed and disappointed at how hard we'd found the climb.

'It's the packs,' Fi said. 'They're the biggest loads we've ever carried out of Hell.'

'It's the lives we've been living,' Homer said. 'Just

11

lounging around watching TV all day. I knew it'd catch up with us.'

We walked along Tailor's Stitch. A lot of the features around the Wirrawee district were named after old trades: Cobbler's Bay, Tailor's Stitch, a hill named Brewer's Mark, and a rock formation called the Old Blacksmith. We kept our eyes and ears open for aircraft, but there were none. About halfway to Mt Martin we turned left down the rough old four-wheel drive track that would take us into the valley. We went right by the Land Rover, hidden in thick bush near the top of the ridge. We'd agreed that it'd be too dangerous to use it until we knew more about what we'd find around Wirrawee. But at least the walking was now downhill.

My place was the first one we came to. Approaching it from the Tailor's road we were in good cover until about a k from the house. By then it was midafternoon. As we reached the edge of the line of trees I signalled to the others to stop while I sneaked forward, searching for a good lookout. I found a huge old river gum and installed myself in it. It was perfect, except for the stream of bees pouring in and out of a large hole in the trunk, about thirty centimetres above my head. I hadn't seen them when I chose the tree. But at the same moment that I noticed them I also noticed a movement out in the paddock we call Bailey's, and I instantly forgot about the bees.

For the first time since the invasion I saw strangers in our paddocks. There was a ute over by the western fenceline and I could see two men working on the fence itself. One of the old pine trees that Grandma had planted must have come down in a storm, and fallen across the fence. One man was holding a chainsaw and the other was dragging away some of the lighter branches. As I watched, the bloke with the chainsaw gave the cord a pull and started it up, then moved in to continue cutting.

It would have been a normal bush scene except for one thing: the soldier with the rifle across his back who was watching from fifty metres away. He was sitting astride a motorbike, a cigarette in his mouth. He looked about fourteen years old.

I studied them for a few minutes. At least the man with the chainsaw seemed to know how to use it; lucky, as it was a big one. We'd all been raised on horrific stories of people slicing arms or legs off with chainsaws. In our district they cause more accidents than tractors and firearms combined.

I went back to the others and told them what I'd seen. In the thicker bush, where they were, the chainsaw sounded like a distant mosquito. But it was blocking our progress and it would keep us there for another hour or more, by the time the men put the fence back up. We agreed to take another siesta; the alternative was doing a serious bushbash to get around them. None of us wanted that much sweat.

While the others settled back on their packs, using them as cushions, I took a walk around the treeline so I could get closer to the work party. I had mixed feelings about them being on our land. I was angry and upset, of course, to see trespassers there, but I was relieved too that someone was at last looking after the place. We'd all been shocked, on our previous expeditions, to see how quickly things were degenerating. Fences were down, sheep were flystruck, horses were foundering, rabbits and foxes were everywhere. The houses, too, were showing

13

signs of wear and tear. A few more years of this and the whole country would be a wilderness of blackberries and Scotch thistle.

In time I got quite close to the men working on the pine tree. I could hear them easily. They'd turned the chainsaw off again and I realised that as they worked they were having a go at the boy with the rifle.

'Hey Wyatt, Wyatt Earp!' one of them called out.

'What?' I heard the boy answer. His voice was much softer than the men's, but sounded reluctant, almost sulky.

'I hope you know what you're doing, sitting under that tree.'

'What for?'

'Well, this time of day, middle of the afternoon, that's when the drop bears get active.'

'That's right,' the other man said. 'Shocking area for drop bears, this.'

'I wouldn't sit under that tree for a million dollars,' the first man said.

'Terrible what those drop bears do. I've seen them take a bloke's face off. Those claws, Gawd, they'd give you the horrors.'

'And you never see the one that gets you.'

'That's the truth.'

'What for, drop bears?' the boy asked.

I'd worked around a bit further, to where I could see his face. He was fidgeting anxiously, but trying to look untroubled.

'You don't know what drop bears are? Fair dink, don't they teach you blokes anything? Fancy sending a bloke to a place like this and not telling him about drop bears.'

14

'They told you about sharks, didn't they?' the second man asked.

'Sharks, yes.'

'And crocodiles?'

'Crocodiles, yes.'

'And hoop snakes?'

The boy hesitated. 'Hoop snakes, yes,' he said after a moment.

'Well, I'll tell you what mate, I'd rather go fifteen rounds with a crocodile than have a drop bear land on my head.'

'What for, drop bears?' the boy asked again. He was showing real nervousness now, standing up straighter against the motorbike and with increased alertness in his voice. The men stopped working and spoke to him directly.

'Mate,' the first one said, with great seriousness, 'it's none of my business if you end up wearing a drop bear for a hat, but if you want to keep that good-looking face attached to your head, I wouldn't recommend you spend any more time under trees.'

The young soldier looked around awkwardly, then peered up through the branches. Finally he said: 'That enough. We go now.'

'Well, whatever you say,' the first man said. 'You're the boss. But it's pretty early to knock off.' To his mate he said, quietly, 'I guess he just doesn't want to lose face.'

Both men sniggered. The boy, flushing red, said angrily: 'Enough. We go.'

He flourished his rifle, then kicked at the starter of his motorbike. But he was off balance from waving his rifle, and he fell sideways, sprawling across the ground and dropping the bike. The men just grinned at each other and walked casually to the ute. They got in and started it, putting it in gear as the boy, humiliated, struggled again with the starter of the bike. By the time he got it going the ute was a hundred metres away, bumping slowly across the paddock towards the gate. The boy tore off after it, his rear tyre sliding around as he accelerated. I wondered if the men would make him open the gate.

I was smiling as I walked back to the others. Seemed like there was more than one way to skin a pussycat.

Chapter Three

My smile didn't last long. As we made our cautious way from property to property we were shocked by the speed with which the invaders had moved. A disease of colonists had infected the countryside.

'You know what it must seem like to them?' Homer said. 'It must feel like the old days, when the whites first arrived, and all they could see was this huge country with no one in it who they cared about. So, after living in pokey little towns or on ten hectare farms in England, they could suddenly spread out and help themselves to thousands of square k's each. You remember that unit we did in history: selectors and squatters? Well, a couple of centuries later, here's history repeating itself.'

We were all silent, a depressed, pessimistic silence.

It took us a few days to work out how things were organised. As far as we could tell there were two or three families who'd moved onto each farm. As well, some places had mini prison camps, thirty or forty people, who were used as slave labour in that particular area. They were locked up each night in sheds or shearers' quarters or workers' cottages – whatever

17

was available. Most of these mini camps were guarded at night by four sentries, one on each corner, and were lit by improvised floodlights. It wouldn't have been so hard to stage a breakout, but I guess the problem for most people was where to go after they broke out. Not everybody had a convenient bolthole called Hell, with a stockpile of food and other stores. It was just another fluke, the way it had worked for us. I still couldn't decide if it was a good fluke or a bad one.

One odd thing was that we didn't recognise any of the prisoners. As we spied on them from different vantage points we thought that most of them seemed like experienced cockies: they moved stock confidently and handled tools well. They were even shearing at a couple of places. But we didn't see anyone we knew and we decided not to take the chance of talking to strangers. It might have made us feel good but the risk wasn't worth it.

Perhaps that, more than anything else, showed how much we'd changed. We'd toughened to such an extent that we chose not to ask about the welfare of our families if it meant any possibility of danger to ourselves. If someone had told me six months earlier that's the kind of person I'd become . . . Of course these prisoners, who we thought were from another area, quite likely wouldn't even know our parents, but there had been a time when we would have asked anyway.

On our third day we were just about out of the Wirrawee district, hiking through some scrubby, very poor country, between Wirrawee and Fletcher East. By staying in the uncleared stuff we were able to make good progress. There was nothing to attract colonists there, just cockatoos, galahs and kanga-roos. And an echidna that I nearly trod on as it grov-elled in the dirt, trying to dig its way to China. We had glimpses of both farmland and the pot-holed bitumen road that wound through the valley like a confused snake. At about lunchtime we saw some-thing that had already become familiar: a group of prisoners at work, with a couple of sentries. It took us a while to figure out what these prisoners were doing. One of them was operating a front-end loader and had dug a big pit; the others were wheeling loads to the pit from a large low brick building a hundred metres further away. We were due for a meal so we stopped and ate our scanty lunch while watching them hard at work.

After a couple of minutes Homer suddenly said: 'I've figured it out.'

'Figured what out?'

'What they're doing.'

I pressed my Vita-Weats together to make the Vegemite come squiggling through the holes like lit-tle black worms. 'OK, what are they doing?'

'It's a piggery and they're taking out the bodies of the pigs. Or what's left of them.'

'Charming.' I squinted my eyes and peered harder. 'Yes, you might be right.' I tried not to think what a stinking mess an abandoned feedlot for pigs might be. And I didn't feel so good about the look of my Vita-Weats.

'Oh!' said Fi, instantly sympathetic. 'You mean they starved to death in there? The poor things. That's awful.'

'The last ones wouldn't have starved for a long time,' Homer said cruelly.

'How do you mean?' Fi asked, not noticing the tone of Homer's voice.

'Don't ask,' I said, too late.

'They would have eaten each other when they got desperate,' Homer said.

'Oh!' Fi said, outraged.

'There goes lunch,' Lee said.

'Lucky we weren't having ham sandwiches,' Robyn said.

'Are they cannibals?' Fi asked.

'Not exactly,' Homer said. 'It's just that they eat everything. They'll eat their keepers quite happily. There was a guy in Peppertown, no one's quite sure what happened, but they think he might have fainted in his pigpen. Anyway, by the time they found him . . . well, they didn't find him, if you see what I mean.'

'Yuk,' Fi said. 'You always know the most disgusting things, Homer.'

'Rats eat each other,' Lee said. 'If you put too many of them in a cage, for example.'

'Just like humans,' Robyn said.

Throughout this conversation I'd been casually watching the prisoners toiling away at the piggery. Now suddenly I stopped eating, a Vita-Weat halfway to my mouth. And not because of the conversation the others were having.

'That bloke just coming out now,' I said quickly, urgently. 'The one with the broom. Tell me I'm dreaming.'

They looked, they stared.

Homer jumped to his feet, dropping his half-eaten biscuit in the dirt.

'You're not dreaming,' he said.

'No, you're not,' Robyn agreed, speaking like someone hypnotised.

'Oh God, I don't believe it,' Fi said.

Lee had the worst eyesight of the five of us, and he alone had to ask to make sure. 'Do you mean . . . are you saying . . . you think it's Kevin?'

'I don't think, I know. That's Kevin. You can bet your sweet bippy on it.'

We gazed, in a kind of trance. I don't know about the others, but I was thinking of the last time I'd seen Kevin, driving away in a big beautiful Mercedes that we'd requisitioned. We hadn't expected it to become an ambulance, but that's what it had become. When my first best friend Corrie had been shot in the back by a bullet from out of the dark, fired by a soldier they never even saw, Kevin drove her into Wirrawee, to the hospital. The hospital – in fact the whole town – was occupied by the enemy, but that hadn't stopped him. We didn't have a lot of clues about what had happened to them since, except that Corrie was in hospital, unconscious, and Kevin was a prisoner at the Showground. We also heard that he had been badly beaten by the soldiers for turning up with someone who had a bullet wound. Presumably the soldiers jumped to the worst conclusions. They may have even thought that Kevin and Corrie had been involved in the destruction of the Wirrawee bridge – the bridge that the rest of us had blown up the previous night.

'What is my sweet bippy?' Lee asked, disturbing my flood of memories.

'Eh? Oh honestly, Lee. I can tell you what it isn't.'

'Kevin,' Robyn breathed. 'It's a miracle.'

I wasn't going to disagree. I was wildly excited to

21

see him. I could feel my eyes growing bigger as I stared and stared. From this distance he looked OK, and he was moving freely. He had always been a big guy, and strong, and although he'd certainly lost some weight he didn't look too bad at all. Not as bad as in my nightmares, anyway. We watched avidly as he put the broom on the back of a Holden ute and picked up a shovel. Then he lifted his head and gazed all around, as though searching for something. He even looked up at the sky for a few moments. We couldn't show ourselves – it was too big a risk – but I knew we wouldn't be leaving this area for a while yet.

We watched them all afternoon. The work party knocked off at about five o'clock. We'd noticed back in Wirrawee that this army kept regular office hours. Or maybe the sentries were getting nervous about the drop bears. The prisoners slouched off in a disorganised bunch towards the farm buildings, which we could see as we edged forwards. The buildings were nearly a kilometre away. The soldiers followed, one in the front seat of the ute and one standing on the tray. Like most of the sentries we saw these days, he hadn't unslung his rifle: it hung over his shoulder.

The five of us moved along parallel to them, but kept well in among the trees. We didn't wear anything metallic these days, in case the sunlight's reflection gave us away. We were taking extreme care. We paced them easily enough though: they weren't exactly hurrying, and it was clear where they were headed.

I don't know the name of the property – we weren't familiar with this country – but it was obviously one of the older ones, probably dating back to the 1860s when a lot of the Wirrawee and Fletcher land was selected. In fact, the Fletchers were the people who'd taken most of it up, but this wasn't their place. I'd been on a school excursion to their house: it was a massive old sandstone mansion owned by the National Trust.

The prisoners were heading for a single-storey stone farmhouse surrounded by heaps of outbuildings. There were six tall palm trees standing over it, and a big white flagpole out the front. Behind it, in the distance, was a great area of water: a lake, probably a natural one, where the river had spread itself across a couple of hectares. It was a pretty sight with the purple–black winter clouds piled high above. It must have been a wonderful home for a lot of different people over the years. Now it had become a home for a new group: we could see colonists moving around the homestead, looking at something in the garden, watching a couple of children kicking a soccer ball. 'It's all right for them,' I thought bitterly. 'They don't have to do any work. They mightn't ever have to work again.'

They certainly had plenty of servants to pick from. Kevin's group had eight members and they looked fit enough, from a distance. Lean, but fit. We watched them swing away to the south when they got close to the flagpole. They walked on down a side track to another group of old buildings, a dilapidated bunch of cottages and sheds. They disappeared into there; the ute pulled up behind them and the two sentries got out. One stayed at the front of the buildings; the other went to the back. By remaining a hundred metres away on either side they had a good field of fire if anyone tried to escape. They could hold the place easily with just two of them.

Ten minutes later an old Commer fire tender

23

drove up to the same buildings. There were two sentries riding shotgun on the back. Four prisoners got out of the cab and went straight into the cottages. These sentries had a short chat to their mate out the front, then went to the homestead. Half an hour later they returned and relieved the two men on guard.

We were very excited by what we'd seen. We were all bursting to talk to Kevin. We wanted to tell him everything that had happened to us, and we wanted to hear everything that had happened to him. We hoped he'd have information on all the people we knew, not just our families, but our friends as well, and especially Corrie. Most of all, we wanted him to rejoin us. Our group could never be complete again, since the death of Chris, but having Kevin back would be fantastic. There were times in the past when he'd irritated me but in the excitement I'd forgotten all that. Anyway, I would have irritated him often enough too.

At first we thought it would be easy to get to him. The security seemed so light compared to what we'd taken on and beaten in the past. But as we waited and waited through the night for our chance, we began to realise that it wasn't going to be such a picnic. There were only two sentries, but they were wide awake. They were relieved at midnight by a pair who were equally sharp. After a freezing night we had to give up, and with the approach of dawn we slipped away through the trees to find a safe spot to sleep.

We realised we had to make something happen. Lee took only a short sleep, then went back and watched to see where the work parties went. He followed them to a dam in a distant paddock, then came back to tell us that they were repairing its wall: it was a newish earthen dam that didn't seem to be holding together too well. We left them there and spent a slow day in the cold woods, waiting for them to return.

Our first aim was of course to let Kevin know we were around. Again that should have been easy. At about 5.30 they came trudging back, but this time, instead of taking the track down to the old buildings where they slept, they took another one, which led around the lake. This brought them fairly close to us, so we followed, keeping inside the treeline. After fifteen minutes they were out of sight of the main house, and at that point the ute stopped and the guards got out. 'This OK,' I heard one of them call. They leant themselves comfortably against the ute and took out cigarettes, laughing as they watched the prisoners. The prisoners were laughing too, making comments to each other that I couldn't quite pick up. Then I found myself blushing a little as I realised what they were going to do.

'Oh golly,' Fi giggled, beside me. She'd just realised what was happening. I took a quick look at her. If I was blushing, she looked sunburnt. Half the men were down to their jocks already. Clothes were dropping like rose petals, and pink skin was appearing everywhere. Not as pink as Fi's and mine though. I didn't dare look at Kevin; I knew that if I caught one glimpse of him I'd never be able to look him in the face again.

I mean, I'd be embarrassed to come face-to-face with him again.

Behind me I could hear Robyn giggling and Homer and Lee making outraged noises at us: 'This is R rated,' Homer hissed. 'Cover your eyes.' We ignored him as a variety of male shapes and sizes were suddenly

25

revealed. It was very interesting. Then there were lots of pale bums as the men ran full-tilt into the lake, yelling and swearing at the shock of the cold water. Some of them were out again in thirty seconds, after quickly splashing themselves; others dived right under. The guards threw a cake of soap in and quite a few guys used that, passing it around like a football. But no one stayed in longer than ten minutes.

It was good to see that despite everything that had happened they could still laugh.

There were no towels. They had to use their clothes to dry themselves. I felt sorry for them doing that: I hate putting on wet clothes. The game of football with the soap that started in the water developed into a game with a shoe on land, as they tried to get warm again. Then, floating across the air towards us we heard one man ask the guard 'Can we run back? To warm up?'

The guard looked at his mate, then back at the prisoner. 'How many?'

The prisoner turned to the others and called out: 'Who wants to run back to the house?'

Four hands were waved in the air. One of them was Kevin's.

'Go like stink,' Homer whispered. He didn't need to tell us twice. We started withdrawing, wriggling back through the undergrowth. When we were well clear of the lake we turned and sprinted, heading for the house and sheds where the prisoners lived. Robyn led. She wasn't the fastest over a short distance, but she had stamina. I stuck with her fairly well, then came Fi, then Lee, then Homer, who was too heavy for long-distance running. Robyn set a cracking pace, yet when we got within sight of the buildings, she wasn't even short of breath. She was getting her fitness back faster than I was.

She stopped behind a big tangle of blackberries in a little gully, and we looked anxiously for Kevin and the others. 'There they are,' Fi said, as she arrived beside us. I saw them then, too. They were slowing down as they approached their cottage, three still jogging, the other two, Kevin and another, walking. A moment later they were in among the sheds and out of sight.

'Let's go for it,' Homer panted. 'We mightn't get another chance for ages.'

'Not everyone,' I said.

'You go,' Robyn said. 'And Lee.'

The others didn't say anything, so I took that for agreement and, with an anxious look towards the lake, crouched low and ran down to the buildings, using them as cover to hide me from anyone up in the main house. We came in through a gap between a galvanised-iron shed and a carport and arrived, breathing fear, quivering like working dogs as they watch their boss approach. We were in a small court-yard, very old, with wallflowers and lavender piled up around a huge well. The stonework around the well was collapsing, but it was a pretty little spot. Lee grabbed my arm. 'This way,' he whispered. I followed him, realising as I did that he could hear their voices. We ran a few metres around an old wall and came to a half-open door. I heard someone say, 'Yeah, but he had an average of sixty in Sheffield Shield, you know,' and then Lee pushed the door open.

Chapter Four

At first I didn't see Kevin. I saw four astonished faces, four open pairs of eyes, four startled mouths. One man, a small middle-aged bloke with a thin moustache, started saying, 'Who the . . .?'

Then Lee shut the door and I saw Kevin, who till then had been hidden by it.

I'll always treasure the look on Kevin's face. Sometimes life really can be like the movies. This time it was. Kevin did one of those dumb double takes that they do in comedy films, and it was a beauty. He was casually asking, 'What's the problem?' but he didn't get to finish the word 'problem'. His chin dropped and his eyes looked like they would pop. His mouth started trying to form a new word but his bottom lip couldn't get around it and just kept wobbling uncontrollably. The only sound that came out was a sort of 'wo, wo, wo –'

I flung myself on him. For a minute he was too shocked to do anything, but eventually he remembered how to hug. Lee joined in and we formed a clump of three, arms around each other, having a good rock. My old hassles with Kevin were all forgotten at that moment.

When we'd had our hug, I took a look at the other men. They were watching and smiling, but as I brushed my hair back and wiped my eyes, the little guy with the moustache spoke up again.

'Sorry to be a party pooper folks, but you'll have to get out of here. They'll be back at any moment.'

'Can we take Kevin?' I asked.

They looked suddenly alarmed. 'No, no way,' one of them said.

'They're right,' Kevin said. 'I can't come with you.'

'But we, we were hoping . . .' I said.

'Look,' Kevin said, 'you've got to go. Tomorrow we're working at the piggery. It's over to the . . .'

'Yes, we know where it is.'

'OK, be in the bush behind it, on the top of the little knoll there, about lunchtime. I'll get away somehow and meet you for a few minutes. We can talk then.'

'OK.'

He hurried us through the door and we ran back past the well and the galvanised-iron shed. Kevin went out onto the muddy brown track, then gave us a signal. 'Hurry,' he called. As we ran past he slapped my back. 'Take care, Ellie,' he whispered. I was moved that he said that. I waved to him when I got into the treeline. Then the little procession of prisoners appeared from the direction of the lake and Kevin immediately turned around and walked casually back to the sheds.

Lee and I hustled on up to the others, who were busting to hear what we had to say. We were all wildly excited. I think we were so sick of each other's company that the possibility of welcoming Kevin back was wonderful for all of us.

'What'd he say? Can we get him out? How'd he sound? How'd he look? He's lost a few k's, hey? What did the others say?'

It took an hour before we calmed down, and then we spent half the night trying to figure out what we could do. At least it helped keep us warm – that night was even colder than the one before. Then, about midnight, it started to rain. We crept down to a hayshed and burrowed in there for a sleep, but it meant we had to post a sentry. That was a drag. I did the first one but didn't sleep much after it, anyway. When dawn came I got up and went over to Homer who was taking his turn. 'You go back to bed if you want,' I said, 'I'm wide awake so I might as well do sentry.'

'I couldn't sleep either. Let's just talk. That way we might talk each other to sleep.'

So we talked, first time in a long time. We'd always been friends – we were practically raised together – but I'd been finding him suffocating in recent months, so I'd given him more room. Sometimes I just wanted to breathe my own air. Wherever there was Homer there wasn't room for much else. We didn't seem to have the time for relationships these days. No, not the time: the energy. That's what we were missing. We were more selfish, I know that much. I used to have strong feelings about Homer but now my strongest feelings were reserved for me, for keeping myself going.

But we talked, mainly about what our world would be like if we ever won back our country. It had always been an article of faith with us that we would win. These days, though, seeing colonists looking so settled, so comfortable, we had to admit that the odds were starting to tip against us. The effect on Homer was to make him more warlike. 'After it's over,' he said, 'we've got to turn this country into a fortress. Everyone should be trained to use weapons, to fight. If anyone tries to invade us again we've got to be ready. And if they do come, we've got to fight for every house, every street, every hectare. That's what we've got to do.'

Me, I had the opposite reaction. I told Homer my favourite story.

'Once upon a time there was a village near a cliff. The road to the village was dangerous, and lots of cars went over the cliff and crashed on the rocks below. The people in the cars got mashed up whenever that happened; some of them even got killed. But eventually the village got a government grant to do something about it. Only trouble then was that the village split into two groups, the people who wanted to build a fence around the top of the cliff, and the people who wanted to buy an ambulance to put at the bottom of the cliff, to cart the casualties off to hospital.'

'Yeah, they shouldn't have waited for a government grant,' said Homer, being smart. 'They should have done something about it themselves. That's a good story.'

'Oh, Homer! You don't have to play dumb any more! You're not at school now.'

'Oh, you mean I've missed something? What kind of fence did they want to build?'

'Very funny. I just think that it's no use having invaders pour into the country and then trying to do something about it. What we need to do is to help other countries get better incomes, so that they don't feel any great urge to rush in here.'

31

'That's easier said than done.'

'How do we know? We never really tried. Anyway, turning the place into a fortress is hopeless. We haven't got enough people to do it properly, even if we wanted to, which I don't.'

'I used to think there were too many people here before. Now look at it.'

'Yeah, they're packing them in. "Populate or perish", that was the motto in Grandma's generation. These guys are carrying it out for us.'

'You and Lee are sure doing your best.'

'What? What did you say?' I started belting him around the head with my gloved hands. 'You take that back.'

'Why, don't tell me he's still got some condoms left?'

'Homer!' I hit him a few more times. When I'd beaten him to a pulp, I said, 'Anyway, I bet Fi's just waiting for you to ask her.'

He looked embarrassed at that. 'I don't want to get too serious,' he mumbled.

'Well, it's either her or Robyn. You don't have a lot of choices.'

'Robyn's a bit of a suck, don't you reckon? She's so perfect all the time. She reckons she's so good.'

'No, she doesn't,' I said loyally.

'Ah well, I wouldn't ever want to go with her. She'd always be telling you what to do. She'd drive any bloke crazy.'

I was shocked at anyone criticising Robyn. She was one of my role models – along with Marilyn Monroe and Emily Dickinson. But Homer always had trouble getting on with strong-minded people. Except me. No, even me sometimes.

We could hear Robyn and Fi talking, back in the hay, so I went and joined them.

'This hay sticks into me so badly,' Fi complained. 'In all those kids' books people used to sleep in haystacks and it sounded really comfortable. But there's nothing comfortable about it.'

We had no need to move until eleven o'clock, so I got back in my sleeping bag and talked to them for a while, before dozing off into a light sleep. We'd been trying to make do on two meals a day, to save supplies, and breakfast was the meal I usually skipped. So there wasn't much incentive to get out of the sleeping bag again.

With the rain still falling and the temperature feeling close to zero we didn't know if the prisoners would be taken off to work. But sure enough, right on nine o'clock, we saw a little bedraggled file of men slopping across the paddock, followed by the guards in their ute. We let them go, glad that we could at least stay dry. Being a prisoner looked worse than working for my dad.

As lunchtime approached my nerves got more and more frayed. Kevin had the answers to a lot of questions that we had been fretting on for a long time. If he could get away on his own for a few minutes we would be able to have our first ever safe conversation with someone who'd been in the Showground. I got so excited I found myself chewing on a corner of my sleeping bag. Of course we all hoped he'd be able to rejoin us, to bring our numbers back up to six, but we knew there was some problem with escaping, or he would have done it yesterday. That was one of the things we wanted to ask about.

We were in position above the piggery well before

noon. The ute was parked there, so we assumed they were all inside, although it was twenty minutes before we saw any activity. Then one of the prisoners came out and got a couple of paintbrushes from the back of the ute. He gazed searchingly up the hill towards us for a minute – they must have all known we'd be there – but we didn't dare show ourselves. He soon went back inside.

The next one to appear was Kevin. He came hurrying out holding a shovel over his left shoulder. He came straight towards us, head down, like a man on a mission. As he got closer I realised what the mission was. He had a roll of toilet paper in his hand. I started laughing.

When he was only a couple of metres away from me I called out softly: 'Not here you don't.' He grinned but he didn't slow down or raise his head until he was well inside the belt of trees, out of sight of the piggery.

Then Robyn, Homer and Fi had the chance that Lee and I had had the day before. There was heaps of hugging. It was only the fear of time that put a stop to it but, even so, the whole time that Kevin was talking Fi stood beside him holding his hand and stroking it. We were very happy to see him. But soon the questions started flooding in, till Kevin had to put his hand up to stop them.

'Whoa, whoa, guys, hold the phone, one at a time.'

'How's Corrie?' I asked quickly, before anyone else had a chance to ask anything else.

'Depends on who you talk to. I haven't seen her since the night she got shot. In fact, I heard that you guys have seen her since I have. Look, I'd say she's about the same, still in a kind of coma. Some people say she's worse, because she's still losing weight, but other people say they're sure she hears them when they talk to her. I don't know. People think what they want to think. No one's got any definite info.'

'How are all our families?'

'Not bad, the last time I saw them. I've been out with these work parties quite a while, but everyone was looking OK a few weeks back. I mean, it's all relative, isn't it? You guys look a lot healthier than anyone at the Showground, but now that people are getting out and working again they're starting to pick up.'

Kevin seemed older and more mature somehow; more intelligent even. He'd never have said 'it's all relative,' or 'people think what they want to think,' when he'd been camping with us in Hell. This war had changed us all, and not always for the worse.

'What's it been like?' Homer asked.

Suddenly, at this simple question, Kevin seemed to fall apart. His face crumpled and for a minute he couldn't get his words out. Fi gripped his hand tighter and I patted his back. He hardly needed to say anything; he'd already answered the question.

'Sorry,' he stammered. 'Sorry.'

'Has it been terrible?' Robyn asked gently.

Kevin just nodded. 'They're OK as long as you do what they say. But the moment you do something they don't like . . .'

I was thinking again of how badly Kevin had been beaten up when he arrived at Wirrawee Hospital with Corrie. I didn't know any details, but my imagination made up for that.

'I'll have to go back in a sec,' Kevin said.

'Can't you escape?' Homer asked urgently. 'What's stopping you?'

Kevin shook his head. 'They keep hostages. Members of your family. If you escape they execute them. They've got us by the balls. The only reason they guard us is to stop us sabotaging or stealing things, and to make us work hard. There's no way anyone can escape.'

He turned to go back. I felt desperately sorry for him. He looked so lonely and miserable at having to return to such a rotten life.

'If it could be managed, would you want to escape?' I asked. 'Would you want to join up with us again?'

He looked shocked. 'Of course. But if you can think of a way to do it I'll say you're a genius, Ellie. I'll even put that in writing.'

I grinned. Privately I was thinking, 'Get your pen out.' I didn't say it, because I didn't want to raise his hopes too much. But I already had the glimmerings of an idea.

Chapter Five

'So, am I a genius?' I asked the others. We were back in the hayshed, sheltering from more rain. It was very dark – probably about ten o'clock – on the night of our conversation with Kevin. I couldn't see anyone's face except Fi's; but I could sense their excitement. I was excited too; I thought it was a good plan.

'I don't know about genius,' Homer grumbled. 'But it's not a bad idea.'

'How would we get word to Kevin?' Robyn asked.

'I'm not sure. Just have to wait for a chance. It shouldn't be too hard.'

'We could write it down,' Fi said, 'and if we get half a minute alone with him we could slip it to him then.'

Privately I thought that was a bit risky, in case it got into the wrong hands, but I agreed to do it. I wrote it early the next morning, with the others adding more suggestions every few minutes. Some of their suggestions were pretty smart, so I chucked them in. Writing it out made me nervous, though. It was like we were going into action again, for the first

37

time in a long while. It was a different kind of action to the other battles we'd fought – this was more a battle of wits – but a lot hinged on it. If it went wrong, things would turn ugly for Kevin's family, back at the Showground. They were the ones actually running the biggest risk and they didn't even know it.

In the end, after we'd waited a day and a half without any contact with Kevin, we delivered the letter in a different way. When the work parties were in the paddocks with their guards, Fi and I slipped out of the bush and, again using the old houses as cover from the colonists in the main homestead, stole into the prisoners' quarters. We found Kevin's bed easily enough: it was the messiest. We got one of his socks and put the paper in it, then made the bed roughly and hid the sock in there. We figured the sentries wouldn't notice if the bed had been made in the morning, but Kevin certainly would. He'd realise there must be something special going on.

The other thing I had to do was check the old well set in the ground in the little courtyard. It was one of the biggest I'd seen but, like a lot of those old wells, was in a dangerous condition. The stonework was crumbling and collapsing around its edges. There was a cover over it: a big steel cap that could be opened in the middle by pulling two handles in opposite directions. While Fi held me by the back of my shirt, I wrestled with the two handles until the cover slowly ground open. A rush of stale, damp air exhaled into my face. The gases were all I hoped they would be; I felt instant nausea at just a sniff of them. I held my breath and leaned forward, peering down the shaft. It was beautifully dark and deep: I couldn't see the bottom. I dropped a pebble and waited nearly six seconds before I heard it hit water, which was perfect. I scrambled backwards. The air had made me so dizzy that I had to get Fi to pull the cover back in place. I didn't want to go near it again.

Nothing happened then until the next morning when Kevin gave the signal we'd suggested in our letter. We'd asked him to wear something green for yes, red for no, yellow if he wanted to meet us and talk it over. I'd been betting that Kevin, who was a cautious guy, would be dressed all in yellow. But he surprised us. He came out with a green cap, a lurid green shirt and an olive pair of trousers. The outfit looked terrible but I realised then, if I hadn't realised it before, just how desperate he was to get away and rejoin us.

We were watching from the scrub and when we saw all the green we looked at each other in a mixture of fear and excitement. For once we wouldn't have much to do. Mostly, we'd have to sit and watch. The only way we'd have a lot to do was if the guards realised that something was wrong and came looking for us. In a way I would have preferred more action. Sitting and watching has never been my style.

We did have one job though: to go get a sheep. Or a pig or roo or calf. But a sheep seemed the easiest. We waited until the work parties set out for the day, then we went in the opposite direction. Out in a distant paddock we found a small mob of two-tooths. We hung around till midafternoon, then Homer and I, helped and hindered by the others, cut out a sheep and got it in a corner. We decided not to kill it there and then because it would leave evidence in the paddock. So we tied its legs and Homer, with a bit of a struggle, got it up across his shoulders and staggered off into the bush with it. There are advantages in having a strong male around sometimes. When we were well into the trees, Homer dropped the sheep and he and I killed it. I cut its throat and he broke its neck, while Fi stood there making little whimpering noises of disgust, as though someone had spat on the floor of her parents' beautiful drawing room.

'Sorry Fi,' I said, grinning.

We left the blood for the flies. Homer shouldered the carcass and led the way back to the farmhouses. The tension was killing me. It's much worse when it's your own plan; the responsibility is too much, too much. I resolved that I'd never suggest anything again, knowing even as I made the resolution that I wouldn't be able to keep it. I talked to Robyn as we walked along though, and that was interesting. She had this great religious theory about how the sheep was a sacrificial lamb, sacrificed to save Kevin's life. I didn't know about that.

Once we were in sight of the farmhouse we had to take a lot of care. It was no easy matter for Homer to carry the sheep all the way to the well. Lee went to a tree which gave him a good view of the main homestead and he waved to us when it was all clear. It took twenty minutes before he signalled, which meant time was starting to get tight. It was 4.25 already. Flies were driving Homer crazy. It's amazing how quickly they sniff out the bleeding and the dead, even in winter. But at last, with a short rush, he was able to hoist the carcass and take it to the well. Robyn and I got the top open and Homer, with a sigh of relief, tossed it in, head first, so it would fall all the way. We slammed the top shut again and raced back to shelter. From now on we were reduced to being an audience.

At 5.19 the men returned. They all went straight into their quarters: apparently this was not a bath night. Was it my imagination or did they look nervous? Wasn't Kevin walking kind of stiffly, grimly? I could hardly breathe. My chest felt tight. But nothing happened till 5.35. Then Kevin began his run for the Academy Award.

First he sauntered out past the galvanised-iron shed and had a bit of a poke around it, as though he'd never seen a galvanised-iron shed before. He looked at the corner post nearest us – and nearest the sentry – then checked the guttering. The sentry called out, obviously asking what he was doing, and Kevin muttered something before dawdling away. He was meant to look like a bored teenager who was going to get into trouble, but he seemed a bit self-conscious about it to me.

After that we lost sight of him for ten minutes, but we knew what was meant to happen. Kevin would wander over to the well, force the cover open, and take a look down it. The crumbling stonework would give way, and Kevin would fall to his death. Either the fall or the fumes would kill him; it didn't matter to us, as long as he was definitely dead. We waited nervously.

Sure enough after five minutes came a sharp cry. It only lasted the briefest moment, seemingly cut off in mid-voice, but it was unusual enough to catch the attention of the sentry. He stood more alertly and turned in the direction of the cry, then did a full circle and looked carefully all around him. He was no fool. In the 'How to Invade Other Countries' textbook he'd obviously read the section on 'Decoys' twice. But a few seconds later a man, one of the prisoners, came running out past the shed and called desperately to the sentry. Without even looking to see if the sentry was following, he ran straight back again. It was nicely done, and seemed to finally convince the soldier. He only hesitated a moment, then quickly followed the prisoner.

We waited in a state of high tension. We could hear a lot of shouting and we caught glimpses of people running to and fro. It lasted about thirty minutes, then seemed to calm down a bit. But it was more than an hour before the sentry came back and took up his position again. And that was the end of the night's excitement. Everything went very quiet and stayed that way. We presumed it had worked, but we didn't know. It was another great night for insomniacs.

Next morning the work parties were late to leave. When they did go they looked subdued and dejected. There was no sign of Kevin, of course. But suddenly I had an awful thought. 'My God,' I said to Homer, 'I hope he didn't really fall down it.'

Another slow hour passed. Then I saw a movement by the corner of the shed. I called out, softly, to the others but there was no need. They had already seen it. We all craned forward. It was an agonising moment. Kevin or not Kevin? Success or failure? Life or death?

He sprinted towards us, grinning from ear to ear. It was as though he were unloading months of misery with this one short run to freedom. I wanted to cheer but it wouldn't have been a good idea. We were still in deadly peril, hanging around there and, more importantly, Kevin's family were in deadly peril. I took a step forward to greet him.

The soldier seemed to come from nowhere. He didn't, of course. There was an old rainwater tank, open to the sky, that had been dumped between the buildings and the bush. It had been there so long that weeds had started to grow through it and over it. It had become part of the landscape and so we hadn't even noticed it. But the soldier must have concealed himself in it sometime before dawn. He was one smart cookie.

He stood with his back to us. Kevin had stopped in an instant and stood there, mouth open, the colour draining from his face. The soldier had a rifle pointing at Kevin, and the rifle was cocked. The only thing we had going for us was that he obviously didn't know we were behind him.

I didn't know what to do, couldn't think of a single thing that might help. All I knew was that I had completely screwed up and people were going to die. I heard the soldier say, 'You think I stupid. They think I stupid. But I no stupid. You stupid.'

I still couldn't think of anything to say or do. Behind me there was a slight movement, a stealthy sound. I turned my head enough to see, not moving my body in case the soldier sensed it. Homer had opened the top of his pack and was in the process of withdrawing his shotgun. He had it half out of the pack already. Further across I saw Lee fishing in his pack for something. I made frantic signals at Homer with my face, widening my eyes and wiggling my eyebrows. I didn't know what the solution was, but it wasn't the shotgun. There were a dozen or more colonists up at the main house; they were sure to be better armed than us. I heard the soldier say to Kevin: 'You walk to house.' At that moment Lee

43

began to move forward. Sick with knowledge, I made myself look at his hands to see what he held. I expected to see a knife, like the one he had used to kill the young soldier back in the Holloway Valley. But he held no knife. He had not found what he'd been looking for in his pack, and now his hands were at his waist. What he was quickly pulling off was worse than a knife. It was his leather-plaited belt.

Lee's eyes were wide open, like spotlights. He moved with the stealth of a feral cat – so quietly that I only heard the slightest crunch as he took each footstep. I somehow found time to be jealous of his grace and lightness of tread. But then I realised I was going to have to do more than watch.

In some ways what Lee had was the perfect weapon. The belt ran through two small rings of steel, and came back between them to get its tension. It was the kind of belt that we all wore: most of us had made our own in Leatherwork. It took Lee, though, to think of using one as a weapon. I had a horrible sick awareness that it was probably going to be perfect. But there was one big problem: Lee was going to try to strangle this guy with a belt while the guy stood there holding a gun. It was probably the bravest, stupidest thing I'd ever seen anyone try to do. I knew I had to help.

The soldier was losing his temper fast. 'Turn round!' he shouted at Kevin. 'You bad boy! You turn round!'

Kevin looked terrified. He had seen Lee moving up behind the soldier and I don't know who he was more scared of: Lee or the soldier. But at least the man was sure he was the one who'd caused Kevin's loss of colour, and shaking lips. He hadn't yet thought that there might be anyone behind him; hadn't yet thought to turn around. I began moving forward with Lee. I knew what I had to do: get the man's gun arm. I tried desperately to move as quietly as Lee. Kevin was turning round as ordered; slowly, but he was turning. 'Hand up, hand up,' the soldier yelled. Lee and I were only a couple of steps away now, and I thought that we should strike while the man was yelling; he would be less likely to hear us while his own voice was filling his ears. I had an awful moment of hesitation when I didn't think I was going to be able to do it; I wanted to freeze but knew I simply couldn't. The only way I could make myself act was to count: I went, 'One, two, three,' very quickly to myself, and dived.

Lee launched himself a split second later. Kevin fell sideways, desperate to avoid the aim of the gun. But the man didn't shoot Kevin by reflex, which is what I'd most feared. He didn't shoot anyone. He didn't even pull the trigger. He did what I suppose most people would do in that situation: he started spinning round to see what was going on behind him. That was the way his reflexes worked. I rabbit-chopped his arm as hard as I could hit, then grabbed the gun and swung it upwards. I'd been hoping he'd drop the gun with the shock of my hit; he didn't, but he lost his grip on it and had to snatch at it to try to get it back. At that moment, Lee knocked the man's cap off and dropped the belt over his head. Now, fighting two battles at once, the man got confused; he tried to push me away and at the same time turned to attack Lee. Then Homer arrived with a rush and, between us, we prised the gun out of the man's grasping fingers. He knew he was in trouble then. Lee was tightening the belt fast. The man tried to get his hands onto the belt but Homer and I grabbed an arm each and dragged them down again. Lee started to put all his weight on the belt. The soldier tried to call for help. Too late. I started getting hysterical myself but some force within me made me hold on. The soldier was pitching to the right, staggering. I lost my grip on his arm and he brought it up to his throat but it did him no good; Lee was implacable. The man's face was mottled now, dark red with patches of white, getting darker by the moment. A horrible gurgling noise came from his mouth, like someone trying to gargle but doing it in the mouth instead of the throat. I didn't, couldn't watch any longer, but looked away, towards the beautiful bush, the bush that I loved. Did these things happen in the bush? Did animals and birds kill each other in cold blood because of fights over territory? You bet your life they did.

I had hold of the soldier's arm again, feeling the strength in it: its desperate struggle as it flailed and writhed and fought. The fight was lasting much longer than I'd expected. I could feel the veins swell in the tortured arm. Then, suddenly, it was over. The arm went limp. A terrible smell filled the air and I realised the man had fouled his trousers. I stole a look at his face and quickly looked away again. It was the most revolting sight I'd ever seen. His tongue hung out like a giant fat bullboar sausage. His skin was purplish black. And his eyes . . . those eyes will follow me to my grave and beyond. They were the eyes of a staring devil; a man sent mad in the last minute of his life by the knowledge that he was dying, and by the manner of his death. Every time I close my eyes, his open in my mind.

Chapter Six

'What do we do now?'

The only ones who seemed able to function at all were Robyn and Homer. I had the shakes badly and much as I tried to stop them I didn't seem able. Kevin was lying on the ground. His face was grey. I'd only seen that colour in a human face once before: when I'd visited Mrs O'Meara in hospital just before she died. She was eighty-eight years old.

Fi was back behind us, in the bush, hugging a tree and crying quietly. Lee was sitting on the ground with his head between his knees. I couldn't see his face and wasn't sure that I wanted to. Compared to the rest of us, Homer and Robyn at least looked like they could still move and think.

It was Robyn who'd asked the question but Homer who answered it.

'Down the well.'

'Eh?'

'It's our only choice, our only chance. Listen to me, everyone. We've got to make this work. Kevin, did you make up a dummy, like we told you?'

Kevin seemed to take five minutes to understand

the question, five minutes more to respond. Then he slowly nodded. 'We stuffed my work clothes with pillows.'

'And what happened?'

Kevin spoke like an old man, a tired old man. He was slurring his words. 'It worked. They looked down there with a torch and they saw it all right. Then they tried to lower one of my mates on a rope, but he started yelling about the fumes and acting all crazy, and they had to bring him back up again.'

'Good,' Homer said. 'That's perfect. Quick, everyone, help carry this guy. Fi, you bring his gun, then come back here and clean up the area, so there's no sign of a struggle.' Because we were too slow to move he got angry with us. 'Come on, damn you all. Get a bloody move on.'

We shambled towards the body and struggled to get a grip on different parts of it. Kevin tried to help but turned his face away in revulsion and let go of the feet which he had been holding. The four of us struggled with the ghastly stinking thing into the little courtyard. With Homer directing, we manoeuvred it towards the well. It had been left open but our problem was to get it down the shaft without falling in ourselves. He was a lot heavier, and a more awkward shape, than the sheep. Just as we nearly had it in the right position, Homer missed his footing and had to let go of the man's head. It dropped onto the rotting stonework with a horrible crack that must have almost split it open. I had the sick thought that if he hadn't been dead already we would have killed him again by doing that. Robyn gave a sob and lost her grip. Homer was furious. He yelled at her. 'It doesn't matter,' I said. 'Pick him up again.' When we were all

48

sure of our footing we gave it a heave. It slid forward over the brink of the well, caught for a moment by a bit of clothing, then came free, and with a floppy rush, kept sliding and went over the edge, dropping into the depths.

I waited for the splash but it didn't come.

'It might have jammed halfway down,' I said.

'Do you know where there's a torch?' Homer asked Kevin. Kevin thought for a moment, then nodded. 'OK, go and get it. Hurry!' he yelled, when Kevin moved away too slowly. Homer turned to us. 'Now,' he ordered. 'We've got to make it look like he slipped and fell in. Fi, chuck his gun on the grass here, like he threw it forward when he felt himself falling. Then go back and clean that spot where . . . where we . . . where we had the fight with him. Lee, go and check the route we brought him in by. Clean up any tracks, any mess we might have left.'

'Let's fake it here,' I said, pointing to a place where the stonework was especially bad. 'If we deliberately collapse a few stones into the well, like they broke away when he stood on them . . .'

'Yes, good.'

Kevin reappeared with the torch. I took it from him and lay full length on my stomach to peer down the shaft. It sure was a deep one, much deeper than any around Wirrawee. Even with this strong torch I could only see, in the distant black depths, a couple of vague bulky shapes that could have been human. The fumes were weaker than they had been, but they were already starting to make me dizzy again. I pulled back.

'Well?' Homer asked.

'Well well well,' I said, remembering an old joke.

Why was I the only one who ever seemed to want to make jokes at times like these? I must have been sicker than even I thought. Homer just looked at me like I really was sick.

'It's not bad,' I said quickly. 'I think the soldier's landed on Kevin's pillows. It's hard to see but. I guess the sheep's under all that.'

'Sheep?' Kevin asked, staring.

'We dropped a dead sheep down there yesterday,' I explained, 'to provide a nice smell in the coming days. Otherwise they wouldn't get sucked in by the dummy. Plus it'll discourage them from trying too hard to get you out.'

He gave a little grin, probably the weakest grin I've ever seen, but it cheered me up to see that much.

Lee and Fi came back. 'All done,' Lee said quietly. 'We found this.' He produced the soldier's cap.

'Good,' Homer said. He put the cap on the grass just beyond the decayed stonework. 'Think it'll work?' he asked Kevin.

Kevin nodded slightly. 'Probably. This bloke was such a drop kick. It's the sort of dumb thing he would do, go peering down the well for a thrill. And because the other sentries thought he was a drop kick, they mightn't waste much time investigating. They all hated him.'

'It's out of our hands now, anyway,' Homer said flatly. 'There's nothing more we can do. Put the torch back and we'll get out of here.'

No sooner said than done. The time was only 10.45. I couldn't believe so much had happened so early. We still had a full day in front of us. Gee, by five o'clock, we could have killed another dozen human beings, if we really set our minds to it.

50

Kevin wanted to bring a few of his most precious things, but we were unanimous in turning him down. It was tough, very tough, but we didn't dare take the risk. 'If they notice a single thing missing, then you're stuffed, or your family is,' Homer said.

'We all might be, if they come after us,' I said.

'You'll just have to hope your mates keep them for you till after the war,' Lee said. That didn't seem much of an offer, to any of us, but it was all we could suggest. To a lesser degree it was going to be tough on us too, because we'd have to share precious things like food and warm clothing. We had a bare minimum as it was. Anyway, wasn't it Kevin who'd stopped us taking lots of extra stuff into Hell, when we first realised we'd been invaded? No, it was Homer. Sometimes I got worried that my memory was falling apart.

With our packs on our backs, and only Kevin unburdened, we set off. Homer was in the lead. He set a cracking pace, but we knew why, and no one raised a murmur. There was no time for shock or horror or grief from the killing. We just had to get our butts a long long way from there, if we wanted to keep our butts attached to our bodies, which we all did. At least, I assumed we did. A couple of us looked like they couldn't care much either way.

We didn't stop for lunch, but ploughed grimly on, no one talking, heads down, human pack-horses on a long trek. In the back of everyone's mind was, I'm sure, the thought of Kevin's family, whom we'd put at risk by our actions. No one suggested that we stay and spy on the soldiers and watch how they reacted when they found one of their number missing. It might have given us some peace of mind if we'd seen

51

them accept it as an accident. But the risk was too great. Anyway, we'd given up hope of peace of mind a long time ago.

Late afternoon we stopped for a snack and a toilet break. I was terribly hungry and I'd been getting annoyed with Kevin because he hadn't even offered to take a pack for anyone yet. Fair enough, he was depressed – in shock, I guess – but so were we all, and these packs were heavy. So I dropped a few hints and he made a few sarcastic comments and then I told him I wouldn't let him carry my pack if he paid me and so it went on. Typical enough stuff when you're tired. I was secretly grateful when Robyn stepped in and told us to grow up, and then worked out a rough roster which meant that we'd all get an occasional break from carrying a pack.

The bush was thinning out again and we realised we were approaching cleared country. This was bad news for us as we would find it much harder to stay unseen, especially now that colonists had spread so far and so fast across the state. Electricity seemed to be on again everywhere, which was another problem. Every house was an island of light at night-times.

Suddenly, at around seven o'clock, we came to the end of the scrub. Without a word being said, we all dropped our packs. We were standing on a slight rise. In the last of the daylight we saw beautiful rich green plains stretching ahead of us. The kind of country that makes your mouth water. The kind of soil you could eat. But of course, being so productive, it was dotted with little clumps of houses everywhere, all with lights on. We could see the road that followed the valley we'd been in. About two k's further on, it joined a major road, a bitumen one, that came across country from our left. Where they met was a small village, with maybe a dozen houses and a service station. There was occasional traffic on the road: two cars and a truck during the time that we were watching. There probably hadn't been much more traffic than that in peacetime.

'We're losing this war,' Homer said flatly.

'Tell me something I didn't know,' Kevin said.

I knew what they meant. Everything looked so normal, so typical, just the way it always had been. It was like nothing had changed. Oh sure, there'd been a minor hiccup, a slight change in the way things were run, and sure, different people were doing the running; but nothing important had changed. The birds still flew, the wind still stormed, the rivers still made their way to the sea. The land hadn't changed.

'We have to keep going,' Robyn said.

I knew what she meant, too. We'd have to keep walking most of the night, maybe all of it. We couldn't travel by day in this kind of country. Darkness was the only safe time for people like us. We'd have to find somewhere safe to rest up during daylight. That would be difficult; difficult and dangerous. But we had no choice.

Of course Robyn, being Robyn, was talking about more than how long we should walk.

In a sense, though, this night travel suited me. I was feeling more comfortable at nights, the longer the war went on. I'd always associated the darkness of night with scary things. It was the time of foxes and dingoes and feral cats. It was the time of witches and goblins, of vampires and werewolves and ghosts. It was the time of evil.

That was why it suited us.

On the other hand, on this particular night, it didn't suit me at all. I was so very tired, so utterly exhausted. I was all in. I knew I couldn't go another step. I hated Robyn for saying that we had to. I waited for someone else to say something, though: I had too much pride to be the one. Then I realised no one was going to say it. Either they had as much pride as me, or else they weren't as tired as me. Grimly, hating them all, I shouldered my pack.

'Not yet, Ellie,' Homer said gently. 'It's still too early.'

'You're unbelievable, Ellie,' Fi said, in quite an admiring voice. 'I don't know how you do it. I couldn't walk another step. I've got to have a rest.'

'Ellie could walk all week,' Lee said, in the same tone Fi had used.

I did feel a bit better then. I didn't confess how wrecked I was. Let them keep thinking I was superwoman if they wanted. I knew the truth.

We waited another hour, not talking, each alone with our thoughts. It was no secret what we were thinking about. I stole a glance at Kevin. He was staring into the distance, lips trembling, as though he were reliving every moment of it in his mind. I wondered about his reactions. How did we seem to him now? How much had we changed? I knew we'd changed a bit, of course, but after seeing the expression on Kevin's face when we killed the soldier, I began to wonder if we'd changed more than we realised. He'd looked at us like we were creatures from another planet. Well, at least I knew that wasn't true. We weren't creatures from another planet. We were just creatures from Hell.

Eventually I was the one who got everyone

moving again. It was because of those dumb comments about my being so strong – I wanted to live up to them now. Plus there was another reason. I never liked it when Homer took command too much or for too long. I always had to assert myself when that happened. It's always been that way, even when we were little kids.

Lee and Robyn were asleep, but they got up when I prodded them. That was one advantage of our way of life – we'd become used to sleeping in short snatches and breaking our sleep to do sentry duty. Everyone except Lee shouldered a pack, and away we went.

That was the start of a horrible night. Fair enough really, to follow a horrible day. I don't know that I've ever been so tired. We just went on putting one foot in front of the other. Minute by minute, hour by hour. First my feet started hurting, then my calves, then my back and neck. My head dropped lower and lower. I soon gave up the occasional effort at conversation. Plod, plod, plod. My muscles ached, my joints ached, my bones ached. I must have spent an hour just thinking about what I could sacrifice from my pack to lighten it. It became a wonderful dream, the thought of having a pack that was two kilos lighter. It seemed that life could offer no sweeter promise, no greater hope. I weighed up the advantages and disadvantages of every item I carried, trying to decide what I could dump. I was sure I'd be able to find something but really there was nothing. Everything had its uses. I couldn't bear to think of doing without any of them. So I kept going.

Eleven o'clock came and went. We walked on. Hours later I looked at my watch. It was 11.12. I could have cried with disappointment. I felt so cheated. Eventually midnight passed and we staggered into the next day. 'That was three hours of my life just gone,' I thought. 'Three hours I'll never have again. I'm three hours closer to my death, and all I did in those three hours was walk.'

I knew my steps were getting shorter and I knew it would be to my advantage to take longer steps. If I could cover an extra twenty centimetres with each step I'd be less tired. I knew that. But I couldn't do it. Instead of my steps getting longer, they got shorter still. Light rain started falling and at first I welcomed it, because it felt refreshing. But then my clothes got damp and sticky and heavy. I got too cold; the first trickle of cold water down my neck was horrible, as though an icy snail was slipping down my bare skin where I couldn't reach it. I think I started crying with exhaustion but I couldn't tell because of the raindrops. I did hear Fi sobbing behind me and I ignored her because I needed all my energy for myself. I didn't dare spend it on anyone else.

As one o'clock approached I kept gazing greedily at my watch. It was just luminous enough to give a reading. I thought that if I could make it to one o'clock something special might happen. Nothing did.

My boots started squelching as the waterproofing began to fail. I tried singing 'Ten thousand green bottles' in my head but got bored with it. At some point Robyn tried to get everyone singing: she did a solo of 'Are You Lonesome Tonight', which was too depressing, then a solo of 'Smoke Curls up Around the Old Gum Tree Trunk', then she started 'Not for the First Time', then she gave up. We stopped not long after that so Fi could go to the dunny, then I realised I had the toilet paper and I didn't know where in my pack it was. It seemed to take half an hour to find; I dug deeper and deeper in the pack, getting everything messed up, letting the rain get in, before finally realising it was in a side pocket. Misery soaked through me and I threw back my head and howled. No one seemed interested; no one seemed to care. 'Can't we camp here somewhere?' Kevin whined, peering around him in the darkness.

'No way,' Homer said. 'We're still in wide open country. We've got to press on.'

There was a grim silence. When Fi came back we picked up our packs and got going again.

The further we went the colder I got. I lost feeling in my feet. All I knew was that they were terribly heavy and seemed to take more and more effort to pick up and carry forward. My head ached and my nose was running continuously. Sniffing didn't stop it and the snot got mixed up with the rain running down my face. My legs were numb, too. I didn't have the energy to lift my arm to look at my watch and it probably wouldn't have been readable anyway. The further we went, the more trouble I had keeping a straight line. I was vaguely aware that I was wandering all the time but didn't seem able to do much about it. I had no idea who was leading but assumed it was Homer, who had a compass. For once – for one of the very few times in my life – I couldn't match it with him.

When we stopped I was too tired to feel any relief, too tired to feel anything. I stood there waiting to be told what to do. For all I knew or cared we might have run into a patrol. After a few minutes Homer came out of the darkness and reached for my hand.

I gave him the wet cold heavy thing. It must have been like picking up a dead fish. 'Come on, Ellie, old mate,' he said wearily. I let myself be led like a help- less child. We walked for about five minutes to a building. I realised suddenly that it was a wheat silo, one of the big concrete ones. I didn't care what it was, but I remember thinking that it was a good choice of shelter, because colonists wouldn't be interested in it until harvest time, in mid-summer.

Chapter Seven

One trouble with the war was that we had no medicines. We'd had the basic odds and ends but we'd used them up pretty quickly. Now we were down to half a packet of Bandaids and a bottle of Alka Seltzer. And after that terrible trudge across the plains we were tired, depressed, and wet to the skin; hair soaked and boots full of water.

We were cases straight out of the medical text-book, in perfect shape to get sick. We got sick.

Robyn, Kevin, Fi and I all went down without a murmur. That only left Homer and Lee, and they weren't too good themselves. We started off with colds, sneezing and dripping, then we got coughs, then we got in serious trouble. We didn't have a thermometer but it didn't matter. You don't always need a smoke alarm to know your house is on fire. One look at the two red spots in Fi's white cheeks was enough. We burned, we shook, we panted, we tossed and turned. I hallucinated so strongly that they had to tie me down. I thought I was the Great Pruner or something; I knew that I held a giant pair of clippers and my job was to go from poplar tree to poplar tree,

59

cutting them into shape. Each tree was OK near the ground; it was the high bits that were the problem. I constantly had to stand on tiptoes, or even to jump with arms outstretched to grab the branches with the shears and haul them down. More and more I realised that the bits to be trimmed were like people; some were beautifully sculptured human forms. It was not very pleasant cutting them in half but I knew it was my duty so I forced myself. Then they would distract me by turning into real people, and I would watch them for a while, before going back to the trees.

It was during the times that I was being the Great Pruner that Homer and Lee had the most trouble with me. They said it was like watching a sort of mad aerobics, with me leaping up and down, grabbing at nothing then struggling and whimpering when they tried to wrestle me back to bed. They had so little energy themselves that they had to go find some rope to tie me up.

'I'll bet that was your idea,' I said to Homer.

'I didn't enjoy it, you know.'

'Sure, sure.'

I have to admit, the two boys were great nurses. I'd wake, burning with fever, and they'd be there within a minute, whether it was three o'clock in the morning or three o'clock in the afternoon. Not that I had any idea of time.

Maybe antibiotics would have cleaned us all up in twenty-four hours: probably. But we didn't have them and so we suffered and our bodies had to do the healing themselves, with a little help from the two boys. They wiped us down with cool damp towels, made us drink, and even eat, a couple of times, kept warm clothes on us, talked to us, soothed our fevered brows.

One day I woke feeling weak as a paper tissue but perfectly clear-headed. I knew it was early in the morning, and I had a vague memory of a moment during the night when I'd felt the fight go out of my body. It had been followed by a kind of sweet peacefulness and, after it, I'd slept soundly and warmly. Homer came in holding a billy and a water bottle and I looked at him lazily.

'What's it like outside?'

'Oh, you're back in the land of the living, are you?'

'Mmm. I don't feel too bad.'

'Good.'

'How're the others?'

'Fi's been on the up and up since yesterday. She's out the back having breakfast with Lee. Robyn and Kevin are still just as crook.'

I glanced across to their beds. They certainly didn't look well. Both were asleep, but Kevin was mumbling and moving around and Robyn looked horribly white.

'God, did I look like that?'

'Worse.'

'How long has this been going on?'

'Four days.'

'Oh yeah.'

'I swear! Lee and I have had about an hour's sleep in the last four days.'

I was silent, for once. I was deeply impressed by the fact that my life could lose four days without my having any awareness of it. Maybe this was a preview of death: continuous visions and dreams and vague glimpses of reality. Only with death you never wake up; you keep having the weird images forever. I thought a lot about death and what it might be like, of course; I still do.

When I tried to get up I realised it was not such a good idea. My limbs had no strength and my mind had no strength to force my limbs to obey. That was unusual for me but I was too tired to care. I went back to sleep.

Next time I woke it was the next day. I was even more astonished by that; in fact, it took Homer and Fi half an hour to convince me. I'd had enough of bed: besides, I was busting for a leak and was enormously hungry. I staggered outside and relieved myself, then got some biscuits and, for the first time in nearly a week, started taking an interest in my surroundings.

We were close to the coast now; I could smell it. I guessed that by the route we'd taken we were probably about twenty k's from Cobbler's Bay. Some time we'd have to start thinking seriously about Cobbler's Bay again. The thought almost gave me an immediate relapse into fever. We were still in quite clear country but nothing like the plains we'd crossed five nights before. The grass was wirier and the trees had a windswept desolate look. There were no dwellings in sight but a line of trees fifty metres away indicated a road. The rain had gone but it was a cold day with a fresh wind; a few clouds scudded across the sky like they were in a hurry to get somewhere.

I went back into the silo and helped Lee do a bit of housework; well, silowork really. 'Where's the water supply?' I asked him, picking up an armful of empty water bottles.

'I'll show you.'

He looked tired and nervous; no wonder, with the work Homer and he had done.

We went across to the road and walked for a few hundred metres. I felt strange walking along so openly, in broad daylight.

'Don't any cars come along here?'

'Four in five days. And there's plenty of cover. You can hear them coming.'

'How are you feeling?' I asked, but I didn't care very much. I was too tired, too feeble and perhaps still too sick about what had happened back at the well.

'OK. Just totally stuffed by nursing you guys.'

'Have a sleep when we get back. Fi and I can take over and give you a break.'

'Yeah, thanks, I think I will.'

I realised quite suddenly, with a sense of shock, that my relationship with Lee was over. I felt nothing for him any more. He seemed like a stranger and this seemed like the kind of polite conversation you have with strangers. Although I didn't admit it to myself then, I think, looking back, that part of the reason was the killing of the soldier when we rescued Kevin. It wasn't the first time we'd killed, of course; it wasn't the first time Lee had killed in cold blood; but this time it had been too horrible, too disgusting. I didn't want to touch Lee; didn't especially want to talk to him, even. I felt sick every time his long fingers touched me.

It's unfair, I know that. It's like making Lee do our dirty work and then blaming him when he does it. But fair and unfair is for the mind; emotions don't know anything about fair and unfair.

We filled the bottles at a wide shallow river,

63

squatting in the gravel and watching the little gurgles as the water rushed in. It was cold though, and the bottles were cold in our hands when we carried them back.

By that evening, Kevin was through the worst of it and Robyn was sensible enough to understand what was going on. The silo smelt terrible, with the stench of us humans having filled it for nearly a week. There were three concrete silos in a row and two steel ones. I checked out the other two concrete ones, thinking we could maybe move into one of them for some fresh air, but they both had a strong smell of chemicals. Probably pesticides. The steel ones had the nice smell of dry grain but they would have been uncomfortable to live in.

I went back to our silo. The first room wasn't too bad. The manager must have used it as his office, where he could peer down through the wire grille into the deep hole and watch the grain slowly filling it. There was a filing cabinet, and a desk and chair where Homer and Lee had spent a lot of time playing cards. There was another room where we sickies had slept, and some little concrete cells, like a medieval convent.

I sat at the desk and played patience for a while.

With Kevin getting better we finally got to have the big conversation that we'd all wanted to have. It was the next day, after breakfast, in the office. Robyn moved her sleeping bag in and lay in it, watching and listening, the rest of us sitting quite comfortably around the walls, drinking cold Milo as a special treat. Homer had the chair.

'So, Kevvy, tell us a story,' Homer said, starting the ball rolling.

'Tell me a story,' I sang, and Robyn and Fi immediately joined in.

'Tell me a story,
Tell me a story,
Tell me a story, remember what you said.
You promised me, you said you would,
You promised me, you said you would,
Tell me a story, remember what you said.'

'Where do you want me to start?' Kevin asked.

'At the beginning,' we chorused.

After horrible times, killing times, we often seemed to regress like this. At that moment I'd say we were about seven years old. Kevin's story forced us to grow up again fast, though. It wasn't a very funny story but it was the first detailed description we'd had of life on the inside.

'OK, I'll go right back, then. After Corrie and I left you guys at Ellie's place – my God, it feels like years ago. That night: it all changed after that night. One bullet, it changed everything.'

He looked down into his cup without drinking from it.

'We got to the hospital about two in the morning. I drove so slowly. I was scared she'd die in the back seat, and I kept looking over my shoulder to see how she was doing. She looked worse and worse; you could see the colour going out of her. But every time I sped up she'd groan, these horrible deep groans like I've never heard before. It was bloody awful.

'By the time we got there I wasn't even thinking about the war and the soldiers. It sounds dumb but it's true. I'd half forgotten there was a war on. All I could think about was getting Corrie to hospital and getting her treated. I drove up to that main entrance with the lights on full beam, the hazards on, and the horn blasting. So they knew I was coming. And arriving like that, I guess they knew I wasn't a threat. They all came bustling out: a nurse and a doctor and a bloke with a trolley – and a couple of soldiers. When I saw them I remembered there was a war on, all right.

'At first it wasn't too bad. The soldiers knew there were still a few people around the district who hadn't been rounded up, so they weren't too surprised to see me. And the hospital staff were our mob, prisoners, so they were cool. The problems started when the soldiers found out Corrie had a bullet wound. The hospital staff tried to keep it secret. They pretended she'd fallen off a cliff, but the trouble was that one of the soldiers knew English and hadn't told anyone he did. I mean, he deliberately pretended he didn't know it, so he could spy on people. They talked quite openly in front of him, and that's how we got found out.'

Kevin paused for a moment. He lifted his eyes from his Milo and gazed up at the funnel of the elevator shaft.

'Well, it was on for young and old then. Corrie was a "bad girl, bad girl," and right away they tried to frame us for blowing up the bridge. The two soldiers had me in a corner, on the floor, and they were bashing me in the back with the butts of their rifles. Going right for the kidneys, and finding them too, no worries. I was pissing blood for a fortnight. Every time I went to the dunny I remembered those guys. Then they brought three sentries in from the bridge – the ones who'd had the best view of you guys – and they were meant to identify us. The only thing that saved us then was that they were so positive it wasn't us. Bloody lucky they were honest. That stopped the soldiers kicking me for a minute.

'They still weren't happy, though. They were telling the doctor that Corrie had to go straight to the Showground; she had to stop treating her. They were really worked up. "No more, no more," they kept screaming. They were waving their rifles around, and trying to wheel the trolley outside. That bloody doctor but, she's a legend. She just said no; like, "Don't even ask, don't waste my time, stop bothering me." I don't think they knew quite what to do about her. There was a full-on tug of war going on over Corrie, and Corrie lying there unconscious in the middle of it. Sort of funny if you'd been in the mood for jokes.'

'Was her name Dr Crassini?' I asked.

Kevin nodded. 'Yeah, that's right, that's her.'

'Figures.' I'd seen Dr Crassini handling my father. She was pretty awesome. Young, but strong.

'Next thing,' Kevin continued, 'two more soldiers came in. The two blokes who'd been there all along had turned their attention back to me, seeing they weren't getting anywhere with the doc. They had me on the floor again and were putting the boot in. The nurse was screaming at them, in between working on Corrie, and I was starting to black out. I was scared they were going to kill me. I'd told them the truth, how she was shot when we were trying to get my uncle's ferrets, but I wasn't convincing them. I had blood all over me and I knew my nose was broken. Every time I breathed I just seemed to breathe blood. I thought I might drown in it. I really thought I was on the way out.'

I glanced around me. There were four pale faces, all intent on Kevin's story. Kevin was looking down at his mug again. I don't know whether he realised the effect he was having.

'So, anyway, in came these other two soldiers. I was hardly aware of them, but the wardsman told me all about it later. He was a bit of a wimp and he hadn't done a thing to help me when I was getting beaten up, but he wasn't a bad bloke. So in came these two soldiers and one of them was hurt, and they made the doctor leave Corrie and treat him. He had a sprained ankle, and how do you think he got it? Chasing two people through the bush out at my uncle's place, that's how. Geez, I tell you, did they ever show up at the critical time. Saved my life. The doc called the two sentries who were giving me the third degree and made the other two repeat their story. When they said they'd fired a few shots at some dark shapes in the bush, the soldiers realised what an honest, respectable person I was. We'd still been naughty, according to them, but we hadn't been sabotaging stuff and that was the important thing. We were just average naughty, instead of highly trained professional naughty.

'"Naughty" is one of their favourite words. "Bad boy" and "naughty boy", that's what they were always calling me.

'But I tell you what, guys, if we ever get caught, don't get lagged for any of the things you've done, the bridge and the ride-on mower, and getting Lee out of Wirrawee. They're still steaming about all those things.'

'What about blowing up Turner Street?' Homer asked, with just a touch of smugness.

Kevin sat up. He got so excited. 'Was that you? Was that really you? Unbelievable! Some people said it was you, but I couldn't believe it. That must have been about a tonne of TNT! How did you do that? My God, it was a hell of a bang. I thought someone had nuked Wirrawee. Wow, I tell you, if they ever bust you for that, you're dead.'

'Thanks a lot.'

But we were proud and excited by Kevin's response. It was nice to be able to boast a bit. That was one of the worst things about our isolation. We felt no one was appreciating or even noticing the battles we'd fought and the risks we'd run – risks that made me go giddy every time I thought about them. The way Kevin went on made us feel, for a few minutes at least, like we were the Foreign Legion, the Green Berets and the Rats of Tobruk, all rolled into one.

'How the heck did you do it?'

We spent ten minutes telling him, tripping over ourselves with corrections and contradictions, having a wonderful time being heroes. But it didn't last too long, as we then had to go on and tell him about the death of Chris. That sobered us up again, fast enough. Kevin didn't seem all that shaken by it, though. I guess he was getting immune to death.

'So, anyway,' I said finally, 'tell us what happened to you after the hospital, and then we'll tell you the rest of our stuff.'

'OK. Where was I up to? Getting my head beaten off my shoulders? OK. So, in the end they generously let Corrie stay in the hospital but she had to be moved to the Prisoners' Block, where you don't exactly get five-star service. And that's where you guys caught up with her. Mrs Slater told me you'd been there and she'd had a good goss with you.'

'Yeah, that's right.'

'Well, I haven't seen her since the night I drove her in there. They wouldn't let me stay – I got chucked in the back of a station wagon and taken to the Showground, feeling like a bloody mess. I was one, too. We had a big family reunion but I don't remember much about it. I got nursed there and eventually I recovered. Took about three weeks. It wasn't easy, though – I guess my nerve had gone, a bit, so I wasn't good for much for a while.

'The Showground was getting ugly. People were so stressed. Conditions probably weren't bad at first but they didn't stay that way for long. I don't think it was ever planned as a long-term residential centre for a thousand people. Most of the buildings are galvanised iron, so they got very hot. The food was OK though, most of the time. Geez, there's enough food in the Wirrawee district to feed a zillion. But these buggers got lazy – they couldn't be bothered going to a lot of trouble to get three course meals for us. Fair enough, I suppose. But it wasn't really the food that was the problem.'

'What was it then?'

Kevin searched his mind, trying to figure out what had caused the build-up of tension. 'It was a mixture of everything, really,' he said slowly. 'The crowding, that was terrible. Not being able to have showers. Especially when we had those thirty-five degree days. And all those dickheads trying to tell everyone else what to do. You know, Mr Rodd and Mr Nelson and Troy South? And Mrs Olsen? Geez, they drove me crazy. I suppose everyone was under stress and that

70

made for a lot of arguments. But some people didn't make any effort. That bloody Mr Rodd, seemed like he was following me around, trying to pick me. I think that's how he got his thrills. I can see why he's had two wives leave him.'

Kevin paused again and sat thinking. We all waited in silence, not liking to interrupt.

'No, that's not what it was,' he said at last. 'It was the boredom, that was the worst thing. Day after day after day, nothing to do. Absolutely totally nothing. People tried organising a few things, but there wasn't much that appealed to me, I guess. They got a school going, for instance, and that was good for the little kids, but for people our age – well, school didn't seem like much of a go. Then some people started classes for adults in a few things. There were cattle-judging lessons, and Chinese, and Indonesian. Old Doc Robbo took first-aid classes – they weren't bad.

'No,' he said, leaning back against the wall with his hands behind his head. 'There was only one interesting thing I learned, the whole time I was there.'

'What was that?'

'Explosives.'

Chapter Eight

'Explosives?' Homer asked politely. 'Did you say explosives?'

'Mmm. I thought you might find that interesting.'

'Explosives.' Homer rolled the word around his tongue, like he was trying it out, to see how it tasted. 'So how far did you get?'

'Well, quite a way. Jock Hubbard taught us. He's got his ticket, his shot-firer's ticket. He got the idea that the time might come when we could use a bit of knowledge. He made up dummies and we practised on them. It would have been better with the real things, of course, but the soldiers weren't too keen to lend us those.'

'OK,' Homer said. 'I know it's possible to make a bomb using fertiliser and diesel, because I remember Dad blowing up tree stumps. The trouble is I never bothered to ask him how to do it. I've often regretted that.'

'Yeah, well that's easy. Ammonium nitrate. For us, in our situation, that's probably the easiest and best way to go.' Kevin had suddenly become transformed. It was the first time I'd seen him like that. It was interesting to see how being an expert changed someone. 'We could expect to find a lot of other stuff in farm buildings too, like gunpowder and dynamite. But the soldiers have probably taken most of that. Yeah, anfo's the way to go.'

'Anfo?'

'Yeah, anfo. It stands for ammonium nitrate fuel oil. That's the stuff Homer's talking about. It's perfect for us because most farms have heaps of ammonium nitrate for fertiliser. It produces oxygen, so it's better even than petrol, cos the more oxygen the better, for a really big bang.'

'So that's all we need? Ammonium nitrate and diesel?' Homer asked.

'It doesn't have to be diesel. Any fuel'll do the job. Charcoal even.'

'But is that all we need?'

'Well, a detonator of course. But again, if we check out the farms we'll find a stack of them somewhere. Jock worked for ICI and he said they sold over a thousand plain detonators every month in Wirrawee alone. What I can do is make a small bomb from anfo, with a detonator, and if we buried that in a big pile of loose anfo, and confined it, well, we'd make a bigger blast than Texas Harbour.'

'What's Texas Harbour?' Fi asked.

'Texas Harbour was an explosion that blew up a port and killed 400 people. There was a ship loaded with ammonium nitrate and they'd been spraying the holds with mineral wax, so that was the fuel. Then someone chucked down a cigarette and the cargo caught fire. They shut the holds, thinking that'd cut off the oxygen, but they didn't realise the fertiliser produces its own oxygen. Being in a confined space, it built up so much pressure that when it blew, it basically blew the whole town away. Oklahoma City, that was anfo, too. Half a tonne of it, and they blew a nine-storey building in half.'

We listened intently. 'You see,' Homer said at last, 'like we told you, we're on our way to Cobbler's Bay. We don't know what we're going to do there; we mightn't have a chance to do anything. But it's probably the most important target we could ever have. All we know for sure is they're not likely to have petrol tankers sitting around waiting for us. If we make our own bomb we at least reduce the problems by one. Then all we have to do is get the thing in there and detonate it.'

'God,' said Fi. 'I don't know about this. We're not professional soldiers, remember. I don't think we should get out of our depth. This is the most scary conversation we've ever had.'

'It may never happen,' Homer said.

Fi looked troubled. 'We've done so well when we stayed in our own district and did what we could there. We can't do everything. This sounds too big.'

'I just don't know if there's any point,' I said, joining in. 'This war looks hopeless. I don't think we're going to make a difference, no matter what we do.'

'Yeah, we're on a hiding to nothing,' Lee said. It was unusual for Lee to have so little fight in him, but he was in one of his depressions. Sooner or later the killing of the soldier at the well had to catch up with him, and I think now it had. Plus he was still really tired from nursing us.

'I remember you guys talking like that the other day,' Kevin said. 'I don't think it's quite that bad.'

I was interested in that.

'What do you know that we don't?' I asked.

'Well, there's good news and bad news, of course. But the good news adds up. This war isn't over yet, not by a long way.'

'Go on,' Homer said eagerly. We were all getting excited. We needed to hear this.

'Don't you listen to the radio any more?' Kevin asked. 'What happened to Corrie's trannie?'

'We ran out of batteries. We left it back in Hell. Anyway, there hadn't been much news of the war at all, and what there was seemed all bad. And then wherever we looked we saw colonists. We've hardly seen any opposition. Except ours.'

'Well, there's been quite a lot going on. They had a radio at the Showground, a secret one, that not even all the prisoners knew about. But Dad listened to it, and he passed on news to me. See, there's not just the international radio stations, there's quite a few guerilla ones, and there's the ones in the Free Zones.'

'What are the Free Zones?'

Kevin looked astonished. 'Geez, you don't know much. There's a few Free Zones.'

'The Outback?'

'Nuh, not really. They control that too, now, because it's so bare they can easily pick up anyone moving around. They use radar and aircraft there. No, the main Free Zones are Cape Martindale, where New Guinea troops landed, and from Newburn right through to the mountains, where the Army had a heap of troops stationed. And Newington and all the Burdekin, where the Kiwis landed. They hold that whole area now.'

There was a pause while we digested all that.

'What else is good news?' I asked.

'The attack on Cobbler's Bay, for one thing. Do you know about that?'

'Yes, tell us,' I said excitedly. 'We saw a bit of it. Well, at least Robyn and Lee heard them, and I saw the smoke.'

'OK, they bombed it pretty heavily. According to the radio they sank seven ships, but there were some casualties taken to Wirrawee Hospital, prisoners who'd been working there, and they said the real figure was three. Whatever, it was quite a success.'

'That might make it more dangerous for us,' Robyn said.

'It could. The rumour at the Showground was that they were putting in more ground-to-air missiles, but that could work in our favour. They wouldn't be expecting a land attack.'

'But they are still using Cobblers?' Fi asked.

'Yeah, apparently. It's a big part of their operation.'

'Let's not get too uptight about it all,' Homer said. 'We're not locked into anything. If we get to Cobbler's Bay and decide it's too much for us, we'll just go quietly away again.'

'Sounds good in theory,' I said. 'But knowing you, Homer . . . I mean, at every birthday party we ever had, you were the one who went around sticking pins in the balloons. Somehow I can't imagine you sneaking quietly away without trying anything.'

'Tell us more about our families,' Robyn said quickly, before I could stir Homer up too much.

Kevin sighed. 'Aw gee,' he said, 'like I told you, they're not too bad. I mean, Ellie, honestly, your Dad, talk about putting pins in balloons, he couldn't walk past a bull without sticking a pin up its backside. Every time a sentry comes near him, he's looking for a fight. What is it with the guy? He's going to get himself in trouble.'

'I don't know what it is with him,' I said. 'If you ever work it out, let me know. He's a mystery to me.'

'And your brother aggravates them, too,' Kevin said to Homer.

'Yeah, the old George doesn't have much sense of humour.'

'How's Tori?' Fi asked.

Victoria, Fi's little sister, got asthma pretty badly.

Kevin made a face. 'Well, there's no Ventolin any more, so she's had a few bad attacks. They got permission to move her and a couple of others into the Show Secretary's Office, because they realised they were allergic to something in the Cattle and Horse Pavilions.'

'Mmm, all that horsehair, and straw, and grass seeds,' Fi said. 'Tori's allergic to everything.'

'She's been better since then,' Kevin said. 'But everyone gets sick at the Showground. It's terrible. You've got no idea. Gastro goes through the place every second day. Like locusts through lucerne. We've had mumps, we've had measles, we've had everything. That's why I volunteered for work parties.'

'Yeah, what's the story with these work parties?' I asked.

'What's the story? They're just a way to get out of the Showground. At first it was all a bit rough and ready but now they're quite organised. You have to be part of a family so they can hold hostages to stop you escaping. You have to have some skills and you have to be fairly fit. That's about all.'

'How come we didn't see anyone we knew around Wirrawee? You were the first person we recognised, and you were a long way from Wirrawee.'

'Yeah, they do that deliberately. Like I said, they're quite organised now. They keep you away from your own district. It's just a security thing. And I think maybe it's because people get too emotional when they see colonists moving into their homes.'

We told Kevin all the other things that had happened to us; and went into more detail about the death of Chris. It was no fun having to recall stuff that I'd started to forget, and badly wanted to forget. But I suppose it was good for us to talk about Chris – we'd never really discussed it among ourselves. His death was so stupid and senseless. Rolling a car when he was drunk – it's the sort of thing that happens in peacetime, and it's bad enough then, but it seemed such a waste when we'd survived so much already. Plus, maybe we all felt a bit guilty about leaving him on his own in Hell, even though that's what he'd wanted.

So we talked about all that, a bit. And that led us on to telling Kevin about Harvey's Heroes: this bunch of middle-aged adults who'd blundered around in the bush, trying to be tough, and nearly getting us wiped out. And afterwards we'd realised that their leader, Major Harvey, had sold out to the enemy.

Kevin got excited then.

'This Major Harvey. What's he look like?'

'Like a forty-four gallon drum,' Homer promptly said.

'With a head on top,' Lee added.

'Like a garden gnome,' Robyn said.

'Like a revolting little pile of sheep poo,' Fi said. I was impressed. At least we'd taught Fi one thing about rural life: what sheep poo looked like.

78

'He's got black hair,' I said to Kevin. I shivered a little as I recalled my first meeting with the Major. We'd stumbled onto his group by chance, and even though we'd felt relieved to be with adults again, I'd sensed from the start that something was wrong about the whole setup. 'He's quite plump in the face. He's got a big nose. And his head, he holds it in a funny way, like he's got a stiff neck or something.'

'Yeah, that's the guy,' Kevin said. He leaned, back nodding his head.

'What do you mean? You saw him?'

'Well, he's not like a personal friend, not my best mate, no. I met him once, before the war. But I've heard plenty about him lately, and I've seen him from a distance a few times.'

'What? That's impossible,' Fi said.

'When was the last time?' Homer asked quickly.

'Oh, gee, about three weeks ago.'

'Oh no!' I cried.

'Are you sure?' Homer asked.

'Yeah, probably a bit less than three weeks. He came round with a group of high-ranking soldiers to have a look at the work we were doing. We all had to stand there seriously and act like we were impressed.'

'We thought we'd wiped him out ages ago,' I explained. 'When we blew up Turner Street we thought we'd got him. That was half the reason we made the attack.'

'Mmm, but remember, you said his car wasn't there that night,' Fi said to Homer.

'Yeah, true, I did say that.'

'So he's alive,' I said. I sat there, stunned. I didn't want to believe it, but I had to. 'Tell us what you know about him,' I finally said to Kevin.

'OK, he's an asshole. What else do you want to know?'

'Everything.'

'Geez, where do I start? He turned up in April, I think. He's from Risdon. He's a teacher, I know that much; in fact, he was Deputy Principal at Risdon High. I remember when we played footie against them. He walked over to me at half-time and yelled at me for tackling one of their players. Reckoned I'd gone in too high. Fair dinks, I thought he was going to hit me. I thought he was a real wanker then, and I know it for sure now. That was the only time I'd met him before the war. When he came to the Show-ground they called us all together and he gave us a lecture on how the invasion wasn't as bad as we might think, and how this country needed a good shake-up, and if we work with these turkeys instead of against them we'll be better off in the long run.

'The soldiers loved it; they were beaming away, but geez, Ellie, if you could have seen your father's face! Lucky Harvey didn't see him or he would have been the first one picked. Cos, yeah, I forgot, you don't know what he's been up to: after that speech they started picking people to be interrogated by him. It got really heavy for a while. Harvey seems to know a lot about Wirrawee. He picked out anyone with military training, plus all the coppers. Some of them were allowed back, if they gave the right answers I guess, but some just disappeared. We only found out a few weeks ago that they've been taken to a maximum-security prison somewhere. But the rumour is that a few of them got shot; like, executed.

'They reckon Harvey's setting himself up to be Governor or something; that he's going to turn him-

80

self into a little dictator. It's probably right. If you'd seen him with these geezers – they were all like the greatest mates, best buddies. It wasn't a pretty sight.'

'After we've finished at Cobbler's Bay we'll go and kill him,' Lee said to me.

I'd given up getting angry with Lee when he talked like that. He did it so often now, whenever he got upset about some bad thing that had happened. He just suddenly said things like he was a robot, programmed to kill, when I knew he wasn't, not at all.

Mind you, I'd gone the same way when I'd seen Corrie in hospital.

Kevin didn't have much to add to what he'd told us. We sat around for another hour or more, talking endlessly about the problems, trying to think of possible solutions. We were depressed to know that Harvey was still on the loose, and Lee's direct approach got quite a bit of support. In the end I got sick of it and went off and started getting lunch ready.

Chapter Nine

Cobbler's Bay was like something out of a war movie. OK, so I'm just a simple little rural who's never been anywhere beyond Stratton in her life. To me, seeing traffic lights was a big thrill. Every time we went to Stratton I grabbed any excuse to ride up and down the escalators, like a six-year-old. So to look out over Cobbler's and see an aircraft carrier, an oil tanker, two small patrol vessels and three container ships was unbelievable. Two long large jetties had been built and all the ships, except the aircraft carrier and the patrol ships, were moored to them. The others were parked at buoys out in the clear water. Prefab sheds had been put up along the shore and huge bitumen loading areas laid down. There were cars and trucks everywhere, and people wandering about in all directions. Around the perimeter was a high barbed-wire fence, very temporary looking, and three tanks just sitting there. There were other things too, like big gun barrels poking out of mounds of dirt: Kevin thought they were the ground-to-air missiles he'd heard about.

One thing was certain though: that air raid had

been a ripper. We could see a long hull over near the rocks to our left, a destroyer maybe, that was a complete wreck, jammed upside down. Lee pointed to a shape we could see shimmering under the water near the heads that looked like another large ship, totally submerged. To the left of the prefabs was the wreckage of a group of buildings; nothing but blackened rafters and a few sheets of torn metal flapping in the wind. Over in the bush even further to the left were two huge craters of torn earth and shattered trees where they must have missed their aim. It looked like the beginnings for a new woodchip industry.

The only entrance to the new port of Cobbler's Bay was a gate with a hut for sentries, and a barrier that they raised and lowered by hand. I'm sure the US Marines would have done the whole thing better, with electric fences and laser beams and electronic security checks, but there was none of that stuff. It looked like it had all been thrown together quickly for the least amount of money possible. This was definitely not twenty-first century technology.

Still, it was formidable enough. It scared the hell out of me. When we were younger, and Dad wasn't around, we sometimes shot up a wasps' nest for fun. You'd get what you hoped was a safe distance away and then empty a .22 magazine or a couple of shells into it. It got pretty wild at times. This place was bigger and meaner than any wasps' nest, and I wasn't in such a hurry to stir it up.

It did make me angry. Cobbler's Bay was among the most beautiful places on Earth. Well, seeing I'd never been beyond Stratton, perhaps I couldn't really go around saying that. 'Yes, ladies and gentlemen, in my vast experience of international travel, after

83

exploring every corner of the globe, I can honestly tell you that Cobbler's Bay is one of the seven scenic wonders of the world.'

But it was beautiful. It was one of those places where the hills meet the sea, so you have the best of them both. There was quite good cover down to the beach, because it was heavily forested right to the road, and the road curved around the bay. Once you cross the road you take half a dozen steps and you're on the sand: fine white sand that runs through your fingers and tickles your toes. You can walk straight on and enter the water, or you can turn left or right and follow the sand around to the rocks. Either way you know you're in a kind of heaven, because of the secret green woods in the background and the rich blue sky above and the dancing blue sea ahead.

The weather always seemed perfect at Cobbler's Bay.

I know it's greedy of me to want it all to myself but even in peacetime when we drove to Cobbler's for a swim and a picnic, I resented finding other people there. I'm sure they resented us, too. So to come in wartime and find ugly growths all over it and great monstrous ships sitting on its innocent water, like big metal leeches, made me both angry and unhappy. I wanted to do something about it but couldn't even imagine how we might. For once, this enemy fortress looked way beyond our capabilities. Those ships and jetties and even the prefab buildings seemed solid and settled and, after all, what were we? Just a bunch of kids, a bunch of amateurs.

'I've only got one idea so far,' Homer said, unexpectedly.

I was deeply impressed. While I sat there thinking black depressed angry thoughts Homer was already figuring out possibilities.

'What?'

'With the bush so close to their buildings we could light a bushfire as a distraction. They'd have to put all their energies into fighting it, because if the wind's blowing in the right direction it'd come roaring down the hill here and land on top of them.'

'That's not a bad idea,' Robyn said thoughtfully. 'It's quite likely it'd end up as more than a distraction. It could do most of our work for us. It could easily wipe those buildings out. Once it jumped the road there's nothing to stop it.'

'As long as we don't burn ourselves up,' Fi said nervously.

'What do we actually want to destroy?' I asked. 'I mean, we're not going to be able to do anything about those ships, are we?'

'Not the ones out there at anchor,' Lee said. 'But the ones at the jetties are possible.'

'That's an oil tanker, Ellie,' Homer said. 'You're the petrol head, aren't you?'

'Mmm, love it. Just point me towards it and give me a box of matches.'

I felt a fluttering in the stomach when I said that though. I never felt comfortable with jokes about the things we'd done.

We sat there looking at it all. The bushfire idea was cute but I couldn't see much beyond it. A bushfire wouldn't hurt the ships, unless we fluked a few lucky sparks landing on the tanker. As a distraction, it might get us into the place, but there was a good chance it wouldn't. And then we had to get away again afterwards. That was the most important thing, and might well be the hardest.

'Did Jock teach you about underwater bombs?' Homer asked Kevin. 'Like, depth charges?'

'No, hey, it wasn't a uni degree, just a few quick lessons.'

I heard a rumbling noise and looked up. A convoy was coming down the hill. There were two green Army trucks in the lead but they were followed by a motley collection of removal vans, tabletops, semi-trailers and petrol tankers. A lot of them had the names of local companies and even big national companies on them. Another Army truck brought up the rear.

We watched anxiously, to see what the routines were for getting through the gate. They pulled up at the entrance and a group of soldiers, eight of them, spilled out of the nearest hut and went trotting along the sides of the convoy. They checked each truck that could have concealed people, ignoring only the table-tops and tankers. It wasn't an incredibly rigorous search, but that wasn't much consolation to us because we had no idea how we could get ourselves aboard the trucks in the first place. There was no need for them to search much if they knew that the convoy hadn't stopped anywhere.

When dusk moved in, we moved out. We went back into the hills to find somewhere to stay. And the way we played it that first night became a routine that we stuck to for the next six days. We camped in a different place each night, for security, and posted a sentry, but by day we spied on Cobbler's Bay and talked about tactics. I have to admit though that the main reason we stayed, the secret reason, was nothing to do with attacking the enemy. It was because Lee, without a word to anyone, went and broke into a holiday shack and came back with an armful of fishing gear.

Well, did that set us off. The little collection of lines, hooks and sinkers gave us the best time we'd had since the invasion. It was like we had ourselves a beach holiday. We could hardly bear to wait for evening so we could start our fishing trips. We fished the mouths of the rivers, soon settling on one place that was both pretty and reliable – and safe. And the fish practically ripped the lines out of our hands. For bait we picked up worms, witchetty grubs and beetles during the day, and with them we caught flathead, bream, mullet and a few other varieties we didn't recognise. I suppose with no one having fished the area for so many months it was easy pickings.

The fishing itself was fun but the major thing was that we suddenly had plenty of food again and it was a change from the monotony that we'd put up with for so very long. Our food supplies had been getting horribly low. We all ate a lot less these days, and we were all nicely slim except Robyn, who was too slim, but now she started to put on weight again. At around two or three o'clock each morning we lit a little fire and either fried our catch straight away or waited with mouths watering for the flames to burn down to coals, so we could bake the fish in them. After months of being starved for fresh meat it seemed that now we couldn't get enough. We never got sick of it. I'll never forget that juicy white fresh fish flesh, the way it fell away from the bones, the way the hot moist flavour gave me new strength and energy.

If you are what you eat, then after a few days of that diet I could have swum the Pacific Ocean.

We always cooked extra, so we could have some cold during the day.

We'd been living like this for four days before we found the weakness in the Cobbler's Bay security arrangements. Homer always said that there'd be a weakness somewhere; we just had to be patient. He was right, although it was only by chance that we picked it up. We were looking for a new fishing spot and at about ten o'clock at night we crossed the road to the bay. Robyn went ahead to check that the road was clear. Instead of calling us on, as we expected, she came slithering back, looking alarmed. 'There's a truck at the corner,' she hissed.

'What doing?'

'Nothing. And it's got no lights. It's just sitting there.'

We all crept up to have a look. We could see it easily, silhouetted against the moonlight. It was a van of some kind, about a four-tonner. After being witnesses to a horrible massacre when Harvey's Heroes had been sucked into attacking an abandoned tank, we weren't about to go rushing up to this thing to investigate. So we left it there and went to another river for our fishing.

At dawn, though, Homer and I sneaked back to check it again. It was still there, looking cold and lonely. We decided to stay for a while and see what happened and sure enough, at 9.30, we heard the grinding of gears as another vehicle climbed the hill towards us. We shrank back into the bushes as this one went past. It was a tow truck, with a couple of soldiers on the back riding shotgun. We wriggled into a better position to watch as the tow truck reached the van and began a three point turn that ended up as a six-point turn in the narrow road.

When it was in position in front of the van everybody got out: the two soldiers, and two men from the cab who were dressed in oil-stained overalls and carried little bags. They looked like mechanics always look: I think it's the way mechanics slouch that gives them their special look. The soldiers went for a bit of a prowl, walking along the road one way, then the other, while the mechanics started poking round in the engine of the van.

But the interesting thing was that nobody thought to look in the back section.

After half an hour, when the mechanics had tried and failed many times to start the van, they hooked it up to the tow truck. A soldier got in the driver's seat to steer, and away they went.

They still hadn't looked in the back.

We couldn't wait to get back to Fi and Kevin, who were spying on the base, to find out what had happened when the tow truck got to Cobbler's Bay.

Chapter Ten

'Yeah, they just went straight through,' Kevin said.

'You sure?' I asked.

'No, I was asleep; what do you bloody think?' Kevin lost his temper, as he did quite often these days. He'd been through a lot, I kept reminding myself. So had we, but maybe what he'd been through was worse than what we'd been through. Or maybe he couldn't cope with it as well as we did. That was no shame, everyone's different; it was just hard to imagine anyone coping with it worse than me, because I don't think I coped with it well at all.

'They went straight through,' Fi said quietly. 'When they got to the barrier they gave a wave to the bloke on duty and he lifted it. They towed it to that big shed on the right; the one with the petrol thingies outside. We think that's a maintenance shed for vehicles, and the one next to it's a generator shed.'

'So that's a way we might be able to get in,' Homer said thoughtfully.

'We can't wait six months for a truck to conveniently break down,' Lee said.

'We could maybe make one break down,' Robyn said. 'Couldn't we?'

'How?'

Three of us asked that question at once and no one had an answer. A flat tyre wouldn't be enough and it was hard to think of any other possibility. Still, it was maybe a step forward.

I took Kevin out to look for explosives. We might have to make a proper bomb this time and, according to Jock, we'd be able to find plenty of ingredients in sheds and farm buildings. I hoped he was right and I hoped he was wrong. If he were wrong, we might then have an excuse to call this crazy thing off. It seemed to be building up so quickly into an enormous operation. I'm sure heroes don't go around thinking: Hope I can find a good excuse to get out of this. I wanted to be a hero but never seemed to quite get it right.

We wandered out into a different part of the country. There weren't so many colonists in this area yet; there were still a number of empty houses. Only the best places were occupied. It was easy to tell which were in use, and to give them a wide berth. The good thing was that a lot of clearing had been going on right through this district before the war, and that made it a certainty that there'd been a lot of blasting. Cockies love messing with explosives, and any big stubborn tree stump was a good enough excuse. It's amazing that there aren't thousands of farmers walking round with only half their fingers, but I never heard of anyone blowing himself up. Dad had a few goes with gelignite when I was younger but Mum talked him into giving it a miss. I wished now that he'd taught me how to use it, and then, remembering that I was meant to be looking for excuses, was glad he hadn't.

We had a mixed morning. The first farm had nothing, the second had a dozen bags of ammonium nitrate – nearly half a tonne – and a couple of 44's of diesel. We decided to leave it all there while we checked other places. The third farm had been thoroughly cleaned out. The fourth was a big place but old and run down. We went straight to the sheds, as we had everywhere else. To my disgust, we walked straight into a miniature battlefield. There were three skeletons in the machinery shed, their clothes still intact, except where ripped by bullets. There wasn't much left of the bodies, mainly bones.

There seemed to have been a full-scale shooting war. We saw many empty shells on the floor and there was damage all around the big dark shed: holes in the walls, shelves shattered by bullets, even the steel plates on the old tractor and header had holes in them. It was frightening to see how much damage had been done. One person had been hiding behind the header, one had been behind a heavy wooden workbench, but the other body was out in the open.

I cried for a bit. I seemed to be doing more of that these days. And there's one thing about Kevin: when a girl's upset, really upset, you see Kevin at his best. He was shaken by the sight of the bodies, of course, but when he saw me in tears he managed to hold himself together and give me a bit of TLC. We'd always looked after each other fairly well I suppose, even at the worst times.

'Come on, Ellie,' he said, giving me a hug. 'You've seen worse than this. You'll be right.'

'Yeah, I know,' I said, sniffling. 'But you never get

used to it. These poor people, just trying to look after their land.'

'Yeah, it's a rotten business.'

'And no one to bury them or have a funeral service or anything.'

'Well, when the war's over maybe that sort of thing'll get done.'

I didn't answer that, just sniffled for a bit longer. Finally I disentangled myself and said, 'Come on, let's go. There's nothing we can do here and it's giving me the willies.'

'No, wait,' Kevin said. 'This is the perfect sort of place for what we want. Let's check it out.'

I was reluctant but he insisted. Occasionally Kevin had these bursts of strength. We did a quick search of the machinery shed but found nothing and with some relief went to the other buildings. We went past some concrete runs that had been built quite recently and fenced off for working dogs. We ignored the skeletons of the poor desperate dogs who'd died in them and, fifty metres further along, entered an old dark hut. And there we found what Kevin had been looking for.

'Wowee,' he said. 'Look at this!' He had a wooden box, about the same size as a box of shotgun cartridges, and he was holding a small shiny aluminium tube, maybe three centimetres long and five or six millimetres in diameter. It was blocked at one end but open at the other.

'What is it?' I asked.

'Plain detonator. Told you we'd find some. Look, there are dozens of them.'

I picked one up and handled it curiously. It had DANGER and EXPLOSIVE written on its side, but it seemed harmless enough.

'Is this all we need?' I asked.

'Well, the ammonium nitrate and the diesel, obviously. But they're not a problem. And the fuse.'

'We could make our own.'

'That's what you think. Anyway, they're sure to have some here. They should have everything stored in separate sheds, but most farmers don't bother. They'll have safety fuse somewhere, which'll be better than anything we'd make. Look, here we go.'

He pulled down a roll of grey–white cord, about the size of the cord in my board shorts, but with black tarry-looking stuff running through it.

'Is that it?'

'Yeah, I'd say so. It's gunpowder wrapped in a waterproof cover, more or less. We shove this in the detonator, then we'll get some pipe, to make our miniature bomb. There'll be some in that machinery shed. And a hacksaw, to cut it.'

By the time we left that farm of death we had enough material, as far as I could tell, to avenge the people who'd died there. Not only did we have the pipe and the detonators and the fuse, we'd also found another six bags of ammonium nitrate. That was three-quarters of a tonne altogether. If we could find a way to blow the lot up in Cobbler's Bay then, according to Kevin, we would cause a tidal wave.

It still seemed a dream to me, though. I couldn't imagine any way we could actually do it. But excited by everything we'd seen that day – even the bodies, in a sick sort of way – Kevin and I talked flat out as we walked back to join the others.

'Look,' I said finally, 'suppose we got a truck loaded with this stuff onto the jetty and set it off. How would that be?'

'I'm not sure. Obviously it'd be a huge bang, probably enough to cause a lot of damage in ships that were close enough to it, and wreck the jetty. But if you could get that truck on board the ship, down in the bowels of the ship then, because it was in an enclosed space, you'd blow the ship to smithereens.'

'Seriously? The whole ship?'

'Yeah! What do you think? This Texas Bay thing, you don't realise: that one ship blew up the whole harbour, the town, and I think all the other ships that were in port with it. This is bigger than a fart in a bathtub, you know.'

'I'm starting to realise that.'

The makings of a plan were coming together, but with a few vital flaws. I ran through the way I saw it so far, to Kevin: 'OK, a truck breaks down. It's there all night and we load it with three-quarters of a tonne of anfo. One or two of us hide in it. That should be cool, because if it's a big enough truck they wouldn't notice a bit of extra weight. Besides, mechanics probably wouldn't know if the truck's meant to be empty or full. They tow the truck into the harbour. A bush-fire starts. Thank God it's been dry again lately. The fire roars down the hill and distracts everybody. We get the truck onto a ship, light the fuse and get out. Bang! End of story, we're legends, and we sell the movie rights the moment the war is over.'

Kevin didn't say anything. Maybe it was still sounding like a daydream to him, too.

'Did you spot the flaws?' I asked him.

He laughed. 'Just a few. How do we make the truck break down? How do we get the truck onto the ship? How do we escape afterwards? That's three for starters.'

'I think we can at least get away afterwards. If Homer and I go in with the truck, well, we're both good swimmers. We could dive into Cobbler's Bay and swim right to the other side.'

Kevin brightened up a bit. I knew why, of course: for the first time he'd had a glimpse of hope, the hope that he wouldn't be one of the people doing the dangerous stuff. I wished I had the same hope, but I'm a very logical person. Swimming was our best chance, and only two of us could swim big distances.

When we got back to the others we found, to my secret fear, that there might be a solution to the second problem, too. Two convoys of container trucks had gone through during the day and the containers had been loaded straight into the hold of a big cargo ship that had come in that morning. It was now tied up at a jetty, next to the oil tanker.

'I'm sure there'll be more convoys,' Homer said excitedly. 'The ship swallowed up those two lots like an elephant eating peanuts. And an oil tanker next to it. Oh Ellie, doesn't it make your mouth water?'

'It makes me water all right,' I said crudely. 'But not from my mouth.'

'But how the hell do we make a truck break down?' Lee worried aloud. He was pacing around, in and out of the trees. We were in quite thick bush, where we could just see splinters of Cobbler's Bay. Robyn was lying on her back eating stale jellybeans that she'd found in a holiday house, Fi was gazing out at the port, Homer was sitting against a tree looking at Lee, and Kevin and I were trying to concentrate on a game of racing patience.

'What can go wrong with a motor vehicle?' Lee asked a small friendly gum tree. 'Flat tyre, radiator boiling, run out of oil, fuel problems, battery, ignition, alternator, carbie, brakes. Oh, it's too frustrating. Why don't the rest of you try to think of something instead of leaving it all to me?'

This was so unfair no one even bothered to answer.

Kevin played a two onto a four and gave a quick furtive glance, to see if I'd noticed. I noticed all right. That tiny little action made me furious. I threw my entire pack into a blackberry bush, screamed a string of swear words at Kevin, kicked his cards over and stormed away through the trees.

Guess we were all pretty brittle.

Chapter Eleven

We started the night with our own little convoy, and a very odd convoy it was. Though we still seemed a long way off a workable plan, we had decided to at least take the next step.

'Every journey begins with a single step,' Lee said gravely, trying to sound like an ancient philosopher.

This journey began with a roll actually. We wanted to shift the ammonium nitrate and the diesel and hide it in the bush near the road, so if anything happened we'd be in a position to swing into action. So we rounded up a mob of wheelbarrows, one for each of us, to collect the bags. It took a while to get six barrows and then a while longer to find a bicycle pump, as all the tyres were flat. Then the hard work began. We had to get not just the bags that Kevin and I had found but also another cache that Robyn and Lee found while looking for wheelbarrows. This was twenty bags, another three-quarters of a tonne, give or take. Each bag was forty kilos. We sure had the makings now.

Pushing wheelbarrows through bush at night is a shocking job. They don't make four-wheel-drive barrows, that's the problem. We didn't dare use the road at all. We hadn't seen any patrols in this district but that's probably because we weren't looking for them. We'd kept away from the road most of the time. Our convoy soon broke up and we found ourselves going at our own various speeds, passing or overtaking each other from time to time.

To keep my mind occupied while I was lurching along with my barrow I thought about our truck problem. It was a good distraction from the hard heavy work. Only when the barrow tipped over, as frequently happened, did I have to come back to reality. But try as I might, I couldn't think of anything that would have the slightest chance of success. Spray oil over the windscreen? Put a bullet through the engine? Jump on the back of a prime mover and pull out the air brakes? There were so many good reasons why those things wouldn't work, and no good reason why they would.

'OK,' I thought. 'Suppose I dig a hole in the road, lie in it, and when a truck goes over the top, I'll reach up, grab the undercarriage, haul myself up and then cut a few lines and drop off again. Should work, no worries.' I suggested it to Fi, who was following me with her barrow, and for a few moments she thought I was serious. Sometimes I really did wonder about Fi.

Then Kevin left me for a few minutes at one of the farmhouses and came back with a white object in his hands, the size of a tennis ball. It was hard to see it clearly in the darkness.

'What have you got?' I asked.

'Stove timer.'

I was a bit surprised but recovered well. 'What's

the matter, your boiled eggs not quite right for breakfast?'

'Yeah, that's right. Listen, there were a few vehicles round this place, weren't there?'

'Mmm, I think so. There's the tractor, and a couple of ag bikes in that green shed. And wasn't there a paddock basher over by the tank?'

'Let's have a look. Leave the barrows for a sec.'

'We can't use a vehicle to take the ammonium down to the road, if that's what you're thinking. Too noisy.'

Kevin didn't bother to answer. I was way off the point. He led me to the paddock basher. It was an old Falcon ute, white, but with a lot of rust, like all the cars that lived close to the coast. And, like all paddock bashers, its keys were in it. Kevin gave them a turn, getting nothing but a tired whine as the battery opened one eye, then went straight back to sleep.

'Give it a push,' he said. He had the driver's door open and started pushing from his side. I still didn't know what this was about but I put my head down and shoved. There wasn't much of a slope so it was hard work. But after fifty metres we were on a roll and a few seconds after that Kevin leapt into the driver's seat and gave it the gun. The engine coughed into life. Kevin brought it to a halt and as I arrived by his window he said, 'Hop in. We're going for a drive.'

'Kevin! This is too dangerous. We can't go fanging around the countryside. If anyone hears us . . .'

'Stop treating me like an idiot, Ellie,' was all he said.

I bit my bottom lip and went round to the passenger side. The door wouldn't open, even with Kevin trying from his side. So I got in the back, the tray. We

U-turned and went along the flat and up the hill, past the silent house, through a gate (which I had to open) and further up an old dirt track till we were probably about halfway up the hill. There Kevin turned the Falcon again, to face downhill, and got out, switching the engine off. He lifted the hood as I came round to the other side. He had a pair of pliers and he'd parked so that he was getting maximum moonlight. With his pliers he cut the lead between the coil and the distributor. I watched, fascinated. He was obviously in no mood to answer questions, but I didn't mind. When the lead was severed, he reconnected it through the back of the timer, each end coming in from opposite sides, so that the lead was now detoured through it. Then he rotated the dial on the timer, setting it for five minutes.

'OK,' he said, 'let's start it up.' He jumped in and turned the key again but the battery was still too flat to turn the engine. With the ute pointing downhill we only needed to give it one shove and it rolled quickly away. Kevin stepped gracefully in, put it in gear and let out the clutch. The engine leapt into life.

I heard a noise behind me and spun round in sudden panic. Homer was looming up out of the darkness.

'What are you doing?' he asked irritably, as Kevin left the ute engine running and stood next to the vehicle, gazing at the bonnet. 'Leaving us to wheel the barrows? You're making enough noise.'

'Fair go,' I said, annoyed. 'We've done our share. Kevin's working out some idea to do with our attack on Cobbler's.'

Homer became a little more interested. 'What?'

'I don't know. He's attached an oven timer between the coil and the distributor.'

'An oven timer? Serious? Is he cooking a cake in there? Kevin, what are you doing?'

He strode down the hill to the ute. I followed. As we got there Kevin said, without looking at us, 'Wait. You'll see. I hope.'

We waited about two minutes. Just as Homer started saying, 'I really don't think we should be making so much noise . . .' the engine of the Falcon cut out. There was no warning. One moment it was throbbing away in good health, the next the cold night air was completely silent. Homer and I looked at Kev in astonishment. 'How did you do that?' Homer asked. 'Just with an oven timer?'

'While you were mucking around in Physics I was paying attention,' Kevin said proudly. He looked absolutely delighted. 'All I've done is create another circuit, to go with the one that's already under the bonnet. The circuit I created is regulated by the timer, OK? So when the timer reaches zero, that circuit cuts out, and takes the whole engine with it.'

I was dumbstruck. I gazed at Kevin admiringly. 'That's so simple,' I said at last. 'And so clever.'

'But how do we get it attached to a truck?' Homer asked. 'Cos that's what you've got in mind, isn't it? To fake a breakdown?'

'Yeah, exactly. And there is a way. What we have to do is create an obstacle for a convoy, so they stop for a few minutes. While they're stopped I'll sneak out, stick the timer on a truck, and set it for whatever time we decide, five minutes, ten, twenty. All I've got to do is make sure it's a petrol engine not a diesel. Twenty minutes later, when the truck breaks down, they won't connect it with the hold-up way back along the road. If it's night-time, and if the drivers

102

aren't good mechanics, I think they'll give up pretty quickly. I don't think they'll be able to figure it out, and they won't want to spend hours looking. It ought to work.'

'Yes,' I said. 'And while we're loading the fertiliser we can take the timer out and make it look like something else caused the breakdown.'

'Yeah, exactly,' Kevin said again.

A wave of fear hit me as I realised that we were steadily solving all our problems. That meant only one thing: that we would go for it. It made me quite dizzy. Dear God, was it possible? We had already reached too far, tested our luck too often. Instead of quitting while we were ahead we were doing the opposite. I didn't say another word to the boys, couldn't. I went back down the hill, got my wheelbarrow, filled it with another heavy load and began another long push back to our ammonium dump. It was all very well for Kevin. He wouldn't be the one going right into Cobbler's Bay. Why did it always have to be me who took the biggest risks? I was scared and that made me angry.

Down at the pile of fertiliser bags I met Fi. She was sitting in her barrow.

'Oh Ellie,' she sighed, 'why's everything so hard? I can't push this thing another inch, I swear.'

'Huh. You think you've got problems.'

I emptied my barrow and collapsed into it beside her, then told her Kevin's plan. As we talked we heard another convoy coming, and soon we could see the big semis through the trees, rolling along pretty fast, considering they were on dimmed lights. Nearly all of them carried containers and the speed at which the trucks went made me think the boxes must be empty. There were fourteen of them and an escort truck at each end.

'How would we stop them to put the timer on?' Fi asked.

'I don't know,' I said crossly. 'I don't want to know. We must be mad. This is much too big for us.'

'Oh, I'm not so sure,' Fi said, as if looking at a difficult line in *Macbeth*, when we studied it last year.

'OK, go on, talk me into doing it and getting killed, and then you can feel guilty for the rest of your life.'

It was a cruel thing to say and almost as soon as I'd finished saying it I was apologising. But I'd really hurt Fi, and it took me ten minutes to get her to talk again.

'I was just going to say that little people can do big things,' she finally said huffily.

'I suppose so,' I said humbly.

'It looks big,' she said, with a bit more warmth, 'because those ships and trucks and jetties are so big. But it's really just people, and they'll be like people everywhere. They'll be careless and they'll be lazy and they'll make mistakes. But you'll be totally alert and concentrating, and that gives you an advantage.'

'Mmm.' I was anxious to have her forget what I'd said, but I was also anxious to believe in what she was saying.

'It's a good plan, Ellie, it really is. We can out-trick these people, and that's all we have to do. Stop thinking about causing a huge explosion; that's got nothing to do with it. It's just a matter of being smarter than a few dozen soldiers.'

A few hundred would have been closer, but I pressed my lips together. Homer and Kevin arrived at that moment, with Lee and Robyn, who they'd found bringing back the last bags of fertiliser. We were all exhausted but Homer wasn't interested in that.

'I think we should do it tonight,' he said.

'Geez, Homer, it's two o'clock in the morning.'

'Yes, but this ship loading containers is perfect for us, and it might be nearly full now. We've got to get it while they're putting them in the holds, before they start stacking them on the decks. If Ellie and I can get in a container with all these bags, and get put on board, we've got the bomb to end all bombs. How else can we get on board if not in a container?'

'There mightn't be another convoy tonight.'

'Yeah, but there might be. They seem to have been running night and day.'

A long silence followed.

'Have you worked out how to stop the trucks?' I asked.

'Robyn has.'

I looked at Robyn. Seemed like she was going to be the one to give me my death warrant.

'OK, what's the deal?'

'It's got to look natural, unsuspicious,' she said. 'Like, a tree across the road's too obvious. They'd be looking for an ambush.'

'Agreed.'

'Well, Ellie, isn't it time you had a chance to get reacquainted with your very best friends?'

Chapter Twelve

It was a big paddock and well stocked, probably a hundred and fifty head. It looked like it had been overstocked before the invasion, because the paddock was dotted with sad little piles of wool and bones. Foxes, feral dogs, wedge-tails, disease; they all would have contributed. The sheep left alive were in poor condition, toddling around feeling sorry for themselves. There certainly wasn't much feed left – it looked OK from a distance but it was poor dry grass, no value in it.

Being so big, though, the paddock was hard to muster. These sheep hadn't seen humans for a long time and they were getting a bit feral themselves. A dozen times as we flushed them out of blackberries, and from behind trees, I wished that we had a dog to help us. Instead we had Lee and Robyn and Fi, who were as much use as a couple of untrained budgies. We didn't need all the sheep, of course, which was lucky, or else we'd still be there, cursing and sweating and trying to make them do what we wanted. We ended up with maybe a hundred and twenty.

We got them out on the road after thirty minutes

work. Then it was a matter of droving them along to a woody section of bush, and holding them till a convoy could be heard. That might sound easy but it wasn't. As soon as the sheep got out the gate they spread along the sides of the road and started eating. We pushed them along slowly but once we got them out of the open country and into the bushy section, the feed along the road disappeared. This upset the sheep and they revved up and started forward to find better stuff. Kevin and I had to head them off fast and then, with Homer at the rear to back us up, persuade them to stay right where they were. We needed that bush for cover, so the sheep had to stay out of open country.

Robyn was dressed entirely in black and had blackened her face as well, with shoe polish from a farmhouse. Shoe polish was one thing that never seemed to get looted. A few months ago we would have thought that blacking faces, wearing camouflage and synchronising watches was a bit over the top, Hollywood movie style, but now we did these things as a matter of course.

I'm not too sure how Robyn got the job of cutting the wire and attaching the timer. The obvious person was Kevin and at one stage he seemed to be volunteering, but somehow Robyn was left holding the pliers. There was a bit of mumbling about Robyn being good with her hands, and Kevin being needed to hold the sheep until the trucks appeared, but I think we all knew that this kind of thing just wasn't Kevin's style. He didn't have the nerve for it. It soon became clear that he didn't want to do it and Robyn said she would and so it was settled.

I think Robyn was always quite keen to do things that didn't directly hurt anyone.

When the sheep settled down and Kevin and I were holding them OK, Homer and Lee disappeared for a few minutes in the direction of the backpacks. I didn't think anything of it until they returned. When I next saw them they were each holding a sawn-off shotgun. This was a whole new move that I hadn't anticipated.

'What are you doing?' I asked angrily.

Homer looked away, guiltily, but Lee was cool enough.

'Don't be stupid about this, Ellie,' he said. 'We're going to give Robyn cover.'

'How do you mean?'

'Ellie, this is dangerous stuff, really dangerous, let's not kid ourselves. These convoys are guarded front and back. If anyone comes up behind Robyn while she's working on the circuit she's got no hope. Well, she will have a hope now, because we'll shoot them.'

'Oh yeah, and what happens then?'

'We all melt away into the bush. They might fire after us but they won't chase us through the bush in the dark. We call the plan off and go somewhere else. We won't have lost anything but we will have saved Robyn's life.'

'Shouldn't Robyn have a say in all this?'

Lee hesitated. 'Yeah, OK, fair enough. Robyn, what do you think? You want cover or not?'

Robyn didn't look at any of us. From out of her dark face a pair of white eyes gazed away through the trees. I was puzzled that she was taking so long to answer. I'd thought that she'd have told them pretty fast what to do with their guns.

'Yes,' she said at last, still not looking at us, 'I think I would like cover, thank you.'

I didn't say anything, just walked back to the sheep, trying to keep my face controlled. I didn't like this situation. I also don't like being surprised by people, especially Robyn, whom I thought I'd figured out a long time ago.

I also like getting my own way.

'What do you think of these guns?' I asked Fi, looking for support.

'I think they're right,' she said. 'Robyn'd be a sitting duck otherwise. If she got shot we'd never forgive ourselves.'

I gave up then. I still thought that it was stupid: that if we ever got involved in a shooting war we'd be massacred. But I'd been outvoted.

We waited about forty minutes and then heard the unmistakeable low rasping buzz of a convoy. 'Oh God,' I thought, 'here we go.' It was still a long way off but it got louder quite quickly. At one stage I almost convinced myself that it wasn't a convoy at all but a low-flying aircraft. Sound does funny things at night.

'We're mad,' I said to Fi.

She gave her little nervous smile.

'Do you think anyone'll ever know about the things we do?' I asked her.

'I know what you mean,' she said. 'It'd be awful if they didn't. I want my parents to know I've tried really hard to help and to do brave things. I'd hate it if they didn't know that.'

I felt better that she understood, that she felt the same way.

We were on a fairly straight stretch of road so we could see the lights of the trucks quite a way off. But these ones surprised me because they were using parking lights. It was a while later that I realised it was a good sign; they must be getting more nervous about air attacks. Up until then we'd seen a lot of convoys with dimmed headlights but never one on parkers only. It meant also that they travelled slowly, which was good news for the sheep.

Kevin at one end of the mob of sheep, and I at the other, were the only people left on the road now. We shook the sheep up and got them onto the bitumen as much as we were able. They weren't all that keen but we had them spread out enough to take up lots of space. At the last moment we slipped into the trees and joined the other four. We heard the brakes of the first truck come on and saw the little parking lights come to a halt. Other trucks quickly stopped behind it, as far back as we could see. It was a big convoy. I saw Robyn sneak forward, followed by Homer and Lee with their guns. I felt sick. I heard truck doors slam, footsteps, voices yelling at the sheep. We figured on having a bit of time, as these guys probably wouldn't have a lot of experience with sheep, plus the sheep only understood English. And the soldiers wouldn't want to leave them wandering all over the road, where they'd be a hazard to other convoys.

A bright spotlight suddenly came on, and swung around towards us. They might have been nervous of planes but they weren't fools either. They'd obviously weighed up the odds and decided the spotlight was worth the risk. Fi and I silently went to ground. I couldn't see Kevin, who was somewhere behind us, but I assumed he was eating dirt, too. I lay there, my heart thudding madly. The sheep were bleating hysterically up on the road, and starting to move away from the soldiers. I could hear the sharp trotters start to accelerate again, tap-dancing on the bitumen. We'd had a cattle stampede, ages ago; seemed that now we were having a sheep stampede. I giggled, and saw Fi's right eye peep at me, startled. That startled me, then: I hadn't thought I'd giggled so loudly. I started worrying that the soldiers had heard.

The spotlight continued to search. It was so bright that it seemed to burn the air, to burn the branches and leaves. A small bird erupted out of a nest to my right and flew away in a wild panicky ungraceful rush. I could see by a reflection in the sky that there was another spotlight scanning the other side of the road.

Then the shooting started. I nearly lifted off the ground with sheer fright. I'm amazed my hair didn't turn white; it felt funny, all frizzy. Shots were being fired at a regular rate, one after another, on both sides of the road. At first they were away to our left but we could tell they were gradually moving closer. I began to realise what was happening: the soldiers, suspicious, were firing methodically into the bush, just to discourage anyone who might be lurking, waiting to attack. I pressed myself down even lower, feeling the cold earth on my lips and forehead. A bullet blasted across my head with horrifying speed and force, rushing away into the darkness. I hoped there weren't too many koalas out there. I was worried sick about Homer and Lee and Robyn but there was nothing we could do, and so far I hadn't heard the shouts of discovery you'd expect if they'd been spotted. I didn't dare move.

The firing continued for several minutes. They must have had tonnes of ammo. They certainly weren't taking risks. Then suddenly I heard a truck

111

engine cough into life. Then another, then another. They merged into a loud purring and I heard the heavy clunks of gears engaging. The convoy was on the move.

I wasn't though. I lay there, waiting for the night to become silent and clear again. But before it did, Homer and Lee arrived, two big dark clumsy figures crashing through the scrub in front of me. Fi and I hauled ourselves up, shaking off twigs and leaves and dirt.

'What happened?' I begged them.

Kevin arrived, behind me.

'What the hell happened?' he echoed.

'They were just so paranoid,' Homer said. Both he and Lee looked wild-eyed with excitement. 'We couldn't do anything. Once they started popping off bullets we hid behind trees and hoped to God they wouldn't come looking for us.'

'Did they see you?' Kevin asked.

'No, no, they were just being cautious.'

'Where's Robyn?'

'I don't know. Up on the road I hope. We didn't dare look out from behind our trees. I don't think she was caught or we would have heard. But I don't know if she managed to get the timer on. It would have been hard.'

We ploughed our way up to the road. There was no sign of Robyn, no sheep either. I was starting to panic. Then I saw a pair of white eyes, and the gleam of white teeth, coming towards us. It proved to be not a wolf, but Robyn.

We engulfed her with questions and emotion.

'Wait! Stop!' she said. 'Let's walk and talk. We can't waste time.' We hurried along behind her, like a gaggle of geese. The first thing we saw was the paddock where they'd put the sheep. Both Homer and I stopped in disgust.

'We can't leave them in there!' Homer exploded.

'We haven't got time,' Lee said.

'We'll have to make time,' I said. 'These sheep helped us a lot tonight. We owe them.'

Homer and I ran to the gate and opened it. I realised we'd have to fake it, so the sheep looked like they'd escaped by themselves.

I called out to Lee: 'See if you can knock the fence down somewhere. Make it look like the sheep did it themselves.'

Grumbling, he went off to do it. Homer and I ran into the paddock and exhausted ourselves rounding the stupid animals up again. The paddock was very small, with no feed at all, and thirty starving tukidales in it already, to go with the merino crosses we'd been droving. We ran them out of the gate so fast that it's a wonder they didn't smother themselves. A few did go down but they got themselves up again. We let them spread out along the sides of the road and graze where they wanted. The road was much wider here and with the sheep off the bitumen I hoped the convoys would let them stay there. Whatever, there was no more we could do for them. At least they'd have full bellies for their next adventure.

We ran off after Robyn and Fi, who were further up the road, talking.

'So what happened?' I asked Robyn, panting.

She was grinning. I got the impression she'd enjoyed herself, despite the danger.

'It was insane.'

'OK, OK, I believe you; but what happened?'

113

'Well, they stopped and I picked one right away, a semi with a container on the back. It was only a short one, about six or seven metres long I'd say, but the long ones were all diesels, I think. I just went straight to it in the shadows before people started getting out of their trucks, and I got in from underneath, like we'd said. It wasn't hard finding the lead, but just after I'd cut it the security guys came past. That's when things got serious. There was nothing to do except crouch there and pray. But they were more interested in the bush than what might be happening in the trucks. The outside, not the inside.'

'Makes sense,' I said. 'They'd be thinking of guerilla attacks, not of one person putting a timer on a distributor lead.'

The others had joined us at this stage and we were walking along fast, hoping to find a broken-down truck. But although the convoy had been travelling slowly we knew we'd have a long way to go.

'Then they started firing,' Robyn continued. 'That was awful. I thought they'd spotted you guys. I turned to stone. I'd thought I was the one in the dangerous spot, then it seemed like you were. I couldn't seem to think or function at all. But I noticed there was no excitement: no one calling out or running like you'd expect if they were suspicious. Then one of the soldiers doing the shooting walked past me firing into the bush, and I realised it wasn't aimed at anyone: they were just playing it safe. I hoped you guys hadn't copped an accidental bullet. But I unparalysed myself and got back to work. It was really hard because my hands were so wet and sweaty. I couldn't get a proper grip. The wires wouldn't do what I wanted, then I dropped the pliers. But I'm pretty sure

I got it right. Then I taped the timer way down and tried to make my move. That's when my real problems started – people were coming back to their trucks and security guys were still wandering around. The truck started and revved up and I still couldn't get off. I thought, "Better flatten myself," and I did. I waited till the truck had gone over me then rolled off the road full speed. I was terrified then. The trucks travel so close together. You should have seen me roll. Still, I survived. Bruises, scratches, scars for life, that's about all.'

'How sure are you that you got it on right?' Homer asked.

'She must have, or the truck wouldn't have started again,' Lee said.

'Yeah, true. If the timer works OK it'll definitely stop it,' Kevin confirmed. 'The problem then will be if they find the timer. At this time of night, and after being held up already, I don't think they'll have the patience to make the whole convoy wait while they look for a reason for one truck breaking down. They sounded tired enough when they were chasing the sheep.'

'I thought you were a long way back in the bush,' I said.

'No, no, I was really close,' he said, but I wasn't sure of that.

'If they find the timer we'll walk straight into an ambush,' Lee said quietly and calmly.

We all slowed down and looked at each other in shock. We'd reached that stage of exhaustion where we were overlooking obvious things.

'But we haven't got time to sneak along in the bush,' Fi said. 'It'll be light soon.'

'We have to,' Homer said. 'Don't forget, this raid is a chance in a million. If anything goes wrong we can call it off, no harm done, no need to feel bad. It's much too big for us, anyway. I think we should put our own safety higher than going on with this.'

I was really staggered. I'm sure Homer wasn't scared. His voice was steady and strong. I think he'd just weighed the risks and made a scientific judgement. For hot-headed Homer this was very cool. Something about it pleased me a lot, though, and not only the fact that it slightly increased my chances of staying alive. I think it was the hope that maybe Homer no longer felt a great macho need to prove himself by leaping wildly into action at every opportunity.

I had strong memories of other amateur soldiers we'd worked with, the adults of Harvey's so-called Heroes, being shot down like skittles as we'd watched helplessly from the bush. They'd been walking towards a disabled enemy vehicle too, taking it for granted that it had been deserted.

So we went bush, we quit talking, we threaded our way through the trees, tripping over roots and rocks, getting bashed in the face by stray branches. Oh, it was hard. 'Won't life ever be easy again?' I begged myself. At about 4.45 in the morning we saw the dull gleam of the stationary container truck, reflecting a little moonlight as it sat at the side of the road.

Chapter Thirteen

I wondered as I looked at it whether I was looking at my own coffin. It was a horrible feeling, to think that I'd be locking myself into that big metal box. We'd crept up on it very gingerly, but everything seemed normal. I know if I were a driver whose truck broke down at that hour of the night I wouldn't want to hang around trying to fix it. I'd leave it to the mechanics.

Kevin took the timer off, wired the lead together again, then pulled the positive wire off the coil. He assured us that they'd think that had caused the breakdown. But he did something to the fuel line as well: ran some water through it, I think. He said they'd have to call a tow truck for that. I took his word for it. I'm good on basic mechanics but I'm not into the deeper mysteries of engines.

We got the container open by swinging one bolt to the right and the other to the left. I'd been thinking – hoping – it might be locked but really that was the easiest part of the whole operation. You could open it from the inside too, which was another thing I'd been wondering about. I didn't want to end up like a possum in a trap.

The inside was a metal cave. It looked much bigger than from the outside. Our footsteps echoed as we tiptoed nervously along its full length. But of course there was nothing to see. It was the same at one end as it was at the other.

'Come on,' I said to the others, knowing Homer was just opening his mouth to say the same thing, and determined to beat him to it. I never wanted to let Homer think he was our lord and master. 'Time to do some hard yakka.'

It was hard yakka, too. Our dump of fertiliser and diesel was about two k's away. We'd calculated the time and speed of the convoy fairly well but I was still whingeing about it. I'd only have been happy if the truck had pulled up neatly next to our pile, had backed up to it even. Homer told Kevin he shouldn't have wrecked the fuel supply, because then I could have driven the truck to the dump and driven it back to the breakdown point after we'd loaded it. Of course there was no way. Those things were too hard to reverse, and in that narrow road, with no good places to turn a semi around, I might have had to drive it right down to Cobbler's Bay to find a place to manoeuvre. That wouldn't have looked so good to the soldiers.

So it was back to the wheelbarrows, back to another trundle through the cold night air, heavy arms struggling to hold up heavy handles, heavy legs wobbling as we tried to keep our balance. We stuck to the road now, listening for convoys and patrols, but knowing that dawn was another enemy for us to beat. But there were no convoys, and there seemed to be no patrols at all in this area.

The hardest part was getting the bags and the

drums up into the actual container. I've got to admit, Homer was good there too. He might be just a big lump of bone and muscle but he did a good job with the sacks. Fi especially had no chance of getting her bags up high enough, and Homer did all of hers. I know he had the strength, but I don't know where he got the energy.

Then suddenly, too fast for my liking, we were ready. I stood on the road behind the truck looking at the others, trying to cope with my flood of feelings. I felt like you do when you realise a polypipe's about to come apart at the join. What do you do first? Try to jam it back on? Rush to the valve? Rush to the pump? It was like that in my head. I'd half thought we might have a mushy farewell scene with everyone kissing and hugging and making speeches. I should have known it wouldn't be like that. In fact what happened was that Kevin handed me the fuse and detonator, and we gave the others our boots, socks and heavy clothes, and the contents of our pockets, so we could swim the bay easily. Then we stood and looked at each other feeling a bit embarrassed, then Homer said, 'Oh well, see you guys at the creek,' which was the meeting place we'd arranged, and Kevin said, 'Yeah, see you,' and I winked at Fi and waved to Robyn and in we went and shut the huge doors behind us.

As soon as we were in that darkness I wanted to rush out again and throw myself around all of them like an emotional boa constrictor but no matter what happened I was going to be as cool as Homer.

It was quite black in there. I held up my hand about five centimetres from my face and could see only the faintest gleam of pale skin. Outside I'd just had evidence that there was still light in the world, with the smudging of grey along the horizon, but in here I could hardly believe it. It was scary in a way that nothing else had been before. This was a totally new kind of venture for us. The other times were kind of local, us doing what we could do in our own neighbourhood, using petrol and gas, stuff that we used every day of our lives. Now it was war and we were soldiers. Anfo, detonators, fuses, trying to infiltrate a harbour and blow up shipping: this wasn't small time. This was a major act of sabotage that we were attempting. This was the Battle of Cobbler's Bay, serious war, real war, the kind of thing that should only be attempted by hundreds of soldiers with uniforms and guns, people who'd been training for years.

'Homer,' I said, suddenly terrified that he'd disappeared and I was all alone in the world. 'Homer, where are you?'

'Yeah, yeah, I'm here.' I heard him move towards me and I felt out in front of my face. My fingers found his face: I was touching the rough skin of his chin. He put his arms around me and I gratefully accepted his big wide hug. Being hugged by Homer felt funny; he didn't do it often and you could feel his awkwardness when he did. He was all sharp angles, not relaxed or comfortable, but it was nice to feel some closeness with him again. I admired him a lot these days, though I didn't ever let him know that.

We sat against the bags of ammonium nitrate and talked in tiny whispers. Although it was amazing how much stuff we'd collected, there was still heaps of room in the container. I was sure the weight wouldn't be noticed. These trucks were used to carrying twenty-five tonnes or more.

We talked about everything: the Deb Ball, embryo

transplants for ewes, a heavy metal CD by a group called Bigger than Boeing, why Robyn sometimes irritated Homer so much, whether stalactites go up or down. We talked about our dreams for the future. Boy, had they ever changed. No more talk now of overseas trips on Rotary Exchanges, hotted up utes for B & S's, courses in hotel management or marine biology. Now it was all small stuff. Having our families back together. Being able to walk around in daylight. Eating fresh fruit. Going to school again. Seeing kids playing on swings and seesaws. That was all we wanted. Little things.

As the light outside strengthened we realised that there were cracks and pinpoint holes in the sides of the container. We could see that the light outside was getting bright and strong. Even without that, we still could have worked it out by the heat in the container, which rose quite fast. Seemed like it was probably heading for a fine winter's day out there. I kept trying to read my watch, wondering when they would come, but I'd say it was about ten o'clock before we heard them. A slow grinding noise of a low-geared vehicle was our warning. We stopped talking and waited, straining every muscle to hear, as though our arms and legs and stomach were as much involved in listening as our ears. We heard the vehicle stop. We heard the opening and shutting of two truck doors. Although there was little point, we crouched lower behind the sacks. Homer thought that our most dangerous time would be getting through the gate into the wharf. I didn't agree. I thought the sentries would take it for granted that the mechanics had checked the container. I thought our most dangerous time would be getting lifted onto a ship, and having the crane driver notice the weight of the load. Homer didn't agree with that. He said the crane driver wouldn't be used to thinking for himself. No one would bother to tell him anything. He'd just sit there all day pressing buttons. If one container was heavier than the others he'd think it was for some reason that he hadn't been told about.

The dangers after that would be of a different type: full of action, physical dangers. But this, this sitting and waiting in the dark, this was all mental.

When I heard those little noises outside, the thumps and bangs, when I felt the container shake a few times, I stopped caring about future dangers. This was danger enough for me. I prayed just to survive this. I heard voices, quiet voices, muttering occasionally to each other. I heard the clang of metal. I heard the rattling of tools. I heard a swear word: not in English, but there's no mistaking the sound of a swear word. Then someone started up the engine. It started OK but it didn't run well: there were a lot of backfires, and it sounded really rough. I heard a shout, the engine went off, and then there was nothing; just a long silence. Soon it started to give me the creeps. I imagined them quietly surrounding the container, quietly raising their weapons, until I was certain that the doors were about to be flung open and we would be caught and dragged away and tortured and killed. I didn't have a relaxed muscle in my body. I could feel trembles running through me as though I'd been wired up to a twelve-volt generator and someone had turned on the power. Only Homer's hand on my arm stopped me from jumping to my feet and screaming. At last the rumble of the low-geared vehicle started again. I whispered in Homer's ear: 'What do you think?' and felt him give an impatient shrug. He didn't like guessing, speculating.

I could hear the vehicle revving and turning. The noise sounded like it was coming from all around us. There were a few shouts, then the engine settled down to a steady throb. And suddenly the container moved. Even though I'd been half expecting it, I took a grip on Homer's arm so tightly that I felt the bone. The container gave a quick lurch, then started moving slowly and steadily forward and upward, until it was at an angle that felt like 45 degrees, but probably wasn't quite so steep. A container of diesel not restrained by the fertiliser bags slid slowly downhill. I grabbed it as though I were drowning and it were a lifebuoy, clutching it hard and hoping the men outside hadn't heard the noise. Homer grabbed me and I realised that on the fear scale we were rating about the same figure. Then we really started moving. There was a clanking noise and slowly we felt ourselves bumping forwards. I wanted to cheer, but didn't. I knew that somewhere Robyn and Lee and Kevin and Fi would be watching, and wondered if they would be cheering, or whether they would be too scared for that. We hadn't talked about covering fire for us, but I'd taken it for granted that they'd have the shotguns out. I'd have lost too much face if I'd mentioned it, but now I prayed that they had them pointing straight at the truck.

The ride down to Cobbler's Bay was uncomfortable and unpleasant. We couldn't see any of the bends of course, so each of them took us by surprise. We used the fertiliser bags to save us from being thrown around too much. They weren't quite the same as air bags but they did the job. It was impossible to guess how far we'd come or how far we had to go: I thought we'd have reached the bay about ten minutes before we actually did. In fact I'd convinced myself that we'd made a terrible mistake and the container wasn't going to Cobbler's; we'd end up in some remote city, not even knowing where we were.

The truck slowed and I could hear gears changing down as we drove along in a straight line for the first time. Then we rocked slowly to a stop. By now my mouth was so dry I couldn't close it. I must have looked like a fish: in the dry coffin I was gasping for air but too panic-stricken to breathe properly. My mind was quite numb. I didn't seem able to think any more. I could hear voices and the throbbing of the engine but couldn't connect them to any meaning. I just sat there waiting for something to happen. After a minute it did: we began to move again, still on a smooth straight road. We swung to the right, then to the left, then went over a series of regular bumps, as though we were driving on a railway track. 'We're on the wharf,' Homer whispered in my ear. His voice was so unexpected that it shocked me back into thought. I realised he was right – we were suddenly breathtakingly close to our target. We'd gone right through the dreaded guard post at the gate without my realising it.

After the shock of this quick change in our situation nothing happened for three hours. The time passed very slowly. We sat in silence, sweat running down my face and stinging my eyes. My neck and armpits and groin became horribly uncomfortable: prickly and damp. I could feel the hair sticking to my skin more and more. There was nothing we could do, of course. We were at their mercy. If they decided to leave us sitting on the wharf for a week, what would become of us? My mind still wasn't working enough to think of any possibilities. I suppose I just vaguely accepted that we'd have to break out and jump off the jetty and swim. I know every time I let myself think about water I longed for a drink with such desperation that I had to try to force a different image into my head. The thirst was certainly the worst thing, so much so that even the danger of being shot got pushed into the background.

A thump on the roof was the first clue that anything had changed. It hit so hard that I jumped up in panic, choking back a scream, thinking that something was about to come right through the roof. I looked for Homer and saw his dark shape opposite mine. He too was standing with equal anxiety, looking up at the thin metal sheet above us, which was still trembling with the shock of the impact.

We lifted, and I did give a small yelp. It felt so strange, to be floating in air, swinging around slightly as we rose. The container was tipping and tilting; I gazed at Homer. I saw the gleam of his teeth as he smiled at me but even in the little light we had I could see that his smile was forced, probably to stop his teeth chattering. I smiled back, an equally fake grin. With the rocking of the box, coming after the twisting drive down from the hills and the long hot wait on the wharf, I was scared I'd be sick. We could have been one metre off the ground or one hundred metres; there was no way of telling. I couldn't even figure out whether we were going up or coming down.

And all at once we seemed to drop out of the bright hard light into a great blackness. It was cold and dark; for a stupid moment I thought we were dropping into Hell.

Chapter Fourteen

This time I grabbed Homer. There was a silence outside and that, with the sudden cold, made me feel we were not in Hell but in a freezer store. A few moments later the container came to rest, landing firmly on its base again. Something loud and heavy scraped across the roof and was gone. I was still holding Homer but he let me go and stepped away to peer through a thin crack in the side of the box. We'd tried peeping through these holes before but all we'd learned was how bright the sun was. The holes were just too small. Now Homer stayed riveted to this one for some time but I don't think he could see anything. There was nothing to tell us what was happening; nothing but the silence of our tomb.

We stayed in there for another hour and a half. We quickly got cold and were soon shivering uncontrollably. I had spasms of intense violent shivering, then I'd go back to normal shivers, but I never stopped altogether. It was just the usual things, of course: fear and cold. I should have been used to both of them.

In all that hour and a half there had not been a

sound around us, and I reached a stage where I thought we had to do something or we'd be unable to move. The cold hadn't reduced my thirst much but I thought some exercise might at least take my mind off that, although I knew there'd be no bottle of ice-cold Pepsi waiting at the end of it. I moved over to Homer and touched his elbow, then whispered, 'I'm going to have a look.' He didn't answer, so I took that for agreement and started clambering over the fertiliser bags. I got to the door and, with numb fingers, fumbled with the handle. It squeaked as I turned it and I waited, heart thudding. Nothing happened, so I finished its turn until it felt loose in my hands. Then I started nudging it down. Inch by slow grinding inch. Without looking round I could feel Homer's tension behind me. At last, with a final rasping stutter, the bolt came free. I leant against it with my head on the cold metal, my eyes closed, holding the pole with both hands so that the doors wouldn't suddenly swing open. We were about to step out into a complete unknown. We could have been in the final moments of our lives.

'Not yet,' Homer murmured into my ear and I waited another three or four minutes before creaking the tall door open.

Squeezing through the smallest possible gap I found myself in a vast dark space filled with containers identical to ours. The slight rocking under my feet, unnoticeable in the container, told me that we were indeed in a ship. I could hear creaks and moans from the steel of the hull. I looked around in wonder. We were seeking to destroy all this. If we achieved what we wanted we would turn our innocent box into a mighty bomb and, in a few hours, all of this would be at the bottom of the sea.

I took a deep breath and stepped forward. The place smelt like fresh air had never reached it. Diesel fumes were mixed with salt and rope and paint and disinfectant. It wasn't pleasant but it was the way I'd imagined a ship would smell. It made a change from the ammonium smell in the container.

There was no one there; that was obvious. The hatch above was closed and we could hear no human noises, nor sense any human presence. I turned to Homer, able at last to see him more clearly.

'What do you think?' I asked.

'Let's get ready. Let's set it up so all we have to do is light the fuse, then as soon as it's night-time we'll light it and go over the side.'

'OK. God, I could use some water.'

'I know. I can't believe we didn't bring any.'

We went back into our container, closing the doors loosely behind us, and set to work, coolly preparing the biggest weapon any of us had ever dreamed of. But it was strange: I did it without thinking about bombs. I could just as easily have been getting feed ready for the poddy lambs at home. We didn't have to do a lot. We cut the bags open and tipped the stuff out so the diesel would soak through it all, then moved the drums of fuel. Then we poured the diesel out. Kevin had worked out the ratio for us: six per cent by weight. We stirred it through the fertiliser. It was like making a tossed salad. I shoved my hand down into the pile and brought out a handful. The little yellow grains were greasy without being wet. It felt right.

The smell of diesel was getting really unpleasant. I tried to ignore it and, with Homer watching, I began to prepare the fuse and detonator. What I had to do was make a small bomb that would set off the big bomb. I used the length of pipe we'd found at the farm and filled it with anfo and the detonator. I had to crimp the end shut, which was pretty dangerous. We hadn't been able to find special crimping pliers which, according to Kevin, is what we should have used, so we had to go with the normal metal ones. The trouble was that one spark would set it off. I just had to be damn careful. I moved the pliers very gently, drying my hands every ten seconds to wipe away the sweat that was making them so slippery. It was a matter of not letting the pliers bang against the pipe. It would have been simple if I'd been doing it with an empty pipe.

At last I finished. We couldn't find anything else to do then. So we shut the container doors, found a corner of the hold, and just lay down and waited. I was leaning against Homer, and he had his arm around me. Neither of us spoke. I enjoyed the feel of cuddling into his strong body and I actually went to sleep for a while. At some stage he produced our food supply, a packet of Morning Coffee biscuits that were broken, stale and soft, and two packets of jelly crystals, one lime and one pineapple.

I got to choose and I chose the pineapple.

The trouble with this lunch was that it increased my thirst to a desperate stage. I couldn't think about anything else and the more I thought, the worse it got. I wondered about drinking diesel, and was sorry we hadn't saved a bit from the bomb. My mouth was hot and dry and my tongue felt large and thick. It was too hard even to talk, and anyway there was nothing left to talk about. I lay back against Homer's ribs again, feeling them rising and falling with each panting breath, and tried to will myself to sleep. But all I could do was long for evening.

Gradually, with sickening slowness, the time moved on. At about half past five, by Homer's unreliable old wind-up watch, we started to get restless. As the air cooled even further we figured it must be close to dark outside. We estimated that the fuse would burn between twenty and twenty-five minutes, so there wasn't much margin for error. We found the exit from the hold: a steel ladder that climbed through the darkness to a metal trapdoor. This was not the main hatch cover of course, but a little one for people. I suppose the sailors used it when they were at sea and wanted to check the cargo. Homer went up the ladder, gingerly, and gave the trapdoor a nudge. It lifted. So it seemed that getting out wouldn't be a problem. What we found when we got out: now that might be a problem.

Homer's watch said seven o'clock. 'Time for the ABC News,' I thought. That had been one of the rituals in our house. Dad always had to watch the ABC News. Now there was no more ABC News and it was time for us to blow up a ship in Cobbler's Bay. Life had changed quite a bit.

'What do you think?' I asked Homer, through dry peeling lips, with my swollen tongue. He looked equally terrible.

'I can't stand this any longer,' he said. 'Let's do it.'

It was much earlier than the time we'd planned, but I was in total agreement with Homer, and that made it unanimous.

We went back to the container. I felt strange, weightless, walking on air.

'Ready?' Homer asked.

I nodded. 'Be funny if we'd forgotten the matches,' I whispered. Homer didn't laugh. He stood by the container door as I rolled the fuse out to its limit. 'There's no point both of us waiting here,' I said. 'You go up the ladder and have the hatch ready.'

He went off obediently and I got out the box and chose a match. It took a few strikes to light it, then it flared up, hurting my eyes. 'Well, here goes,' I said out loud, but I waited for it to burn down a little before applying it to the fuse. The flame was at my fingers, scorching them slightly before the fuse caught alight. I shook the match out quickly, and stood watching to make sure the fuse was burning. It was. I ran for the ladder.

It had been cool in the hold but when Homer raised the trapdoor a fraction the night air felt really freezing. With our light clothing – shorts and T-shirts, nothing else – we had no protection against the chill. 'Ready?' Homer asked, lowering the door on our heads again. We were jammed in together on the top of the ladder, our feet on the same rung. I nodded. He couldn't have seen my nod but he must have assumed it. 'Straight to the left-hand rail and over it,' he whispered.

'Port,' I said, but I don't think Homer heard. He lifted the hatch again and I shivered once more at the cold unfriendly air that blew in so quickly. I could see the dark sky; not a star in sight. Homer's head was now almost clear of the opening, looking around cautiously. All I could do was huddle in behind him and wait. I hated being so helpless, so dependent on someone else. I was nervous about how long we were taking, hanging around in this massive ticking time bomb. But suddenly Homer took off. He went so fast I almost thought he'd been lifted out of the hole by a hand grabbing his collar. But no, he was self-propelled. When I followed him I could see that. He ran across the deck and took cover behind a steel mast. I closed the hatch, as carefully as I could, hating him for leaving me with that job, then joined him, trying to orientate myself. Which was the front of the ship and which was the back? Or the bow and stern, or whatever they call them. I looked to the right – starboard – and saw the long wide deck tapering as it disappeared in the darkness. So at least I knew where I was. But there was still a fair way to go to get to the side. Homer started out, and I followed straight away, but running at an angle, aiming for a different part of the rail.

We got halfway there, and that's where things started to go wrong.

With a horrible lurch of my stomach I saw a sentry, with a rifle slung across his back, appear suddenly from the left. He was walking quickly along by the rail. I nearly called out but realised I couldn't. Homer saw the sentry a fraction of a second later, but by then the soldier had seen him. The man moved with amazing speed. Swivelling, so that his back was to the rail, he began to unsling his rifle. Although his eyes were on Homer I was actually closer to him. I ran straight at him. He was bringing the rifle up so quickly I thought he would be able to fire it into my stomach at point-blank range. I covered the last three metres in a frantic dive, not having any idea of what I was going to do, just desperate to stop him pulling the trigger. What I did was to hit him somewhere between his chest and stomach with my head. I felt a hard impact, hurting my head and jarring my neck, but above that I felt relief as he fell backwards. He hadn't been able to fire. I was all over him as he fell but, to my horror, we kept falling. I realised that we'd both gone over the rail. I was beating my arms in

132

panic, trying to get away from him. We fell and fell. I just couldn't believe how far we fell. How high was this ship? I thought maybe we were in dry dock and I was about to land on steel and concrete.

I heard a choking scream and realised it was the soldier, then there was a volley of shots right next to my head. His rifle was firing; I guess by accident. The sound completely deafened me. Then we hit the water. It felt like concrete: I hit it with my shoulder, and thought I'd broken my collarbone with the impact. I was about a metre from the sentry and I twisted by instinct and wriggled away under water to get a few more metres away. As I surfaced, I saw Homer enter the water in a perfect racing dive, about fifteen metres away. 'Bastard,' I thought, jealous of him for having such an easy passage. I swam awkwardly towards him, looking all the time for the soldier but seeing no sign of him. Maybe he'd sunk straight away. Maybe he'd accidentally shot himself. Maybe he'd swum under water and was about to come up right in front of me.

The shock to my shoulder was starting to wear off, although my neck was still hurting. As I got to within two metres of Homer there was a sudden spitting and foaming of water in a long line to my left. I thought of sharks. 'What is it?' I yelled at Homer. He looked equally shocked and confused. Then he took a funny sort of backward stroke, as if I'd slapped him in the face. 'Bullets!' he screamed. His voice sounded thick and muffled through my deafened ears. I looked around in panic. Had the soldier resurfaced? Was he now firing at us? Impossible, surely. 'Go under!' Homer yelled, and disappeared. I gasped at some air and turned turtle, swimming down deep deep deep, till my ears started to hurt. As I did so I realised the

133

obvious: that the bullets must be coming from the ship or the wharf. I swam as far and as hard as I could, ignoring my sore neck but not able to go very smoothly or quickly. My lungs were empty, my chest was contracting, my stomach cramping. I had to go up. I did so, popping out of the water into the cold night air and taking an immediate swift look around, even as I wheezed for air. I couldn't see anyone: the soldier or Homer. I couldn't hear anything. Then a strong light caught my eye. It was lifting into the sky. It was a helicopter leaving the wharf and heading my way. They sure weren't wasting time. At the same time, another row of splashes in the water ten metres to my right proved that bullets were still flying, even if I couldn't hear them. I could hear the chopper though, and could see the white searchlight from its belly turning towards me. I cursed and dived again. There was no time to look for Homer; I had to get going. The ship was due to blow up in fifteen minutes and it was going to be bloody dangerous to be anywhere near it. I again swam as fast and far as possible, only coming up when my body was leeched of every molecule of air. I knew I'd breathe water if I stayed under a second longer.

I could see the white of the searchlight through the water and I avoided that, but the helicopter was coming right in over my head and very low, buffeting the water violently. It was churning up waves and making me even colder. I gasped for air, shivering with terror, took a deep breath and went under again. I'd got some second wind and was able to make better progress, but it wasn't like swimming in the Wirrawee pool; I seemed to be getting waterlogged, and not going nearly as fast as I'd have liked. My energy was going in all directions: I was worrying about the explosion, worrying about Homer, terrified of the bullets and the chopper, and trying to swim, all at the same time. What a mess. Maybe if we'd eaten and drunk more I'd have had some energy.

Surfacing again, away from the helicopter light, I looked back at the ship. There were soldiers lined along the rails with weapons trained at the water. One of them actually saw me and shouted and pointed: I was shocked, as I'd thought I'd be invisible in the darkness. But there was a lot of reflected light from the spotlight. His gun turned towards me and I duck-dived fast and deep. I thought they'd expect me to swim away from them so I went back towards the ship, hoping that the explosion was a long way off. The helicopter light swept through the water and past me; it was almost vertical, so I knew the chopper was very close. I turned again and headed for the ship's stern, then, taking one quick breath, set out across the bay, fast, hoping I'd thrown them off. 'Flat out, Ellie,' I begged myself, 'go harder, never mind how much it hurts.' I knew there was no more time for strategy: that backtracking had been the last throw of my dice. If they saw me now, they saw me. I just had to get well away from that ship before it blew.

I ploughed on grimly. I'd gone maybe eighty metres when I nearly lost my head. I was coming up with bursting lungs, not a wisp of air left in my body, when a huge grey churning shape screamed through the water just metres in front of me. Again, stupidly, I thought it was a shark but it would have broken world records if it was. I realised then that it was the hull of a boat, some kind of gun boat, probably. If it had been a bit closer I really would have lost my head. The wake hit me and threw me backwards. I grabbed a breath as I went, but half of it was water. I had a glimpse of more spotlights as I twisted and went under again. I couldn't see any clear path to the other side of Cobbler's Bay but I knew I had to keep going in that direction, no matter what. If Kevin was right about the explosive power of anfo I'd need to be out of the water and well into the bush when it blew up. There didn't seem to be much chance now that I'd get that far – I'd lost too much time already – but I just had to get as far as possible. In my mind was the image of that container filling and filling with oxygen; the fuse steadily snaking its glowing way towards it; the massive blast that now might be only moments away.

I was helped and hindered then by something else I hadn't counted on. Some force, like a silent invisible underwater wave, hit me and threw me forward. I couldn't swim with it or against it; it was too powerful. My first thought was that the ship had blown up and this was the shock wave. I went tumbling through the water like a plastic bag in a windstorm. My arms and legs were thrashing around trying to get some control, but failing. I forgot about breathing but at least had the sense to try to get to the surface. Without knowing how I suddenly realised I had broken through into air and was lying on the surface gasping and sobbing. My head felt funny, all numb and stupid. As the wild waves rocked me I got a glimpse of the ship, as large and secure as ever. It didn't look like it had just blown up.

White water sprayed up around me. Bullets again, only metres away. The sharp cold wind they made brought me to my senses. I took a roll and went under, having no energy to go deep, but at least striking out in the right direction, towards the wooded shore. I felt a thud on my back, like someone had hit me with a stick, or a stone, but I kept going.

The grey hull raced past again, to my right, a bit further away than last time. I thought they must be throwing bombs or hand grenades or something in the water. Depth charges maybe. When I came up for air this time I risked everything on taking a quick look. There seemed to be only one patrol boat looking for us and that had its back to me. The helicopter was screaming angrily across a patch of water a hundred metres to my right; its searchlight showing every white fleck, every grey–green ripple. I hoped they hadn't found Homer over there somewhere. I glanced back at the container ship and checked again that it showed no signs of an explosion. It looked very comfortable. But for the first time I felt that I was making progress. Although the shore seemed no closer, the ship was now quite a long way away. I was just sorry to see it was on its own; the oil tanker must have left harbour. At least the quick sighting gave me the encouragement I needed to keep my effort going. I freestyled a fast twenty metres before diving again, breaststroking down deep. There was a dull ache in my back but that wasn't slowing me; my neck, where I'd collided with the sentry's chest on the ship, was the biggest problem.

The main fear I felt now was of sharks. If I were bleeding anywhere, which seemed quite likely, I would attract sharks like shit attracts flies. The ironic thing was that the helicopter and the gunboat, in hunting me, were my best chances of keeping the sharks away. They were so loud and big and alien that they must surely frighten sharks as much as they frightened me. I kept that grim hope firmly in my head as I ploughed on through the choppy water.

I was alternating freestyle with under water. I was too tired to go under water all the time. As I felt the boat roar up behind me again, I dived and went as deep as I could. The wash this time wasn't quite as violent: the boat must have turned a bit further away.

I surfaced, trembling with cold and exhaustion and fear. Rolling onto my back I looked for the container ship again, hoping it would now be so far away that I would feel good, be encouraged to battle on for the shore. For a moment I couldn't see it, because the swell was above me. Then the swell lifted me and I had a grandstand view. There was the ship and there was the helicopter, wheeling to the left above the stern, obviously about to charge back across the water and sweep another stretch.

At that moment the ship simply lifted out of the ocean. One millisecond it was there; the next it was up there. It actually seemed to hang in the air for a moment and I saw its back start to break. And then came a light: a huge bright light, like a phosphorescent flower, so white and blinding that it hurt my eyes. Briefly, night became brightest, sharpest day. I was hit by a tremendous noise, a crack, like the biggest stockwhip in the universe. It seemed to break the sky apart. It felt like it was vibrating through me. It was like a concert I'd gone to at Wirrawee Showground, when I'd been right near the speakers, and I'd felt my body was resonating with the music.

A million shooting stars, some of them huge, were flying in all directions. I couldn't believe how far they travelled. Quite a few whooshed loudly over my head then fell and sizzled in the ocean behind me. Others went way way up in the air.

There was an awful rumbling, like the sea was about to vomit its darkest secrets. Then a crash that went on forever. The trees, the shoreline, the water – all seemed to rock, as though they were being re-organised. My mouth opened in fright. Something caught my eye, something up high, almost out of view. I looked up. It was the helicopter, tumbling out of the sky. It looked like a huge wasp that had been hit by a spray of Mortein. With the scream of a tortured soul it fell and fell. The sound was so high-pitched that I could hear it even above the booming of the explosion. The chopper hadn't seemed to be up very high but it must have been, because it took forever to fall. It went end over end, three times I think, till it was obvious that it couldn't recover, could never pull out. Then it hit, in an instant volcano of white water. I couldn't see what was happening in the middle of the volcano. The water went up so high, then fell back in slow motion. When I could see through the spray again there was nothing, just a great wild boiling of white water. The rumbling of the exploded ship was as loud as ever, rolling around and around Cobbler's Bay. I glanced to my right in terror, expecting to see the hills collapsing in on the bay, the whole world blown up. But the dark hills did not seem to have moved. They were the only things that hadn't.

Then came the most frightening sight of all. When I looked back to where the ship had been, once again there was nothing to see. It was like a giant grey paintbrush had suddenly painted everything out. It took me a split second to realise what it was. I wish I hadn't taken that second; I'd needed it to get ready, to take some evading action, to defend myself. There was a wave bearing down on me, a wave so vast that I cowered in terror, waiting to be crushed. It was sucking the water from under me, building itself into a gigantic wall. As it towered above me it blocked out the very sky. I know that I screamed: I felt my mouth open and my throat tighten with the effort of making a great noise, but I didn't hear a trace of it. I was picked up like a bit of old seaweed, like a scrap of driftwood, and hurtled so fast that I could have been travelling in a car. I was sure I'd be broken into splinters of bone and shreds of flesh by the wild force of it. It was like being in a washing machine gone mad; an out-of-control washing machine about to shake itself apart. It was like being in the world's fiercest dumper, every bad wave I'd ever caught multiplied a thousand times. I don't know what I did for breath; I don't think I had any in my lungs, but the pain from there went unnoticed as my body got tossed and tumbled in this wet tornado. Amazingly, I did have time for one clear thought and even more amazingly it was a joke, sort of. I thought, 'Well, at least the sharks won't find me in this.' I didn't get around to laughing, though.

Then the wave smashed itself against the shore. The land held; the wave didn't. It flung itself to pieces on the rocks, the trees, the ground. I felt myself touch bottom with my hip, then bounce, hit again, get turned over and over, hit again, this time with the back of my head, get scraped along dirt or gravel or something, hit something else with my bad knee and then get rolled along, bashing everything I could find. I was deaf and blind and concussed; I could hear the thundering noise continuing to crash and vibrate around me, but I didn't know if it was in my head or if it was really happening. I lay there thinking I was probably dead.

Chapter Fifteen

I felt like I'd been beaten with truncheons on every inch of my body. I had so many aches and pains that I didn't know which part of myself to feel sorry for first. When I realised I was alive I hauled myself up onto all fours, then used a small tree trunk to get on my feet. I hung on to the tree, willing myself to find some energy. Behind me, wave after wave was crashing onto the shore. It was a long time before they started to quieten down. By then I was back on all fours, unable to stand without feeling sick and dizzy. I didn't give a moment's thought to what we'd done. It seemed unreal, and irrelevant. All I could do was survive the next moment, the next minute. It was impossible to tell where I was: just somewhere on the shore of Cobbler's Bay, and probably a few k's from Baloney Creek where Homer and I had arranged to meet the others. I didn't think about Homer though; he could have been alive or he could have been dead, or he could have been somewhere in between, but there was nothing I could do for him.

My mind just wouldn't work: nothing would connect. All I knew was that I had a terrible craving for fresh water and that I was terribly cold and that I couldn't cope with the pain. I heard a gurgle of water near me, striking quite a different note to the roar of the waves behind, so I crawled to that. But when I found the little stream and sank my face into it all I could taste was salt. It had probably been flooded by the tidal wave that Homer and I had created.

I had another go at getting upright and this time was more successful. I started to wonder about the chances of soldiers finding me, but thought they would probably be too busy back at the wharf – if any of the wharf was left, which was unlikely. My thirst forced me forwards. I took a couple of hesitant steps, trying to work out which leg was the better. There wasn't much in it, but the left one seemed to at least have a functioning knee. I put more weight on that and hobbled uphill into the bush.

I don't know where I wandered that night. I found some fresh water eventually and lay with my face soaking in it for ages, cold though it was. I drank like a dog, lapping noisily and greedily, coughing when I swallowed too much, but gulping down more even while I was recovering from the coughing fit. After that I staggered on for a while, holding my head in both hands and wishing it would stop hurting. I had enough sense to know that I shouldn't stop and lie down when I was so wet, so I kept walking till my clothes were just damp, then lowered myself carefully between two logs and lay there shaking. I couldn't sleep, but spent most of the time trying painfully to get into more comfortable positions. My hips got really sore on the hard ground. I think I probably did have a couple of short uneasy dozes, but I really don't know.

I felt my back as best as I could. It was sore and tender, but the skin wasn't broken. It didn't seem like a bullet had hit me, so that was one less worry.

Some time before dawn I started out again. I hadn't given any thought to where I should aim; my only ambition was to put as much distance between me and Cobbler's Bay as possible. That was sensible considering the uproar that would be raging back there. I crossed a road at one stage but it never occurred to me that I could use it to navigate to our meeting point. I was just so scared to be on it that I stumbled quickly across and ran into the thicker bush on the other side.

My headache was better after the brief rest I'd had, but now I had another urgent need. I was desperately hungry, so hungry that I felt dizzy for need of food. I couldn't find any energy without food to charge me up. As the light grew better I started looking for something, anything, to eat. I found a few late blackberries, sad wizened little fruit, but I ate them. I was trying to remember the occasional TV shows I'd seen about bush tucker but the memories had all gone and nothing I saw looked edible.

Then came a big distraction, a sound I'd become familiar with over the months. It was a throbbing roar like a giant lawn mower or food processor. It was the clatter of another helicopter, another ugly bird of prey searching for a meal. I was like a rabbit beneath its vicious rotor and if it caught me I would die like a rabbit. I was in quite open country when I heard it and I ran crazily for a tree, pounding along on my bruised knee, my sore ankle, my aching feet. I dived under the tree at the exact second that the huge chopper appeared above the clearing. Its glass front seemed like a giant eye; the whole machine seemed like an eye, peering in every direction, seeing everything. I lay among the leaves and mud, begging it to go away, praying that it wouldn't see me. I remembered how they'd hung around Corrie's house and how they'd later destroyed it with a single missile. I realised how easily they could kill me, just by dropping a bomb in the clearing. I closed my eyes and clenched every muscle in my body, gripping two tufts of grass with my fists, my heart thumping like unbalanced windmill sails. A blizzard of leaves and dust from the downdraft stung my bare legs and arms as it blew over me. I was more helpless than I'd ever been. If I moved I was dead; if I didn't move I might be shot from the air without even putting up a fight. I was especially disgusted by the thought of dying like that.

I was hoping that the leaves blowing across the clearing would cover me, hide me from the great goggle eye. I heard the thing move a little, then it abruptly shifted sideways, across a line of trees to my left. The trees changed the sound of the engine, making it less loud, less threatening. But the engine note kept on changing. I lay there trying to work out what was happening, trying to second guess the flying monster. The rough rasping noise was quietening now, but I still didn't know what it meant till another gale of leaves came blowing dustily through the trees. The helicopter was landing; that's what was happening! Only a thin row of trees separated me from it, a row of trees and maybe fifty metres.

I had to assume that they'd seen me and that's why they were landing. Maybe they thought I was a dead body, lying there face down. The time had come to stop planning every move; instead I ran. I kept low but I went fast. I was aiming for a patch of scrub that wasn't far away, thirty metres, but it seemed a kilometre. Even when I had just one step to go I still never believed I'd reach it. I crashed through, tripped over a log, rolled sideways down a long slope and twisted into another patch of scrub, thinking now that I had a chance. I knew they couldn't see me here; I also knew I was more at home in this environment than they'd ever be.

Behind me I heard a shout and some running feet, but no shots. I swerved again and jumped a small creek, starting to feel renewed pains and aches in my body. There was a short slope ahead; I pounded up that, feeling very exposed again, struggling for a good clean lungful of air. As I reached the top they had a good view of me for a moment. I knew they would, but there was nothing I could do about it. Speed seemed more important than anything. I had a stupid faith in my sore legs, my wrecked body, to get me away from this. I crouched as I went over the little hill, hearing more shouts, but looking at the same time for a good route to follow. The best way seemed to be between some trees to my right, so I swung to the left, figuring again that I had to do the unexpected. There were rocks and rabbit holes; somehow I managed to miss them. Across another ridge and I came to an old fence, rickety and rusty but all barbed wire. Sobbing and gasping I tried to get over it but the fence posts were too old and wouldn't stay still. My right hand tore on a barb; finally I decided I had to get over no matter what it cost me, so I did a sort of roll across the top strand. I landed awkwardly on the other side. My shirt caught in the wire. I ripped

145

at it madly and it came away with a sound like a velcro fastener.

As I got up I saw for the first time the soldiers chasing me. A woman appeared on the skyline. She was in uniform, carrying an automatic rifle of some kind and looking around anxiously. Even from my distance I could see the sweat on her. Another soldier came up behind her – man or woman, I couldn't be sure – and at that moment they both saw me. They called behind them as I took off again. I hoped the fence would hold them up and I bolted down an eroded gully, praying I wouldn't trip in one of the holes. It was the end of me if I did. There was a small dam blocking the gully. I skirted round that and went through a thick stand of eucalyptus, thinking that might give me a bit of cover. Beyond it was a patch of long grass. I was only a few metres into it when I nearly died of shock. Wherever I looked I saw large figures rising from the grass, jumping to their feet. Tall grey figures starting up in panic. I thought, 'It finishes here.' Then I realised they were kangaroos who'd been having a morning nap. Now, as startled by me as I had been by them, they were splitting in all directions, bounding away into the trees, leaving behind the flattened grass where they'd been sleeping. I almost laughed; it was such a relief.

It gave me more energy somehow. I ran on faster. I had a bit of a breeze behind and that helped too. I was thinking of the cross-countries at school, and how I'd never done very well in them. If they were holding one now, I would have won it. I got to another fence and took the wimp's way, going under it. I heard a few more human cries behind me, which probably meant that they'd seen the roos, then I went through another stand of trees. To my surprise I then saw a hut, a half-built cabin that was open to the weather, with a galvanised-iron roof. Next to it was a caravan, old and patched, badly needing a coat of paint. I ignored that and rushed on, looking for a way out, a safe route that would get me away from the human dog pack. I just couldn't see any possibilities. A track led away from the hut to a gate. I ran along it but I knew I couldn't stay on it for long; it was a death trap. At least the gate was new and strong and I could climb over it easily. I did that, hesitated, then, hearing the soldiers again, chose to go to the right. They sounded close, probably at the hut already. I heard another aircraft, very low, and started sweating even more heavily, feeling that a net was closing in fast. Seemed like they were sparing no effort to get me. As I ran, the noise of the plane grew louder and louder: it sounded like it was coming straight at me. Sure enough it suddenly did appear right in front, a silver-grey jet flying very low. I swore and almost ran off to the side to get away from it, but realised at the same moment that I was being stupid, that they wouldn't have time to shoot at me when they were travelling at that speed. The plane, ignoring me, swept straight over my head with a scream. As it passed, I glanced up and saw an unmistakeable red kiwi on a white background, with a blue circle around it. I almost shouted out loud with joy. There was still hope! Friends were out there! We hadn't lost! We hadn't lost yet!

Just a moment later I heard a tremendously loud whoosh, then a dull thud. I took a moment to glance crazily over my shoulder, having no idea what I would see. Somewhere, way back in the bush, something was burning. A huge cloud of black smoke, bending a little towards me because of the breeze, was rising quickly in the sky. The plane was behind it, banking sharply and climbing, looking perfectly intact. With a bound of excitement I realised what had happened. The plane had caught the helicopter on the ground, a true sitting duck. The chopper wouldn't have had a chance. It was a wonderful unexpected score.

I ran and ran as the plane banked away and disappeared into the distance. I ran for another ten minutes. In all that time I heard no more human sounds. I thought I was safe, that the attack on the helicopter had stopped my pursuers. Finally the point came where I had to stop, no matter who might be following. My lungs had taken on their own life and were rasping and groaning, desperate for air. My legs were cramping up and my knee felt like it was full of fragments of bone. Looking down I was shocked to see how swollen it was. I slowed to a walk, staggered over to a tree and fell on the ground behind it, hoping it would hide me. I lay there grunting. My stomach was cramping up again and I couldn't get enough breath. I really thought this time I was going to die, and die in agony.

But as the minutes passed and no soldiers came I started to recover a little. It was a sweet feeling. I had survived. I had no food or drink, my body was wrecked, I'd lost my friends but, for the moment, I had survived.

Chapter Sixteen

Hunger's a funny thing. It goes in stages. First you're so hungry you think you'll faint. Your stomach is one huge empty refrigerator: the light's on, the door's open, but there's nothing in it. Then that stage passes and it gets better. You don't think about food nearly as much, and the idea of food actually makes you a bit sick. You can go on for quite a while when you're in that stage.

I kept walking for a long time, avoiding any clear spaces, any roads or fire trails. I stuck to the thickest bush, trying to stay invisible, not just to anyone on the ground but to people in the sky too. It was extra tiring, having to concentrate so hard all the time.

When you're lost in the bush you're meant to go back to your last-known point and start again. I'd had that drummed into me often enough. I couldn't do it though, because I didn't really have a last-known point. Or if I did, it was the wharf at Cobbler's Bay. I could have gone back there, but would they have lent me a map and a compass? I didn't think so.

I just kept walking, though my walk soon became a limp – eventually a very slow one indeed. I was looking for any place I could recognise. I'd arranged to meet the others at a river crossing on Baloney Creek, on a logging track that came off the main Cobbler's Bay road. It was a good fishing spot that a lot of Wirrawee people knew about, but now I didn't have a clue where either the creek or the road might be. I crossed so many creeks as the day went on, some of them quite large, but they didn't have little signs telling me their names.

When the sun got higher I crept into a spot under a bank, shaded by a creeper, and had a sleep. It was a warm sun for winter; seemed like we'd had a lot of warm winters the last few years. The hard walking had made me uncomfortably hot and sticky, but I'd rather have had that than rain and cold winds.

I slept only half an hour but I lay there a lot longer, too tired to move. When I did move it was only to slide back into the sun, as it got cold too quickly in the shade. I propped myself against a tree and sat, looking in frustration at my swollen knee. Apart from soaking my hanky in cold water and tying it on, there wasn't much I could do. I wished I had some Aboriginal friends: they would have found a bush remedy in the nearest tree and fixed me up in no time. Or they might have had a packet of Panadol in their pocket. I would have settled for either.

I tried to walk on but letting my knee get cold had been its kiss of death: it just wouldn't function at all. I started to realise that it might be better to spend the night there. It wasn't a very interesting place, or an attractive one, but it would do. I put my little remaining energy into making myself comfortable. I used a sharp rock to gouge out a hollow that I could lie in, and collected a heap of creeper that I could crawl under for a bit of warmth. I don't know what kind of creeper it was, but there was plenty of it around, and I could pull it down from the trees fairly easily. The trees were probably grateful – a lot of them looked like they were close to choking with the stuff. I just hoped I wasn't allergic to it.

There was a creek flowing fast about a hundred metres away, so I waddled over there and had a drink. Growing in it was some green stuff that we'd always called water lettuce at home. It looked harmless so I ate a few leaves, deciding that if I didn't die of it during the night I'd try a bit more in the morning. It didn't have much flavour: it tasted like lettuce that had been soaked in water so long the flavour had been leeched out of it, which is probably exactly what it was.

Already it was getting dark; no daylight saving here. I went back to my bush bed and sat on the pile of creeper, thinking deep thoughts about life, and trying not to get depressed. 'You have so much to be proud of,' I lectured myself. 'You've destroyed a huge container ship, and probably the jetty as well, judging by the size of the explosion. You wiped out one helicopter and indirectly accounted for another. I'll bet the plane was sent to check out the blast at Cobbler's, and it was because of you the chopper was sitting on the ground. So that was a bonus. You've done more fighting than anyone could have thought or hoped or expected. You shouldn't feel so bad.'

But none of that stopped me sinking slowly but surely into depression. I missed everyone so much. Homer, with his strength and leadership and planning; Fi, with her courage and grace; Kevin, with the new energy he'd brought to our little group; Robyn with her wisdom and goodness; Lee with his sexy body . . . 'Whoops, where did that come from?' I wondered. I thought I was off Lee for life. Still, he was a good looking guy . . .

Most of all, though, I missed my mum and dad. Deep down inside, Ellie, the tough jungle fighter, was a baby, a five-year-old wanting to be tucked into bed, read a story, kissed good night. The nicest times I'd had with Dad when I was little was when he read me bedtime stories. He'd lie on the bed and start a book, then fall asleep beside me, more often than not. Of course, we worked together on the farm a lot, but he always seemed stressed then. If a calf got out of the cattle yards or a dog scattered a mob of sheep or it rained during shearing he'd get so mad. There'd be a flood of swear words; he'd be red in the face and cursing the stock and the dog and the government and the whole farming industry and the heavens above, and me too if I was stupid enough to get in the way. Then Mum would upset me sometimes by telling me how worried she was about his blood pressure and how his father had dropped dead in the middle of changing a tyre on a tractor, at the age of forty-five, and she was scared Dad would go the same way. I never really wanted her to talk to me about things like that – and yet I sort of liked it in a way. I felt like an adult, like we were talking on equal terms.

It's one good thing about being an only child, I guess. Your parents do treat you like you're on the same level. Sometimes, anyway. Sometimes Dad treated me like I really was five years old. Once I left the gate on Cooper's (that's our biggest paddock) open, and the joined ewes that were in there wandered into One Tree (another paddock) and got mixed up with the unjoined ewes. Dad went birko that time. I thought he was going to hit me. Mum had to get between us, to save me. I don't blame him; it was an extremely dumb thing to do, but he always acted like he'd never made a mistake in his life. After all, it wasn't me who sprayed Round-up on Mum's raspberries when she wanted them given some fertiliser.

Sometime in their marriage, Mum decided that she would stay sane by not getting caught up in Dad's moods. She did all the things that farmers' wives do in our part of the world – in fact she did them better than most – but she didn't give the impression that there was nothing else in her life, the way Mrs Mackenzie and Mrs Brogan did. Mum seemed able to step away from it all. She often looked a bit amused by the things she found herself doing. When Mrs Mackenzie won the jam section at the Show for instance, she'd get very excited and talk about it for weeks. When Mum won the Best Sponge Cake she just gave a little sly smile and didn't say anything in public. But when we got home she'd laugh and celebrate. One year she even danced me around the kitchen.

She had mixed feelings about it all; I guess that's what it boils down to. Maybe it was to do with her being a city girl originally. Her father was an accountant and she'd never been out of the city in her life, until a friend talked her into going to the Motteram B & S. The friend had a ute, and they took that because they thought it would look more rural. Some time during the B & S, Dad, who must have been legless, staggered out of the hall looking for a place to sleep. Of course he never admitted to being legless; he said he'd had a long hard day marking lambs. Anyway, he curled up in the back of Mum's friend's ute, under the tarp, and had a good nap. When he woke up it was ten o'clock in the morning and he was still in the ute, 300 k's from Motteram and doing 100 k's an hour. He had to bang on the back of the window to get the girls' attention – it was the first they knew that they had a passenger. I can imagine the shock when they heard the banging and turned around to see a pair of blood-shot eyes staring at them through the glass.

Four months later they were married. Dad was twenty-three; Mum was three weeks away from her nineteenth birthday.

I didn't arrive till eight years later. I think they had a bit of trouble having me, but I never asked them about that. There are some things about your parents you really don't want to know.

From the first I loved the land. I don't know whether Dad wanted a son – most places around Wirrawee are run by men, and handed on from father to son – but he never gave me any sign of that. One time when a bloke at the Wirrawee Saleyards was talking to us he said to Dad, right in front of me, 'If I had daughters I wouldn't let them do stockwork.' Dad just looked at me for a minute while I waited to see what he would say. Finally he said, 'I don't know what I'd do without her.' I went red with pleasure. It was the best compliment he ever paid me. I was nine years old.

I'm not saying I enjoyed everything about my life. When Dad was in one of his moods it was no fun being at home. I didn't like some of the jobs, like mulesing – well, you'd have to be sick to like that. But I also didn't like feeding poddies on cold mornings, chopping kindling and lighting the Aga, putting the dogs back on their chains after they'd been for a run, finding mice in my bed during mouse plagues, and finding spiders in my gum boots a few minutes after I'd put them on.

The best time of the year was definitely shearing. We only had a small shed, two stands, and as the economy got worse Dad did a lot of the shearing himself. It was more fun when contractors came in, but I didn't mind either way. As soon as I was old enough I became the roustabout. That was a big moment in my life, being able to do that. Another big moment was being strong enough to throw a fleece onto the table for the classer. Again, Dad had been doing his own classing lately. It was something I wanted to learn; I'd been planning to do a course when I finished school.

I loved the activity in the shearing shed. The sheep milling in the pens. The dogs lying in the shadows panting, their bright eyes watching the sheep, hoping they'd be called up again to run across their backs and shift them to the next yard or back to the paddock. I loved the oily feel of the classing table, the soft whiteness of the fleeces, the quiet bleating of the waiting sheep. I was proud to see our bales, with our brands on them, on the back of a truck heading for the sales. I knew they were going halfway around the world to be made into wonderful warm clothes that would be worn by city people, people I'd never meet. Even the really hard-bitten farmers, the ones you'd think had as much poetry in them as a sedimentary rock, got a bit emotional about shearing. Dad used to look at photos of models wearing wool, in Mum's fashion magazines, with a kind of wonder in his face, like he could hardly believe that our great heavy fleeces could travel so far and be turned into things of such beauty. It was a long way from Wirrawee to Paris and Rome and Tokyo.

But I don't want to give the impression that Dad was a rural redneck, like some of the men in our district. When Mum decided she wanted to do things that would extend her mind, he backed her all the way. She did a course in Art Appreciation, then one in Medieval History, then one in Mandarin Chinese. And she joined a public speaking group in town. Dad was really proud of her and boasted to everyone about how smart she was. Some farmers didn't like their wives going to town more than once a week. When Mrs Salter got offered a job as a part-time debt counsellor with Community Services her husband wouldn't let her take it. So it was pretty gutsy of my dad to stand up in front of his mates and take their jokes about his feminist wife.

I have to admit, we are a few decades behind in Wirrawee sometimes.

But despite all that, Mum was happiest in her kitchen. It was the warm heart of our house, and I think she felt comfortable in it. It was her territory and she was in control. She was a good cook, a creative one, who never followed a recipe exactly. She'd add a touch of basil here, a dash of Tabasco there, and a large swig of wine just about every time. Somehow it always seemed to work out. I can't remember any disasters, except when she sprinkled salt instead of castor sugar on my twelfth birthday cake. She was so good in the kitchen that she intimidated me a bit; I kept to the simplest cooking: scrambled eggs, lamb chops, pasta, anzac biscuits.

There was never much doubt in my mind that I'd run the farm one day. We never talked about it, but I think we took it for granted. All I worried about was how I'd get Dad to give it up without him hanging round for twenty years afterwards telling me what to do.

All of that seemed like a movie to me that night, though, lying under my mat of creepers, waiting for the long lonely hours to tick away. I could call up these images of life as it used to be, but they seemed to be things that happened to other people, happy-looking people in an artificial world, on a big screen. It seemed unreal. I cried myself to sleep, but it wasn't much of a sleep anyway. I was just lonely and scared and lost, and the morning seemed a long way away.

Chapter Seventeen

In the morning the hunger had come back. I felt dizzy and light-headed. When I sat up I thought I would faint. I ached all over: my knee was bad, but it was just one of many pains, mostly from sleeping on a cold uncomfortable bed.

But I was still terrified of being tracked and caught, so I made myself get up. I hobbled into the clearing and looked up at the hills. I'd worked out my tactics as I'd lain there in the dark – I had to get to the highest point and see where I was. Once I knew where I was, I could get to where I was going, if that makes sense.

Of course I now had the extra worry of not knowing if the others would be there. They could have been captured or killed, or they could have given up and gone. Stupidly we hadn't made all the alternative arrangements we normally made for a rendezvous; I suppose we'd thought Homer and I would swim straight to the creek and wade up it to meet Robyn and the rest. We hadn't counted on all the distractions. Plus there'd been so many things to think about, and we'd done everything in such a rush.

The people who kept popping up in my mind were Burke and Wills, from the history books. They'd struggled back to Cooper's Creek, sick and starving after crossing the continent, and found their support party had given up and left seven hours before. That had been a death sentence for Burke and his mate. I was scared I might follow their example.

I kept hobbling round till my body was in some sort of working order. The sun still wasn't up, which meant that the ground was very cold, and that made it even harder to get myself going. Eventually I shoved my arms into my armpits and, hugging myself to try to get warm, I set off, head down, eyes half closed against the cruel sharp breeze.

Once I got started it wasn't too bad for a while. The hunger pains left me again and the slope wasn't too steep. It was annoying having to keep a lookout as well as walk; I hoped that I'd hear any soldiers before they heard me, but I couldn't count on that. Navigation wasn't such a problem: I knew that as long as I went uphill it had to be the right direction.

The big problem soon became obvious. The higher I got, the less cover was available. The trees thinned out and there was more and more rock, outcrops so hard to climb and so bare that I was afraid I could be seen from k's away. I had little enough energy for climbing, let alone for trying to stay concealed at the same time. But it was no good avoiding it; with a groan and a few curses, and a feeble push of my hair out of my eyes, I worked my way around to the right where there were more trees. It probably added twenty minutes to the climb.

I was sweating hard by the time I got to the top. It was a couple of hours after sunrise. There wasn't much heat in the day but I was creating my own heat by this slow hard stagger up the hill. I resented having to keep worrying about aircraft and ground troops, and although I kept looking for them, it was by a sort of reflex: I could hardly remember what I was looking for.

Someone had built a little cairn of rocks at the top. There was no obvious reason for it, but at least when I saw it I knew I must be at the summit. I skirted around it and went back further into the shade of some trees. Then at last I was able to turn and look at the view.

There was Cobbler's Bay spread out before me. And away in the distance, beyond the heads, was the blue and beautiful ocean. I longed to be on it, sailing away. As much as I loved my country, it was not a happy place to be these days. I didn't know whose fault it was that it was so stuffed – the invaders, our politicians, or we ordinary people who hadn't taken enough interest – but right now I was too weary from the strain of surviving to enjoy it any longer. I could still admire the beauty of the coastline but I wanted a holiday from it.

My eyes swivelled a bit to the right. When I saw what was there I sat up fast and made a little 'Oh' noise out loud. I was looking at the wharf, or what was left of it. It was the first time I'd seen the results of one of our attacks so soon after it happened. The only other one I'd seen was the Wirrawee bridge, but that was ages later, and it was hard to think of it as something we'd done. By then it looked more like an archaeological ruin.

The Cobbler's wharf was a bloody mess. The ship Homer and I had been on had disappeared completely.

The wharf itself had lost all its middle section and the rest of it was black and charred; there was no part wide enough to drive even a car along. It seemed like it had caught fire and burned fiercely. Two cranes had collapsed and were lying on their sides like stick insects. Another big ship was still moored at the wrecked wharf but it was burnt all along its deck and half sunk; it was virtually a floating hull. It didn't look like it would be going anywhere for a long time.

Beyond the wharf, a couple of hectares of bush had been demolished and burnt. It looked like someone had gone through it with a giant whipper-snipper.

No wonder the New Zealand jet was able to fly around as much as it wanted. There was nothing left there worth defending.

It was the most exciting view I'd ever seen. It gave me new energy, wonderful energy. I wanted to dance and scream and shout. If we did nothing else for the whole of this horrible war we could at least say now that we had made a major difference. We hadn't just damaged the enemy in our own little area of Wirrawee; we'd damaged him in a way that would make a real difference to his ability to take over our country.

I turned my gaze to the left, searching. Sure enough I soon saw what I was looking for: another blackened patch of burnt bush, the crowns of trees brown and scorched. In the middle of it was the twisted wrecked metal of the helicopter, a black skeleton. Looking at it I gave a savage grin, a wild grin. I could take some credit for the chopper too, I reminded myself again. By God, we had made a difference.

I sat there smirking. For a few moments I felt free to enjoy what we'd achieved. I forgot the hunger, the fear, the aches and pains. For a few moments I don't think I'd have cared if I'd been caught. I knew we'd been lucky a lot of times – we'd been lucky we weren't caught in the first place, when they invaded – but we'd made the most of our luck and we hadn't let our families and friends down. We'd done a lot with the freedom we had.

Back to the right I at last saw Baloney Creek, where we'd agreed to meet. I could see no sign of life, but of course I didn't expect to. All I knew was that it was still a long way off. I worked out my bearings. There was the logging track, a dirt road that cut through the bush and crossed the creek about a k from its mouth.

I was too tired to resist the temptation of the track. There was no evidence of any pursuers, anyone looking for us. I think the Kiwi bird had scared them off. So I figured that if I made for the track and walked along beside it, in the bush, I should be safe, and that way I wouldn't get lost.

I made the big effort to get going, standing with a big sigh. At least the first part was downhill, and so would be the last part.

At that moment, as though it had been waiting for me to show myself, a helicopter came over the rise behind me. I squatted fast and covered my head. It swept across the hill, travelling fast and low. Just as I hadn't expected the earlier one to see me, and it had, so I expected this one to see me, and it didn't. Murphy's Law. I felt a cold dark shiver as its shadow crossed me, but it continued down into the valley. It was searching all right, combing the valley in long passes just metres from the treetops. I bet its crew was nervous, being able to see the wreck of the other one.

I waited till it had its back to me, searching nearer the coast, and I put my head down and ran like a rabbit. Not till I was well into the treeline did I stop again and stand there hugging a tree – well, leaning against it, anyway. My calves and lower legs were shaking, trembling, and it took a long time to stop them. Now that I was deep in the bush, the chopper was just a faint humming sound, and that made me feel a bit safer.

My hunger was making my stomach cramp and I had to bend over for a while to make the pain go away. So it was ten or fifteen minutes before I felt well enough to start out for the dirt road. I'd thought the downhill would be easy, but before long I was wishing for some uphill. It hurt my calves too much going downhill; I had to use them to brake myself on the steep slope. But when I did hit an uphill section I wasn't happy with that either. It was hard on my knees, the good one and the bad one, and soon the backs of my legs were hurting like crazy, too. It got to the point where any slight slope seemed like the Swiss Alps. I'd start trudging up it and after a while I'd lift my head, expecting to see that I was almost at the top, and find to my anguish that I wasn't even halfway. That happened with every hill and was very frustrating.

When I came to the road I'd almost given up hope that I'd find it. I had convinced myself that I'd made some terrible mistake in navigation. The only reason I kept going was because I couldn't think of anything else to do, didn't have the energy to stop and reconsider. I'd thought I heard a vehicle at one time, but it was either a very quiet vehicle or it was a long way off – or else I imagined it. Occasionally the buzzing of the helicopter would send me stumbling under the trees, but I never actually saw it again.

But suddenly there was the brown dirt strip under my feet and I was on the edge of the track.

I turned right automatically and, with a faint feeling of relief – forgetting that I'd planned to stay in the bush – started to tramp along it. Now that I was there I could see what a rough old track it was. Long grass grew in its centre, so it was obvious from that alone that it hadn't seen a lot of recent traffic. As I walked I did notice one thing though: that the grass was freshly bent over and bruised in quite a few places. Sometimes you could even see it slowly standing again as you walked past. Seemed like that vehicle I thought I'd heard mightn't have been an illusion. I started getting nervous all over again.

The roar of the helicopter came loud in my ears and I ducked into the trees and waited. This time it sounded like it was heading straight towards Cobbler's Bay. It had abandoned its searching pattern. Perhaps they were going home for lunch. I came out and kept walking.

Round a long bend, a bend that curved and curved long after I thought it should have straightened out again, I found the vehicle. It was a fawn-coloured Holden Jackaroo, quite a new one, but with the look of a car that wasn't going to live to a ripe old age. It was very dirty and had lots of scratches and marks, including a smashed tail light and a broken side window. Not that I stood there studying it for a long time. I got such a shock that I felt like I'd been woken from a long sleep by someone putting ice blocks down my back.

I did a double take, then dived into the bush

again, my heart thudding hard. But there wasn't any movement from the car. I stood there watching for several minutes. Gradually I realised that something was very wrong. The Jackaroo was in fact at our rendezvous spot. I could just see the track drop down to the gravelly river crossing in among the trees. It was Baloney Creek. There was a vague possibility that Lee and the others had stolen a vehicle, but if they had they'd never park it in the open like this. No, there was only one reason there'd be a car parked here.

I started creeping along to get closer to the vehicle. There was no sign of life in it at all. I kept going, waiting for some warning sign that would make me stop but, as there wasn't one, I kept going till I was level with it. I crouched furtively behind a gorse bush, wondering what I should do, looking for a cue. Then I got one. A shot rang out behind me; a single shot, though not sounding like the shots I was used to. It was followed immediately by a girl's scream: a girl who sounded awfully like Fi.

I'd been so scared already that the sound of the shot frightened me out of my boots. I burst out of the bush, running away from the shot, thinking for a crazy moment that someone was firing at me. Of course this meant that I practically crashed into the Jackaroo. That little fact, the fact that I went onto the road instead of in another direction, changed all our lives. Because as I stood, shaking, next to the car, having no idea where to go or what to do, but realising that no one seemed to be chasing me, two things happened. One was that I heard Homer's voice, unmistakeably, call out something like 'No way!' I got instant goosebumps on the back of my neck to hear

165

that voice. He could so easily have been shot or drowned or blown up, but he had survived. He had survived! It was wonderful to hear those two words, even in these conditions.

There was some shouting then, that I couldn't pick up. But at the same moment, the other vital thing happened: I saw a revolver sitting on the driver's seat of the Holden. I reached through the window and grabbed it without hesitation. It was an ugly black thing, all hard edges, no curves or smooth surfaces. I checked it quickly. It seemed to work on the same principles as every other gun I'd fired. A switch under the trigger guard released the magazine. I slipped it out. The little holes showed two bullets but, when I pulled back the slide, I found another one in the chamber.

All that took just three or four seconds. I flicked the safety catch up to 'on', and walked through the trees towards the voices.

Chapter Eighteen

I'll never forget the next minute. The image I most remember is the first view I had of the soldiers and my friends. They were all gathered around the creek in a little cleared area. They looked like they were having a meeting. There were three soldiers, all men and all on my side of the creek. Two were standing to my left, the other on my right. They looked tense but excited, very happy with themselves. The two on my left held rifles, but the one on the right, who was an officer, seemed unarmed. I guessed it was his revolver that I carried.

I could still smell a trace of gunpowder in the air but none of my friends seemed hurt. They were standing in a line on a big flat rock, across the other side of the shallow gurgling creek. Their hands were on their heads. Fi was white and trembling uncontrollably; Robyn had her chin out, defiantly; Lee's face was totally expressionless. Homer looked desperate, thin and tired, with his dark eyes sunk deep in his face. But I was so relieved to see him at all: I'd had the worst fears about what might have happened to him.

Kevin was standing a little apart from the others and he looked absolutely terrified.

I didn't even think about what to do. It was a relief, not having to think: for once the choice was made for me. I stood very still, feet well apart, lifted the revolver, held it with both hands, aimed carefully at the chest of the first soldier, and squeezed the trigger. Gently, gently, squeeze, squeeze. I thought it would never fire, it took so long. Then the bang, the explosion, the smoke, the smell. The gun kicked up hard, like it had been given a jolt of electricity, and the empty shell shot out, to my right. I saw the soldier go staggering backwards, dropping his rifle, his hands to his chest as though trying – unsuccessfully – to hold himself together. But I had no time to think about him. I aimed again, fired again: shot the second one before he had his rifle halfway to his shoulder.

Then I turned to the officer. He was facing me now. He didn't seem to know where to go. I fired for the third time. My hands were shaking badly and the bullet went a little low. The slide locked back; the gun was empty; useless scrap metal. I threw it away, quickly, as if it was contaminated. It fell in the creek.

It had all been very quick, kind of clinical, not at all like our other killings had been. Just popping down targets, with no emotion.

Or maybe that was just a measure of how much I'd changed.

The others handled it pretty much in the same style though. Lee went straight to the bodies and checked each one quickly. Robyn and Kevin grabbed the rucksacks: seemed like they were the current packhorses. Homer ran over and gave me a quick kiss. 'Thank God you're all right,' he said, and I was amazed to see tears in his eyes.

Fi followed him and gave me a longer hug. 'Thank you, Ellie,' was all she said.

Without any discussion we ran straight out to the dirt track. We didn't need any discussion to know that speed was going to save us or kill us. 'Take the car,' I yelled to Lee, who was well in front of me. It was a calculated risk, but I thought it was the best thing. If we could get a few k's away and dump it, we'd at least get a decent start.

No one argued. When I got there Robyn and Lee had already piled into the back, Kevin was following them, and Fi was waiting her turn. Homer had gone around to the passenger side. Seemed like I was driving, though God knows how I was meant to find the energy. But I didn't stop to discuss it. I jumped in. The key was in the ignition. The Jackaroo started straight away, but it was facing in the opposite direction to the one we wanted. In the narrow track it was hard to see a place to turn; I just shrugged and shoved the car in reverse and drove it hard back along the road.

'Goddam!' Kevin gasped, as we careered along, probably doing sixty in reverse. The others didn't say anything but they looked more scared than when I'd been shooting the soldiers. We were going around the long curve and were nearly through it when I thought I saw a spot coming up that would do to turn; a clearing on my left. I hauled on the wheel but misjudged it badly, missing the clearing and thumping into a small tree. I remembered the damage this car had already suffered to its rear end and realised grimly that I had just made it ten times worse. Kevin was rubbing his head where he'd hit it on the roof at impact, but he didn't say anything. I was grateful for that. Fi was biting her lip anxiously. Thankfully the car didn't stall, and still seemed to steer OK. I swung the wheel and we took off again, this time facing the right way.

I was pretty confident that we wouldn't meet any traffic, and at the speed we were going I had to hope we wouldn't. Apart from Kevin's 'Goddam' no one had said a word since we started. I was terrified of helicopters but we'd have little chance of seeing or hearing them if they came. I just kept my foot down and moved the car along at speeds that gave me hernias.

After twenty minutes we hit the main road. There was no warning – suddenly we burst out of the bush onto bitumen and I was spinning the wheel again, putting the car into a squealing skidding turn that nearly tipped us over. I straightened it, but it took a hundred metres to get it back on an even keel, steering a straight line. I got it over to the left-hand side of the road and wiped my face, not daring to look at the others.

We raced on, up into the hills. 'How far do we want to take this thing?' I asked.

'Not much further,' Homer said.

'They'll know we've got it,' Robyn called from the back. 'So we've got to dump it where they won't find it. And the further we get the better, because that'll give them a wider area to search.'

'We dumped that BMW in a dam,' Fi said.

'I'm just worried we'll meet a convoy,' I said.

We were in thick bush now, but still on the main coast road.

'Do you want your stuff?' Robyn called out suddenly.

'What?'

'Your packs are hidden just around the next corner. Do you want them?'

I thought quickly and decided that I certainly wanted mine. We screeched to a stop and jumped out, grabbing the heavy packs from under piles of leaves and bark. I found I didn't have the strength to pull my pack into the back of the Jackaroo, and had to ask Robyn to do it for me. She looked at me anxiously. 'It's OK,' I said. 'Just find me some food, please.'

We drove on, and a minute later her hand appeared in front of my face. She was holding something. I was too busy driving to look at it but I opened my mouth and she pressed a date into it. I love dates. I have no idea where she got them – I didn't know she had any – but she was always coming up with little surprises like that.

We sped on through a couple of big intersections, turning right at a third one to confuse them when they started the next search for us. We were on a road which, according to a sign, led to Stratton via Garley Vale. At least there was less chance of convoys now, but we were all anxious to get rid of the car. We'd pushed our luck hard enough. Our chance came at last when Fi spotted, of all things, a wrecker's yard.

'There!' she said.

'What?'

'If you want to hide a book, put it in a bookcase.'

'What?'

'Over there, that wrecker's yard. If we hide the car in there they won't find it for ten years.'

I looked at Homer and we both laughed. He shrugged. 'Why not?'

I turned off the road into the driveway. The yard was called Ralston's Wreckers. It looked funny: several hectares of smashed cars stuck in the middle of the countryside. The ones at the back were old rusted wrecks, most missing their doors and bonnets. Ivy and blackberries, and in one place a passionfruit vine, were growing all over them. With some, it was hard to tell what make they were, or even what colour they had been. But closer to the front were the newer models, some still glossy and bright, spoilt only by a crumpled rear end, a smashed side or a dented roof.

I drove along the rows until I found a gap where the Jackaroo looked at home. I drove it in nose-first so that the wrecked rear was showing.

And at last I could let go. I was in worse shape than the Jackaroo, but I didn't have to run and fight and starve any more, not for a few minutes anyway. Maybe not for a few hours. I turned off the ignition and leaned forward, resting my forehead on the steering wheel. 'Someone get the number plates,' I said, closing my eyes. No other vehicle in the yard had number plates, so we had to get ours off. But I let the others do that. I just sat. I wanted to lie down somewhere and sleep but I was too tired to go find a place. I could hear them unpacking the car and talking to each other, just occasional mumbled comments, but I couldn't hear what they were saying – not because they were talking too softly or because I was deaf, but because I was so tired I couldn't turn the sounds into words. The stuff was coming in my ears but not reaching my brain. The energy required to push the words the last millimetre into my brain wasn't there. I've never been that tired before.

I started lying across the front seats of the car: not exactly lying, just letting myself fall sideways. All the bruises and aches and pains were hurting hard now, now that I didn't have to ignore them, fight them off. But then there was a cold draft as someone opened the door.

'Don't,' I whined, 'don't.' I huddled up a little tighter, trying to keep warm.

'Come on, Ellie,' Fi's voice said. 'You can't stay there.'

But I didn't want to move, couldn't move. I was like that five-year-old again, wanting someone to carry her into the house after she'd fallen asleep on a late-night ride home.

'Come on, Ellie,' Fi said again. She didn't even sound sympathetic, just bullying and irritated, too tired herself to have sympathy for me.

She tugged on my leg and I kicked out angrily and connected pretty hard with something. Fi squealed, in anger or pain or both, and I realised I'd have to move now. I'd put myself too far in the wrong. So without a word of apology to Fi, who was holding her side and scowling, I stumbled out of the car and along the row towards Robyn, who I could see in the distance.

They were setting up a rough camp in the back of a Nissan E20 delivery van that had been whacked severely right where the driver had been sitting. He would have got a hell of a headache: it was really a mess in that corner. But the rear section was whole, and dry. I didn't say anything to anyone, just dragged myself in there and lay like an old sleeping bag. I was still very hungry but had no energy to eat.

It turned out that I didn't have the energy to sleep, either. I probably did sleep a bit but I didn't feel like I had. Fi and Homer squeezed in beside me after a while, but I ignored them. Lee and Robyn were doing sentry. I knew sooner or later a patrol would come around, but I had to trust the others to be ready for them, to take the precautions.

At least the patrol didn't come till the next morning. I slept a bit during the night. It was warmer with the bodies of the others to snuggle up to. I let them do all the sentry duties; no one asked me and I couldn't have got out of the van. Fi brought me some food quite early in the evening and again at dawn. I ate both times, and gratefully too. It wasn't until I was busting for a leak that I finally left the van, and even then I put it off until I was desperate.

At about eleven o'clock Robyn arrived at a run. 'They're coming,' she said.

We all came writhing out of the back of the E20, like a nest full of snakes.

'This way,' Lee said to me. I followed him down to the back row of cars, and beyond them to an old overgrown collapsed fence. We climbed over that and ran on down to a patch of bush. We grovelled in there till we were well out of sight.

'How long do you think they'll keep looking for us?' I asked Lee, as we lay there. We were so close that we were nearly touching, but I wanted to keep his mind on other things.

'Until they find us,' he answered grimly.

That seemed to kill off any romantic thoughts.

'Did the helicopters wake you?' Lee asked after a while.

'What helicopters?'

'There's been three this morning already. The first one was just after dawn.'

'Looking for us?'

'I guess.'

I couldn't think of anything else to say that wasn't too personal or too frightening. So I just lay there. Ten minutes later, Robyn appeared in front of us.

'Anti-climax, guys,' she said. 'They drove in, drove round the yard, and drove straight out again.'

'They didn't see the Jackaroo?' I asked.

'No, they didn't go near it.'

We went back into the yard, where I at last had

174

enough energy to start taking an interest in my surroundings. I saw Homer, who was on his way to have a poke around the house at the end of Ralston's yard; presumably the home of the Ralston family.

'Do you want to come?' he asked.

'OK.' I was really just tagging along for the ride, something to do.

'What happened to you in the water?' Homer asked.

'Not now, please,' I begged. 'I don't want to talk about it now. I don't want to talk about anything.'

He shut up.

We approached the house from the back, which was on the gully side. Then we realised that it was actually the front; that it had been built with its back to the road. The effect was strange: it was facing nothing much. It was an old weatherboard place, with a galvanised-iron roof. A verandah ran right around it, and a grapevine ran along that, as thick as a telegraph pole in some places. There were no electricity poles, but there was quite a modern generator almost hidden around the back. The house really was a dump, though. It wouldn't have been much of a place when it was first built and years of neglect had made sure that it was more of a dump now. The verandah was bowed in the middle, and swayed and sank as we stepped onto it. A row of starter motors was neatly placed along the wall to the left; a dozen of them at least. Half a bird's nest lay near the front door, and the mat was fraying on all four sides. Stencilled on the mat in faded black letters was the message: TAKE YOUR BLOODY SHOES OFF.

Yet, after all that, we were surprised to find a big gleaming lock on the front door. It looked expensive, and tough to crack. The door itself was quite solid, so we didn't bother with either. I picked up a stick and went to break a window. 'Hope there's not a burglar alarm,' Homer said nervously. 'Someone on the road might hear it.'

I thought for a moment. 'Doubt it. Why put in a burglar alarm when there's no neighbours to hear it?'

I smashed the glass out in one pane, then, when there was no sound of sirens and ringing bells, smashed out the other panes, too.

'Anyway,' I said to Homer, 'There's no power line. It'd have to run off batteries and they'd be flat by now.'

I knocked out the rest of the glass and the cross-pieces of wood, then swung a leg over the sill and climbed inside. It was dark and smelly, like going into a laundry full of over-used socks. Rain had leaked down one side of the wall and stained the wallpaper; it was all mildewy and musty.

'Imagine living here,' Homer said behind me.

I went on into the kitchen, where it was too dark to see much. There was a fridge, but I wasn't going to open that, and an old meat safe with cans on the top that looked worth investigating. It was obvious that no looters had been here, probably because the house was so run down it didn't look worth the trouble. Homer went through another door into the back of the house and I had a look at the bathroom. There was an old claw-foot bath, a bit like the one at home. I peered into it and was disgusted to see two little grey furry things with tails sticking out of the plughole. It took a moment for me to realise what they were: mice that had died in there, probably so desperate with thirst that they'd stuck their heads down the hole looking for water.

Homer came in but before I could say anything about the mice, he said, with a sort of quiver of excitement: 'Come and look what I've found.'

Chapter Nineteen

I followed Homer through an old crimson curtain that served as a door. It was like we'd suddenly landed in an electronics showroom. I couldn't even recognise most of the stuff. There was a computer and a printer, a couple of video recorders and a monitor, and a fax machine. That was standard enough. But the whole of the far wall was communications equipment. There seemed to be a variety of radios, two microphones, and a lot of little gadgets, like a walkie-talkie and a mobile phone.

'Amazing,' I said.

'Looks like a branch of Tandy,' Homer said.

'Talk about a double life. Living in the nineteenth century half the time and the twenty-first century the other half.'

'Yeah, toys for the boys,' Homer said. 'They say no matter how old guys are, they have to have their toys.'

That sounded so funny coming from Homer that I had to struggle not to laugh.

'This one's like the rural firefighting sets,' I said, walking over to a big radio unit in the corner.

'Yeah.' Homer was looking thoughtful. 'I think this

guy's a real whatever they call it, ham. Short-wave radios and all that stuff. I tell you, Ellie, we could probably talk to other countries using this gear.'

'E-mail with voices.'

'Exactly.'

'You just want to play with these toys yourself.'

'Yeah, maybe.'

'What exactly are you thinking? Giving yourself the pleasure of some French practice?'

'New Zealand. If we could get in touch with the Kiwis, if they knew we were the ones who blew up Cobbler's Bay, they might, I don't know . . .'

I began to realise where Homer was heading. My mind began to jump at some of the possibilities.

'They might come and rescue us?'

'Well, they might.'

'We'd need to start the generator. I don't think the noise of that'd be too good.'

'Mmm. But we've got to take some risks. At night we could see them coming from a good way off.'

'It's possible, I suppose. I do like the idea of a holiday in Milford Sound. But surely they'd have too much on their minds to worry about a few kids.'

'Probably. But still . . .'

The thing was that once Homer put the idea in my head, I knew I was stuck with it. For months we'd had no glimpse of even the slightest hope. We couldn't see any end to this war in the near future; maybe not even in the distant future. So what was to become of us? Were we doomed to wander the countryside, having smaller and smaller areas where we could hide, until one day we were caught? That seemed our only choice. At one stage I'd even had a dream of making a raft and sailing to New Zealand, like ship-wrecked mariners in old adventure stories.

But at least if we could talk to someone, to anyone, really: well, at least they'd know we were alive. That would be comforting, even if they didn't send a VIP jet to rescue us.

'We'll have to ask the others,' I said at last.

'Look,' Homer said, showing me an old exercise book. 'This is the key. It's all the call-signs and frequencies and things.'

I took it and had a look. A lot of it didn't make any sense, just lists of numbers. But it was obvious that this guy could tune in to the emergency frequencies: he had numbers for police, ambulance, fire authority, different airports, air force, state emergency. I had a vague idea that it was illegal to listen in to some of these channels. Oh well. Not many of them would be broadcasting these days.

We climbed back out the broken window and went to find the others. Lee and Fi had joined Kevin and Robyn on sentry duty and they were talking earnestly. It turned out they were discussing the same subject that was starting to obsess us all: our futures. They'd been trying to recall the news Kevin had brought of the counter attacks: troops from New Guinea were holding an area around Cape Martindale; the Kiwis had recaptured much of the southern coastline: the Burdekin and the area around Newington. Trouble was, that was weeks ago; a lot could have changed since. What Lee wanted to do was to get through to Newington. It was a thought that horrified me.

'Lee, I don't know what a full-on war zone would be like – none of us do – but I can't see how we could possibly get to a place like that. I mean, surely there'd be tanks and rocket launchers and all that stuff. If it was easy just to waltz through it all, the Kiwis would have done it.'

'But they wouldn't be expecting anyone to come from the other direction,' said Robyn, who seemed to be agreeing with Lee.

'I don't see that we have any choice,' Lee said. 'The one thing we all agree on is that we've got no future here. The war's not going to end in a hurry, and we're running out of options fast. We've got to make something happen, not sit around and wait to be caught. Take the initiative, do something decisive, that's what I reckon.'

I mentally cursed all those videos that Lee had watched over the years. Stallone had a lot to answer for.

'But Lee, we can't take on an army. All we've done so far has been sneaky stuff. We've been like rats in the dark, keeping ourselves invisible. That's why we've been so successful – well, one reason, anyway,' I added, not wanting to give up all the credit I thought we deserved. 'We can't go into a battle zone. We just aren't prepared for that. They'd knock us over in thirty seconds.'

'So what do you want us to do?' he said angrily. 'Sit on our bums and wait? Start making white flags that we can wave when they come for us?'

'I don't know what to do! Stop acting like there's one right answer and all we have to do is find it and that'll be the end of our problems! This isn't a Maths test.'

That killed off the argument a bit. Homer and I told them about our discovery, and that got everyone excited. We agreed it would be too dangerous to start the generator in day time, but there was no hesitation about having a go that night. Lee went off to check it out. Robyn and Kevin still had an hour of sentry to do, and Fi wanted to show me an old lube pit that she'd found. She had the clever idea of turning it into a bolt hole by covering it with iron and parking a vehicle over the top. We sweated for a while doing that. It was quite fun, and the result was perfect. After we'd covered it with galvanised iron we scattered dirt over it, and a few bits of exhaust pipes, a broken windscreen, and an empty soft drink can. Then we pushed an old Commer delivery van over the top of that, and brushed away the tyre tracks so it looked like it had been sitting there for twenty years.

Homer and Lee had taken over as sentries by then, but we challenged the other two to a game of hide and seek. We made it easy for them by telling them which row of cars we'd be in, then we ran down there, slipped into the pit through a little hole we'd left open, and pulled the galvanised iron in place above us. It was a dark little cubby but dry, and we sat in there quite comfortably, giggling at our own cleverness. After five or six minutes we heard Kevin and Robyn searching; Robyn opened the back door of the Commer and we heard her say 'Not here.' We gave them a couple more minutes, then crawled out. They were already four cars further down the row. We were delighted. It wasn't a place where we'd want to spend six months of our lives, but it was a good retreat for emergencies.

Helicopters continued to be our major problem, though. We got buzzed twice more that morning, then in the afternoon one of them returned, and went

over the yard really carefully. Backwards and forwards, backwards and forwards, patient and relent-
less. The noise shook through me: there was no
keeping it out. We were all in hiding but our problem
was the Jackaroo. If they saw that they could call up
ground troops and surround the place, then pick us
off at their leisure.

The helicopter spent more than ten minutes scanning the yard. Then it tilted and turned and moved
off to the north. It started inspecting a set of sheds
that we could see about a k away. We had to assume
that this meant we were safe; that we had survived
again.

If only we could relax.

Just before five o'clock, a formation of jets
screamed past, but there was no other action in the air.

When it got dark, Homer went off to the old house
to fiddle with the generator. Despite the danger, we
were all looking forward to having a go on the short
wave. We didn't know whether it would achieve anything, but it was probably worth the risk. We had an
idea that any listening enemies might be able to trace
us if we talked on it for too long. That was our biggest
worry.

At half past ten we got ready for the big experi-
ment. We had the notebook with the frequencies. All
we could work out from it was that we probably
needed to be in the VHF 30 to 300 MHz frequency.
That seemed to be where all the big operators were:
the police and the airports and the ambulance. We
weren't expecting to have a nice friendly chat with
Constable Jones at the local cop shop, but we were
hoping to reach New Zealand, and we had to hope
that they used a similar range of frequencies to us.

I didn't know what VHF 30 to 300 MHz meant, but it was easy enough to see on the dial where those figures were. We used a candle for light and turned the tuner to 300. Lee and Robyn were on sentry but Lee was just outside the back door and Robyn outside the window of the room, so they could listen in to whatever happened. Kevin was standing by at the generator and Homer was operating the radio itself. We were ready.

'OK, fire her up,' Homer called. Kevin gave the cord a pull. It was a pull-start Honda generator, and it started on the third try. Pretty impressive. What we hadn't counted on – and what we should have checked before we started – was that half the lights in the house slowly started coming on too.

'Turn it off! Turn it off!' Lee shouted at Kevin.

A moment later we were back in silence and darkness.

Robyn jumped in through the window. 'If there was anyone on the road they would have seen that,' she said.

'Head for the lube pit,' Homer ordered.

We ran like hares straight for it, and squeezed in one by one, leaving only Robyn outside, ready to follow if she saw anything.

With exaggerated caution we decided to wait in there a full hour. Homer was raging. 'I can't believe we didn't check those bloody switches,' he kept saying. He made me feel guilty, though I don't know why it should have been my job.

Finally I said: 'It's done, Homer. Shut up about it.'

We sat in the dark, sweating to think of some enemy patrol about to descend on us. But after a while I think we all dozed off. I know I did, and apparently Homer did, too. I'd been going on nervous energy for many hours and it suddenly seemed to run out. And the others decided to let us sleep. We were meant to have gone on sentry duty at 5 am but they split it up between them and let us sleep till dawn. Sure it was a cramped uncomfortable sleep but it was better than nothing, and it was a lot better than sentry.

I crawled out of the hole at about seven and found the others sitting around drinking tea that they'd boiled on a little fire in a sheltered corner of the junkyard. Although they'd put the fire out and buried it, the billy was still hot enough to make me a cuppa.

'You should have woken me,' I said, but without much conviction.

'We were going to, then Lee figured out about the time difference,' Robyn said.

'The time difference?' I asked, still not functioning above twenty per cent.

'If we'd tried to call New Zealand at midnight, it'd be about two o'clock their time and they'd all be asleep,' Lee explained.

'Oh yes.'

I drank my tea.

'So what are we going to do?' I asked, when my mind was starting to rev up properly.

'Try again, and do it about now,' Robyn said. 'We can't leave it much later. Today's the most likely day for them to come looking for us. So we should go into hiding pretty soon.'

She went to wake Homer while I threw out the tea leaves and followed the others to the house. Although Lee swore he'd checked that the lights were off this time I couldn't help but double check, which must have annoyed him out of his mind. Still, he was tactful enough not to say anything. I was so flat and tired I could hardly move. I was thinking about those action war movies Lee liked, where the hero goes from a martial arts fight to a ski chase to a gun battle to a wrestle with piranhas, and all that time he never seems to slow down or need a rest.

Every time we did anything dangerous I took ages to recover – not because of the physical effort, which sometimes wasn't much, but I think because of the emotional backlash. The episode at the river – I call it an 'episode' because it helps me not to think of it as killing or murder – overwhelmed my mind so much that it left me an emotional paraplegic for a long time.

So checking the light switches was about the most energetic thing I did. For once I was content to take a back seat. Homer came in looking shocking and rubbing his eyes, shivering in the cold of the early morning. But he was desperately keen to make the transmission and no one else seemed to mind, so we took up the positions we'd been in the night before. I found myself shivering too: from the cold, from the risk we were taking, but most of all from the exciting feeling that we might be about to talk to a friendly adult again – a rare opportunity in our lives.

Kevin pulled the cord, the generator started first go, the lights didn't come on, but, when the output reached 240 volts and Homer threw the switch, things lit up all around the room. The computer made a birrrkkking noise, the video recorder flashed zeros, the printer went baddup baddup, and several radios emitted static that sounded like rain on the roof. Robyn and I went around quickly pulling plugs out, until the only thing left functioning was the short-wave transmitter. Homer was intent on its dial, slowly turning the tuning knob. The main sound was static, but occasionally we heard foreign voices mixed in with it: nothing but unintelligible mutters constantly interrupted by crackling noises. Some of the bursts of static were so loud and unexpected that they sounded aggressive: they made me jump.

After ten minutes of watching Homer spinning the knob backwards and forwards, Robyn asked: 'How long are we going to risk doing this?'

Without looking up, Homer said: 'Ask Lee how it looks outside.'

I went out the back window and found Lee, who was keeping watch from the top of the water tank where he was almost completely hidden by ivy.

'How's it looking?' I asked.

'Nothing to see. What's happening with the radio?'

'Just static.'

'Let's give it another fifteen minutes,' Homer said, when I reported back.

'That's nearly half an hour all together,' Robyn said. 'That's a long time if they have tracking equipment zeroing in on us.'

No one seemed willing to make a decision. We stood watching Homer as he continued to try, with his head on one side, listening intently.

At twenty-one minutes we hit something, a couple of words in English. Homer frantically backtracked, trying to bring the voice into focus. It took him a couple of goes, crossing backwards and forwards above the voice, then suddenly he had it quite clearly. We all leaned forward.

'. . . but a foxskin has to be perfect,' a man said.

186

'Prices are that low, it's not worth your trouble. There's too many of the buggers. Over.'

We couldn't hear the reply, but after a few moments of static Homer made his move. He pressed the transmission button and said, 'Hello. Can you hear me?' He said it three times, then released the button again.

The reply was immediate. The man said, 'Hang on, Hank. I missed the last bit. There's a gatecrasher around. Mate, get off the air would you? Learn some manners.'

I whispered to Homer, 'Say "mayday".'

I knew it was a powerful word to use. And it sure was. Homer said it three times. Suddenly we had an ally.

'Hank, I've got a mayday. Call you tomorrow. Go ahead, mayday. What's your problem?'

'Are you in New Zealand?' Homer asked.

'10–4, over.'

We were all leaning forward, crowding around the microphone, as though we were trying to get inside the transmitter.

Homer started. 'There's six of us, trapped in the Cobbler's Bay area, near Stratton. We've managed to stay free since the invasion but it's getting really hard. We're hoping to get some help to get out of here, before they catch us. It's pretty hot for us at the moment. Um, over.'

The man's voice came back straight away, quiet but confident. 'OK, got all that. First thing, don't give any more details about your location. You don't know who might be listening. Second thing, don't stay on the air long. You can be traced. Now mate, as you can imagine, you're not the first Aussies to call for help.

All I can do is record your details and pass them on to the military. I've got to tell you, I don't think there's much we can do for you. That's been the story with the others I've talked to. But if you call me back in two hours, by then I'll have had a wee chat to military intelligence and I'll tell you what they say. Over.'

'Where are you?' Homer asked.

'South Island. Thirty-six k's out of Christchurch. Now are there any details you want to tell me about yourselves? But be careful, ay. Over.'

'We're just a bunch of teenagers,' Homer said. 'We've done the best we can but I don't know how much longer we can keep going.'

Homer sounded tired and defeated, almost like he was going to cry. I was shocked. I didn't think Homer would ever sound like that. Robyn grabbed the microphone.

'When you talk to the military,' she said, 'tell them we're the ones who blew up Cobbler's Bay. Over.'

'Cobbler's Bay, OK. I'll tell them. Anything else? Over.'

'No,' Robyn said. 'I guess that's all. We'll call you back in two hours. Over and out.'

'Good luck, kids,' the man said. 'Take care over there. We're with you a hundred per cent, you know that. Over and out.'

Chapter Twenty

The two hours took forever. All of us had been through the same emotions, I think. We'd started pinning a lot on our call to New Zealand, though we didn't know exactly how they could help us. It had been so exciting when the man responded to our mayday. But it hadn't taken him long to curdle our little cup of hope. Our reactions after that were about what you'd expect. We wandered off in different directions – the four of us not on sentry, that is – no one wanting to talk to anyone else. The thing was, now I couldn't see any hope at all. What could we do? Where could we go? The only option was to return to Hell, but I couldn't stomach that idea at the moment. I thought I'd go mad in that claustrophobic cauldron of rocks and trees. I never wanted to see it again. I wanted to see escalators and traffic lights and sky-scrapers and crowded crowded streets. I wanted to mix with millions of people, in the world's biggest city. I was sick of our lifestyle and the five people I had to share it with.

I landed in the room with the electronics gear fifteen minutes before we were due to call back.

I thought it was getting dangerous. Anything in the bright daylight scared me now. We should not be out in the light. I told Homer to keep it quick if we did manage to re-establish the contact. But Homer just got offended and said he'd worked that out for himself, he wasn't stupid. I sighed and sat there, gazing at my watch, then going out every couple of minutes and looking anxiously at the road. Robyn and Fi were our sentries but they couldn't bear to get too far away, which meant in fact that they were practically in the room with us.

With two minutes to go Kevin got the generator running and as soon as the output reached 240 again he rushed in to listen. Homer had left the transmitter on the right frequency and he began to broadcast. To our relief, and excitement, he got an answer almost straight away. There was more static this time, but we could hear the man quite clearly.

'OK, I'm receiving you,' he said. 'I've got someone here who wants to talk to you. Whatever you people did at this Cobbler's Bay seems to have stirred up some interest. I got the quickest response from the military that I've ever had. Stand by now.'

Almost immediately another voice came on. Quiet but crisp and forceful. I have to admit he did put me off a bit by managing to sound like Major Harvey. Maybe anyone with military training sounds like that.

'I'm Lieutenant-Colonel Finley from New Zealand Army Intelligence. We're aware of recent damage to enemy installations at Cobbler's Bay and we understand you're claiming responsibility. I'd like whatever information you have, but bear in mind that enemy intelligence might be monitoring this conversation. So is there anything you can tell me? Over.'

Homer took a deep breath, sat up straighter and began.

'We've been free since the invasion,' he said carefully. 'I won't say how many of us there are, or who we are, or give our ages. But it's true that we were able to get into Cobbler's Bay and do a lot of damage. We used nearly two tonnes of anfo and sank a container ship. The explosion also damaged two cranes, blew a helicopter out of the sky, and set fire to the wharf. This is the fourth attack we've done since the invasion, but we're now on the run and we need help. We're getting hemmed in and we haven't got much future. We need to get out, and we want to know if you can help us. Over.'

Colonel Finley came on again straight away.

'What is your assessment of the present operating capacity of Cobbler's Bay? Over.'

Homer struggled for words. Finally, all he could say was, 'What do you mean?'

'Is the wharf still able to function? If so, to what extent? Over.'

Homer looked at us helplessly. I grabbed the microphone. 'We can't tell that. We're not experts. It looks a mess, that's all we can say. Most of the wharf was destroyed, so it'll be very hard for them to load or unload till they rebuild that. Over.'

'Do you know the name of the container ship you sank?'

'No.'

'Do you know its nationality?'

'No.'

'Do you know what its cargo was?'

'No. Just empty containers we think.'

'Is there any chance of you going back in there to

have a look at a few things for me? If I give you a list of questions, things we need investigated?'

My blood boiled. 'No! No way! We're not heavily into suicide. Over.'

'All right, I quite understand. You've obviously done very well, and I congratulate you. Keep up the good work. Now, hang on a moment and I'll put you back to Laurie. Over.'

'Wait!' I yelled. 'Wait!' I tried to find the words. 'What are you going to . . . I mean, can't you get us out of here?'

'Regrettably, no. We just don't have the resources. We're at full stretch as it is, as I'm sure you'd appreciate. You sound as though you're looking after yourselves very well, though. I'm sure things'll change in a few months, but until then we can't help you. Keep in touch with Laurie, and anything else you can do to help the war effort will be much appreciated, believe me.'

I didn't say any more, and in a moment Laurie came back on and wound up the conversation. He said he'd keep listening at 8 pm, their time, every night, in case we needed to get in touch. And that was all anyone could do for us. We were on our own again. We'd had our hopes raised so much for that short time, then, just as suddenly, nothing.

There was silence in the room. No one seemed able to speak. We were all too depressed. I was way overdue for some sentry duty; so was Homer, but he looked too devastated to think about it. I went out to take over from Robyn, not because I'm a martyr but because I wanted to be on my own for a while, and going on sentry was as good a way as any to do it.

I found a possie on the top of a wrecked pantech

that I reached by climbing a tree and dropping onto it. The light branches of the tree draped over the pantech and hid me well enough. The van looked like it had rolled: not only was it bent and crushed all along the passenger side but also the roof was creased and crumpled. Grass was growing in the roof; a little dirt was lodged there, probably from when it had rolled, and weeds were growing happily from it. I wasn't in a good position to alert the others if enemy troops suddenly appeared, but I thought I'd worry about that if and when it happened. I sat there hugging my knees, wondering what we should do next. Maybe hijack a jet and fly to New Zealand. I gazed at my arms and hands. They looked pretty rough. There were scratches and scars everywhere. The knuckles on my left hand were swollen from where I'd been bashed into the rocks by the tidal wave at Cobbler's Bay. I tried to work out how long ago that was, but had to give up. It felt like weeks, but I knew it wasn't. Probably only a few days.

There was a scar on the right thumb that went way back to the time we'd got Lee out of Wirrawee, using a front-end loading truck. On the inside of the right arm was a long scar that I'd picked up blundering through the bush, the night of the Harvey's Heroes' massacre. I don't know how I hurt my arm; I was too upset at the time to notice. Just a stick, I guess.

On the tip of my left elbow was a mosquito bite, on the back of the hand a bruise that I'd picked up when I'd tripped in the dark. My fingernails were a manicurist's nightmare, ripped, bitten, cut, torn. There wasn't one that was undamaged. I seemed to bleed easily around the fingernails these days. Maybe lack of vitamins, I don't know. I've never been much into skin care, but I'd had the usual collection of moisturisers and creams and lotions and I used them on special occasions, like going to socials. I didn't use them much on school days. I never had time anyway: I was too busy in the mornings. But what I would have done now for my little line-up of jars and tubes! I'd love to have rubbed the soft white fragrant cream slowly into my skin, making it supple and smooth, bringing it back to life. Such a little luxury, but I longed for it.

Somehow Lee tracked me to the pantech. I don't know how. He must have had the nose of a border collie. But he saw me there and started climbing the tree to come up with me. He didn't say anything, just climbed slowly to the truck roof, then crawled along the deformed metal.

'Hello,' I said.

'Hello.'

'Looks like we're not going to New Zealand, hey.'

'Looks that way.'

'I was hoping so much . . .'

'I didn't know if it'd be good or bad. I never thought they'd pick us up anyway, and I don't know about walking out on my family.'

'Yeah, that was what I was worried about. But there doesn't seem to be anything we can do for them. Not yet.'

'You don't like me any more, do you?'

He'd caught me by surprise. I knew it was coming, but not like that.

'Yes, of course I like you.'

'But not the way it was.'

'No, I guess not.'

194

'Why?'

'Dunno. It just happened.'

'What, you mean that one minute you liked me and a millisecond later you didn't?'

'More or less, yeah.'

'That doesn't sound very likely.'

'I don't care what it sounds like, that's the way it was.'

'Did Fi say anything against me?'

'Fi? No, why would she?'

'I don't know, but you're always talking to her and you take so much notice of what she says.'

'I don't know about that, but she didn't say anything to put me off you. She's not a backstabber, not like me.' I grinned, but Lee wasn't into laughs today.

'Is it something I said?'

'No, no, really. Nothing dramatic happened, I swear. Maybe we'd just seen enough of each other for a while. I mean, God, we're only young, we're not meant to be getting married, you know. At our age we're meant to have lots of romances.'

'My father was seventeen when he was married.'

'Well, whoopiedoo, I'm very happy for him, but I've got no plans yet, believe me.'

'Are you having it off with Homer?'

I lifted my arm fast, to hit him, then changed my mind. But I don't know how I didn't push him straight off the roof. He had such a hide, saying that. I know he was only saying it because he was upset, but that didn't make it all right. What a dickhead. It made me really pleased that I'd dropped him, because at that moment I didn't care if I never saw him again, and I had no interest in continuing the conversation. So we sat there in silence for a couple of minutes.

He knew he'd gone too far – I mean, you didn't have to be a Nobel Prize winner to work that out.

I could feel him getting ready to apologise. There wasn't much else he could do. But I wasn't going to make it easy for him. He could stew for a while yet, as far as I was concerned. Eventually though, after he'd cleared his throat a couple of times, he managed to struggle through it, taking about five minutes.

'OK, OK,' I said at last, 'don't worry about it. But honestly, Lee, nothing special's happened. I just want some time and some space. Let's not make a whole big issue of it, please. We've got on pretty well so far – we haven't had too many fights. But I've got the feeling that our toughest times are still ahead. I think we're in for a really rough stretch now, because there's no obvious path for us to take, and I think it could get seriously depressing. So we've got to keep cheerful and not get too hung up about stuff like this.'

He didn't answer and the two of us kept sitting there for a long time, until it started raining.

'Come on,' I said at last, 'let's get down. I'll have to find somewhere else to watch for the bad guys.'

Chapter Twenty-one

Late in the afternoon we had a meeting in a parked car where I'd sat for hours. It was an old white Rover 2000 with leather seats, in quite good condition. I don't think it had been in an accident; it probably just died of old age, but I figured I might as well be comfortable, so that's why I chose it. Plus it was one of the few cars that still had its windscreen. There were a couple of leaks from rust spots in the roof but I sat far enough away from them and stared out through the scratched and dirty windscreen at the grey road beyond.

The others had been back in the middle of the car yard, lounging around doing nothing much. Most of them seemed asleep when I went to check on them. I rigged up a long cord with a can of pebbles on the end of it, so that if any soldiers appeared I could yank on the cord, making a noise which would alert the others. And at 3.30 I got to use it. A couple of trucks appeared on the road, going much slower than the other traffic which had sped past from time to time. I pulled the can over straight away. By now I knew the look of a patrol when I saw one. Then I slithered

197

out of the Rover and did a stomach crawl back to the gang. We made a quick decision – there was no time for any other kind – they would hide in the pit and I would go up the tree above the pantech and watch from there.

So I shinned up the wet trunk, trying not to hug it too tightly, to keep as dry as I could. Then I huddled in among the dripping leaves and watched the patrol. They turned straight into the gates of the yard then stopped, and eight soldiers, six of them women, got out. The encouraging thing was that there was no sense of purpose about the trucks or the people. They didn't look like highly trained commandos launching a search and destroy mission. They looked like a bunch of part-time soldiers who'd been dragged out into the rain to do a job that they didn't have a lot of enthusiasm for. There was an officer with them, and she yelled and pointed for a few minutes, and then they split up into pairs and went off in different directions.

It was all a bit casual. They poked around and under cars, and looked in most of them. But that was the extent of it. One of them went to the back door of the house, which he probably thought was the front door, and broke the pane of glass in it. I heard the tinkle of it falling. He peered through it, but came back almost straight away wrinkling his face and saying something to his partner. I could guess what it was: this place stinks. It did too; I didn't blame him.

Within half an hour they were gone. I waited ten minutes, then went and got the others out of their hole. No one was too excited. We'd seen it all before. It was another escape, not a particularly close one, but of course it could easily have been different. It

198

would only have taken one curious soldier to notice the galvanised iron over the pit and call the others, and that would have been the end of us. One day it would happen. One day we would be caught. Seemed like it wasn't going to be this time.

I went back to the Rover to continue my watch, and it was there that the others came, half an hour before sunset. Robyn sat in the front seat beside me, with Fi on her lap, and the boys squashed into the back. It was so crowded that they had to leave the back doors open to fit themselves in. Kevin sat right under a leak and got dripped on every few seconds.

The most unexpected thing about our meeting was that it was Fi who took charge. Everyone else seemed too tired and depressed. Homer looked terrible, like he'd been to a B & S and was the last one left at the Recovery. Lee was sunk in his own private thoughts. Kevin looked so jumpy; he kept blinking all the time, as though he had dust in his eyes. Robyn was OK, I think, but quiet, but Fi seemed strong and determined, like she could be sometimes.

'Seeing nobody else seems to have any ideas,' she said in a firm voice, 'I'm going to say what I think.'

'Onya, Fi, go for it,' I said.

'Well,' she said, 'I think we have to take care of ourselves for a while. The best thing would be a three-week holiday on the Barrier Reef, all expenses paid and a thousand dollars spending money. I don't think we're going to get that, though. But even in World War Two the pilots only had to fly a certain number of missions, and then they'd be rested. Battle fatigue I think it was called. Well, we've got our own battle fatigue, and we need to take a rest. If we try and do any more for a while we'll just wreck ourselves. The last few weeks we've been going steadily crazy, and part of going crazy is that you don't notice you're going crazy. Whether we do it for our own sakes or whether we do it because it'll make us better fighters doesn't matter; the fact is we have to look after ourselves.'

'So do you think we should have a holiday?' Homer asked.

I was so relieved that Homer was showing some life again that I could have cried. I think the thing that mattered most was that Fi was giving us permission to take a break. There were no adults to say such things to us, and we'd stopped saying them to ourselves. We'd got ourselves into a state of mind where we couldn't think clearly; we were just driving onwards until, like overworked engines, we broke down. As Fi talked I realised that it was OK to take a break, that we didn't have to win the war all by ourselves.

'Yes,' said Fi firmly.

'I don't want to go back to Hell,' Robyn said.

'Likewise,' I said.

'I wouldn't mind,' Kevin said. 'It's so long since I've been there.'

'I was thinking of the Isthmus,' Fi said.

'Yeah!' Lee suddenly said. We got such a shock at the way he blurted it out that we got the giggles. I could see Lee in the cracked rear-vision mirror; he looked a bit sheepish, but he was grinning.

'You like the idea, huh?' Homer said to him.

'Well, I like the Isthmus,' Lee said.

The Isthmus is a long neck of land that connects the town of Ferris with Blue Rocks National Park. It's actually called Webster's Isthmus, but no one ever uses its full name.

There's no access to the National Park by car; you have the choice of foot or boat, because there's no road across the Isthmus. That made it ideal for us, of course. The park is beautiful, but it's the Isthmus itself that's extra beautiful. I'd been there once with Fi's family, staying at a cabin that some friends of theirs owned. I didn't know Lee had been there at all.

'When did you go there?' I asked his reflection in the mirror.

'With the scouts,' he said.

'I didn't know you were a scout.'

'Well I was. For more than a year. There's a scout camp about a k from Ferris, and we spent five days there one Easter. It was great. They made us hike our little butts off, but I enjoyed it. What a place.'

'Mmm,' I agreed, remembering that wild rocky landscape, and the water exploding against the cliffs. 'We'd be safe there for a while. I think the colonists'll be too busy colonising to go bushwalking.'

'It means staying away from Wirrawee quite a bit longer,' Robyn said hesitantly. 'I feel guilty when we're not near our families, even if we can't do anything to help them.'

'Of course,' said Fi. 'We all feel that. But honestly, what can we do for them? We all know the answer: nothing. We've got to think of this as a holiday. Let's say we'll go there for two weeks, and at the end of the two weeks we'll go back to Wirrawee and check out the situation. We've got enough food, easily, with the cans we scored here, but too much to carry. We'll have to take the Jackaroo. I think it's worth the risk. If we go in the middle of the night, drive slowly, don't use lights, we should be safe. Surely they'll be thinking that we're out of the district by now. All the

201

search parties'll be coming back to Cobbler's saying they found nothing, and I guess their bosses'll never know what sloppy searching they do.'

'Hope they never find out,' Robyn said, with feeling.

There was no real opposition to Fi's idea. The only problem was the timing. No one felt comfortable about leaving straight away. It was still too soon after the attack. We decided we would wait four days, and see whether they had stopped combing the district by then. It would be boring, but boredom was better than death, any day.

So we fiddled around, doing nothing. I spent the time sitting and thinking, looking out across the paddocks. I'm embarrassed to say that I went back to thumb-sucking in a big way, till the thumb on my left hand looked soft and white and wet. But at least it was clean.

We looked in the house for books, but only found two, apart from technical manuals. I thought it was amazing; a house with just two books. One of them was *How to Win Friends and Influence People*, and the other was *Gone With The Wind*. No one wanted the first one but Fi and Robyn argued over *Gone With The Wind*. In the end, they compromised. Fi's the faster reader, so she started it, then as she finished each page, she tore it out and gave it to Robyn. It was a good system.

Homer and Kevin started mucking round with the Jackaroo engine, trying different parts that they salvaged from the wrecked cars. They claimed they were making it faster, quieter, cleaner, smoother. By the time they finished, I was just grateful it was running at all.

Lee disappeared for hours on end. I mean many hours, like eight or ten. I think he just roamed across the countryside, going wherever his mood took him. He was so restless. I wondered if he was turning into a wild animal, a lone wolf maybe.

It was four o'clock on the third day when our plans changed. I was on the top of the pantech, sucking my thumb, watching Lee come back across the paddock. He was sticking close to the treeline, slipping quickly from tree to tree, a shadow among many shadows. When he was climbing the fence into the wrecker's yard, I went down to meet him.

'Get everyone,' he said as soon as he saw me. 'Tell them to meet at the Jackaroo.'

I took one look at his face and ran to find the others. In just a couple of minutes we were gathered there, facing Lee. He said one word, and that was enough.

'Dogs,' he said.

'How do you mean?' asked Fi, but the rest of us knew.

'They've got a pack of dogs,' Lee said. 'Two alsatians and a couple of beagles. They've knocked off for today but I reckon they'll be back tomorrow. And they're not mucking around. They know what they're doing.'

'Tell us the whole story,' Homer said.

'There's not much to tell. About 3 k's from here, there's a church and a hall, and a farmhouse across the road. I was just coming over the hill behind the church when I heard dogs barking. I dropped down and crawled forward a bit, and there they were: searching the church and hall. Four soldiers, each with a dog. When they finished, they went over to the farmhouse and did the same thing there. Only took them ten minutes. And I forgot to mention: there were two others with rifles, just watching. Then they all got in a truck, and drove along to the next place, looked like an old primary school. Same thing there, then they had a bit of a conference, looked at their watches, hopped in the truck and drove back the way they'd come.'

'So they look like they're working their way along the road?' I asked.

'Exactly. And if that's what they are doing, they'd be here by tomorrow lunchtime. At the latest.'

We all looked at each other.

'Well, who's for the Isthmus?' Homer asked, when no one else said anything.

It seemed the most sensible thing to do. We had to go by car now, because if we tried to walk the dogs would pick up our scent. We had to move the Jackaroo, because it was such a fatal piece of evidence against us. Seemed like the time had come to get way out of this district.

After that it was all action.

We didn't have any maps but we thought we could scam it. If we kept to the south of Stratton we should hit the Conway Highway, and that went through Ferris. I figured on a three-hour drive. Petrol might be our biggest problem. Here we were surrounded by hundreds of cars and not a drop of petrol to be had. The Jackaroo was three-quarters full and I could only hope its tank would be big enough.

We decided to leave at 2.30 am, but in the end we got so bored and impatient sitting around that we went a few minutes before two o'clock. Robyn and Fi had been sitting in the car for an hour already: they said they were doing it to make sure they got the front seat. The boys grumbled a bit but finally sorted themselves out in the back; I jumped in the driver's seat, and a moment later we were on our way.

The rain was blowing in again and the temperature was dropping; not a great start to our beach holiday. But we were in a better mood. Just being on the move again was good.

We crawled along on the edge of the bitumen, without lights. A few times when the bush thinned and the road curved I stopped. We took it in turns to walk up to the corner, check it out, and wave the car on.

Random patrols seemed to be a thing of the past, and we felt we would see any convoys before they saw us, even if they did have their lights dimmed. It struck me that since our attack on Cobbler's Bay we'd hardly seen any convoys. I mentioned that to the others and it cheered them up even more. Maybe we really had achieved something special with our anfo. Certainly Lieutenant Colonel Finley's reaction had been encouraging. He wouldn't have come rushing to the radio to speak to us if we'd just let down some-one's tyres.

We started talking about it all. It seemed a new compulsion: everyone suddenly gushing about what they'd done and what they'd seen and how they'd felt. It had been the same after our other big hits, talking about them over and over until we didn't feel the need any more. But we hadn't really done that with Cobbler's Bay. Maybe we'd been too tired, or too depressed. For me, it was because the whole thing was too big. I couldn't cope with the enormity of it. Especially the last bit, shooting those soldiers. That was way too big. And the biggest thing of all was that in another way it had hardly affected me. I'd put bullets through their guts, shot them dead and left them there with their blood pouring out onto the bright red sand, and I'd hardly noticed I'd done it. Just another moment in my life, an 'incident', like drenching sheep. I was numb about it.

So we drove on and I talked about all that, a bit. Not a lot, mainly because it was so hard to get a word in. Everyone was cutting across everyone else, jumping in before the other person had finished what they were saying, finishing their sentences for them, even. It was like some of our drama rehearsals at school. Homer was still the quietest but he did say a few things, each of them making me realise how much the time in the container and the escape across the Bay, into the arms of the enemy, had affected him. I remember hoping desperately that he wouldn't get caught again, because I didn't think he'd be able to stand it. It had really fazed him, the swim, then being grabbed by those guys at the creek. It had damaged his confidence.

'I'd given up,' he said, when I asked him about the time in the water.

'You'd given up?' I said, shocked.

'They'd seen me, and I was too tired to dive anymore.'

'Who'd seen you?'

'The guys in the boat, and the ones in the chopper.'

'So what happened? Were they shooting at you? How'd you get away? You hadn't really given up?'

He shrugged. 'I was just floating there, watching them come for me. Then the ship blew up.'

He wouldn't say much more. I asked the others: 'What happened at Baloney Creek?' But none of them really knew how they'd been caught.

'It must have been the chopper,' Kevin said.

'We were pretty slack,' Fi confessed. 'We didn't . . .'

'I didn't even hear their car,' Lee said.

'I guess we were talking too loud or something.'

'I heard you scream,' Robyn said to Fi, 'and that's the first I knew they were there.'

'God, I'll never forget it,' Fi said, shivering.

'And what you said to them,' Robyn said to Lee, laughing.

'What?'

'He told them to piss off.'

'You what?'

'It was the shock,' Lee said. 'I said it before I knew I'd said it. It just blurted out.'

'I don't think they heard it,' Homer said.

'They heard it,' Kevin said, 'but they didn't take it in. It was just part of all the shouting and carrying on.'

'Yeah, what was all the shouting and carrying on?' I asked. 'What was the shot?'

'It was lust,' Kevin said, but the others didn't laugh, so neither did I.

'They were after the two girls,' Homer said.

'And the two girls weren't moving,' Lee explained.

'The shot was to make me hurry up a bit,' Robyn said.

Then I started to understand what had been happening, and how lucky I'd been to arrive when I did.

We ploughed on. The only sign of life was a cream-coloured van that looked as though it might have once belonged to an electrician or plumber. It was parked in a truck stop with its parking lights on, but because it was well away from the road we didn't see it until we were almost level with it. The bad weather didn't help either.

There was nothing we could do but accelerate and keep going. We went four k's as fast as I dared, with Kevin looking fearfully through the back windows for signs of pursuit. Then we pulled into a side track and sat there for ten minutes. But there was no sign of anyone and we couldn't afford to waste much more time if we were going to reach the Isthmus before daybreak. I started the engine and we kept going towards Ferris.

'It was probably a patrol and they were having a nice quiet sleep,' Homer suggested. 'In this rotten weather they wouldn't feel much like wandering up and down the road.'

Even though it seemed odd, we still thought that was the most likely explanation. I sure thought so, anyway. That's why it was such a complete and utter shock when we were caught.

Chapter Twenty-two

They'd chosen the spot well. It was a narrow stretch of road crossing the old Huntleigh Bridge. The road twisted around, then turned on itself to cross the bridge. Beyond the bridge it started to climb again, in a long sweeping bend that led to the Stratton turn-off. It was nearly four in the morning when I dropped a gear to poke the Jackaroo slowly round the bend and onto the bridge. Everyone was asleep, or I would have asked for a volunteer to walk down and check it out. I saw out of the corner of my eye the NO PASSING ON BRIDGE sign, a dim yellow diamond. Then we bumped across the old wooden roadway. It was like driving down a railway track.

We crossed it and I started to accelerate again, into the long bend. I thought I was imagining things when I saw a big grey obstruction in the middle of the road. A huge dim grey boulder. Stupidly, as I began to brake, I started wondering if there'd been a landslide. People were waking up. Then Homer was yelling something, I don't know what, in my ear, so loudly that the fright of it paralysed me. But I saw what it was in the middle of the road: a dirty great tank with its huge grey gun barrel pointing straight at us.

My next rational thought was that they might be asleep, like the people in the van we'd passed earlier. I still thought we were in with a chance. I stood on the brake and shoved the gear stick into reverse, not even looking in the rear-vision mirror, thinking there was no need. But I saw enough through the windscreen to realise the trouble we were in. A line of soldiers suddenly appeared either side of the tank. About eight of them in all. Each one carried a gun that I think could fire a shell or missile: the barrels on these guns must have been a metre long, and as big as drainage pipes. I don't know how the soldiers carried the weight of them. Then Homer yelled again in my ear, and this time I heard him clearly. He said, 'Stop, stop, they're behind us.' Then he said quietly, 'No good.' Looking in the rear-vision mirror for the first time, I realised what he meant. They had us all ends up. There was a whopping great Army truck, a proper green Army truck, right up our bumper bar. And an instant later, before I'd had time to digest what I was seeing, a soldier was at my window and a rifle muzzle at my right cheek. The soldier was breathing hard, his face shiny with sweat, and his eyes wide open, as if he was on drugs. I guess he was just hyped up at making a bust, but I was scared by how unstable he seemed. I slowly, carefully, very carefully, raised my arms. By moving my head fractionally to the left I could see Robyn and Fi. They were still waking up, struggling to understand what was going on. That's how quickly it all happened. Their hair was all mussed up and Fi's mouth was open as she looked around and realised that our good luck had come to a sudden bitter end.

210

She too raised her arms, then Robyn did the same. I couldn't see much of the back seat in the rear-vision mirror, but guess it was the same scene there.

The soldier beside me opened the door and I slowly got out. He turned the engine off and took the keys then, with a nod of his head, pointed me to the side of the road. I went there and stood next to the three boys. Robyn and Fi, with a soldier escorting them, came over to join us a moment later. I said to Homer, 'Some holiday this is turning . . .' but didn't get to finish the sentence: the soldier who stood next to me hit me across the side of my face with the back of his closed fist.

He was a tall man and he swung hard. I felt like I'd slammed into a wall. The side of my face went instantly numb, and I couldn't hear anything more in that ear. Everything started tingling, my eye, my cheek, my ear, as though it had all gone to sleep. Tears stung my eyes, not crying-because-of-pain-and-shock tears but reflex tears from my tear ducts. I just hoped the soldier wouldn't think that I'd gone all girly and was crying from being hit. I didn't want to give them that satisfaction. I didn't want my friends to think I was weak, either.

Standing by the side of the road I knew all too well there was a good chance we were about to be shot. It was something about the way they had us lined up. It looked chillingly like a scene from movies where they have firing squads. I don't know if the others thought that, but I certainly did. No one spoke again. We just stood there with heads bowed, feeling our own fears. Then Kevin farted suddenly and, unbelievably, we all got the giggles. It was such a loud rattling fart and so unexpected and out of place that we couldn't cope with it.

211

I thought we would get our faces smashed in for sure. I stood there almost waiting to be hit, but then I noticed a couple of the soldiers trying not to laugh, too. I guess some things are universal. But an officer, one of a group of officers standing talking on the other side of the road, shouted something, and the soldiers hardened up again. By then we'd got over our initial sniggers and when we saw the soldiers getting serious we controlled ourselves. But I still remember that moment. It made things just a fraction easier to bear.

There was no firing squad. After ten minutes we got marched to the back of the big Army truck. We stood there a few more minutes watching the tank crawl away and then a soldier motioned Homer to climb in the truck. As Homer got onto the steel step the man hit him hard across the back of the head, so that he half fell forward. Kevin was next and he got bashed too, then Robyn. Seemed like it was a part of the routine. But it hurt me when he hit Fi. In all my life I've never seen anyone hit Fi. It was like hitting a beautiful water bird. I watched as the fist smacked against her. Her head dropped lower and her shoulders too but, of course, I couldn't see her face. When my turn came and I got in, getting the same treatment, Fi was already sitting turned away, her face towards the front of the truck.

It was dark in there and smelt of canvas, and something else, creosote perhaps. A couple of soldiers got in behind us and spent a few minutes tying our wrists to crossbars that ran the length of the truck. When they were done they sat at the back watching us. It made it difficult to do anything, or even talk. All I could do was think.

212

Robyn tried to speak to the soldiers, but she didn't get far. She said to one, 'Did you know we were on this road?', but he just looked away. I don't know if he understood English.

She tried the other one but he said: 'Shut up. No talk.' That didn't allow a lot of possibilities for conversation. Robyn, who was opposite me, looked at me and made a face. I grinned back, hoping I looked like a hero, but feeling so wild with fear inside that I could hardly make my face work.

'Does your face hurt?' Robyn asked.

The soldier who'd told her to shut up made a movement forwards, towards Robyn.

'You shut!' he shouted. 'You bad girl.' Then to all of us he shouted 'You bad people. You kill my friends. You all die, now you die.' And he sat back again, trembling.

I felt sure then that we would be shot. I felt sorry for the man a bit, too. I'd never really thought about these soldiers having friends, being friends with each other. It must have been as awful for them to have their friends killed as it was for us. It had been a long time since I'd thought about all these issues of right and wrong. We'd become used to doing the things we did, to attacking and destroying and killing, without thinking whether there was right on both sides. Sure in the early days of the invasion we'd thought about it – I remember writing about it. We had so much in our country: so much food, so much space, so much entertainment. But we'd resented sharing it with anyone, even refugees. The longer the war had gone on, the more we'd become used to thinking of the soldiers as the baddies, and us as the goodies. As simple as that. As dumb as that.

I thought about it all now again, though. And without caring what the soldier would think, or what the others would think, I said to him, 'I'm sorry about your friends.'

He looked like I'd hit him. His eyebrows rose and his mouth went into an 'O' shape. He looked shocked, angry, then for a moment he stared at me like he was a real person again. For that brief time I saw that he wasn't a mechanical killer, just someone as young and confused and under pressure as we were. Our eyes met almost like friends.

It didn't last long. His face went back into the sulky aggressive expression he'd had before. But I was glad I'd said it.

A male officer got into the cabin of the truck, on the passenger side, and a woman soldier on the driver's side. She started the engine and away we went. I could see the tail-lights of another vehicle through the windscreen and behind us the parking lights of the Jackaroo. There was another vehicle behind that. I began to realise how impossible escape was going to be. Yet I was determined not to go passively to my death. I'd rather be shot trying to escape than just walk to a wall and stand there while they filled my body with bullets.

We drove for over an hour. I spent the time shivering with cold, speculating about what might happen to us, while glancing from time to time at the faces of my friends to see how they were going. We all looked so white, so tired, so strained and frightened. How could they ever believe that we were dangerous? How could they send all these trucks and the tank just for us? Yet I knew all too well that we had done more damage to these people than anyone else in this whole district, in the whole state, maybe. We were public enemies, no doubt about it. We were probably public enemy number one.

In the dim lights of the trucks I saw a green and white road sign: STRATTON 14.

So that's where we were headed. It figured. It was good in a way; it gave me something other than death to think about. As we got closer I peered through the windscreen to see how Stratton was looking. It was so long since we'd been in a city. We passed a deserted truck stop that seemed to have been smashed to bits, as though a giant had attacked it with a giant sledgehammer. Then we were in the suburbs. It was a shocking sight. There'd been some damage in Wirrawee, but nothing like this. You could see that a lot of cleaning up had been done, but it would take years and a billion bucks to clear it up properly. In some blocks the buildings were pretty much untouched but in plenty of others every one had been flattened. The roads were clear but nothing else was. It was all rubble: bricks and wood and stone, and sheets of galvanised iron sticking out and flapping in the breeze, like cold metal leaves.

My grandmother lived in Stratton, but a long way from where we were now, in a big old house up in the hills. Thinking about her sent a tear rolling down my cheek; a real tear. I brushed it angrily away. I didn't want to show any fear. I wanted to keep my fear all to myself: a storm inside but a desert on my face. That was the only way I could maintain any kind of strength.

We drove straight through the CBD. It was a bigger mess than the suburbs. I didn't know if the damage had been done by the enemy during the invasion, or by the Kiwi air attacks after it. But big bombs had been used. Tozer's, the department store that had been three-storeys high, covering the best part of a block, now looked like it'd make a good car park. The back wall of the electricity building was still standing, but there was nothing else of Stratton's biggest building.

The saddest sight was the Cathedral of the Sacred Heart. It had been a beautiful old stone church, quiet and peaceful, with glowing stained-glass windows. I wouldn't have liked to be standing near when it was blown up. Those huge stone blocks had been thrown around like bits of Lego. One of them was a hundred metres along the street, where it had fallen on the iron-railing fence of the Mackenzie Botanical Gardens.

We accelerated up the hill then turned abruptly right at the top. I suddenly realised where we were going. To the most obvious place: the prison. I almost smiled. Many times we'd been past its grim grey walls on the way to visit Grandma, but I guess no one had thought that I'd end up in it before I'd even finished school. What a disgrace. We'd never live it down.

Then the fear got hold of me again. I'd been hoping that we'd go to some camp, like the Wirrawee Showgrounds, and I'd already dreamed that we'd escape from there in a blaze of glory. But Stratton Prison was different. It was a maximum-security institution, designed for the toughest offenders. We wouldn't be escaping.

Our convoy came to a halt at the huge steel doors of the prison. There was much shouting and slamming of car doors. Only the soldiers in our truck didn't move, just sat there watching. An officer came and spoke to our driver through the window of the truck. The driver put the truck in gear and we began to move forward. The steel doors rolled silently aside and we drove through. They closed behind us just as quietly. We were in a dark concrete chamber, like a big garage, but completely bare. We only had to wait a second before a door at the other end opened and we drove on again. I glanced at the others. They were all sitting forward like me, as far as our cuffs would let us, gazing through the windscreen, wondering what horrors would be revealed.

What we saw was a vast area of buildings and lawns. A high fence enclosed the whole place, but it was like a little village inside; a village of concrete and wire and steel. There were covered walkways connecting the various buildings. They looked like extended aviaries, long cages that prisoners could be moved along without having any taste of the free air.

In the few open spaces were a swimming pool and two tennis courts, but I had the feeling we wouldn't be getting much of a chance to use them.

The truck was only moving at walking pace, and it stopped now on a big bitumen square near a building marked 'Administration'. I wondered who we'd be sharing Stratton Prison with – prisoners of war, or the 'normal' criminals from before the invasion: the murderers and rapists and bank robbers.

We continued to sit in the back of the truck and wait. I became aware of a lot of movement around us, and looking out the back I realised what it was. Soldiers were coming from different buildings. I could see fifteen or twenty of them. But they were not aggressive soldiers with rifles, coming to torture or shoot us. It took me a while to figure out their mood. But finally it hit me. They were tourists. They were spectators. At last I understood something that only the radio conversation with Lieutenant Colonel Finley had given any clue to: we were celebrities. This was like the arrest of Ned Kelly. Not that these people would have heard of Ned Kelly, but our capture was on about the same scale.

We sat there in shock as the soldiers crowded round the back of the truck, staring at us and talking to each other. Their voices amazed me. They were so hushed, like they were in church. They pointed to us and made comments, then people at the back of the crowd pushed their way through. They were all shoving and crowding, trying to get the best views.

I just hoped we wouldn't get the same punishment as the Kelly gang. I cursed the Jackaroo. If we hadn't been caught in it we might have been able to bluff, to pretend we were normal kids who'd been hiding in the bush since the invasion. But now we had no hope, especially when we weren't getting any chance to put a story together, a story we could all stick to.

After twenty minutes sitting there shivering, being studied like specimens in the zoo, a senior officer appeared. He had more gold on him than you'd see in a jewellery shop window. The crowd parted and this man, a little guy with oiled black hair, walked up, took one look at us and rattled off a series of orders. Our guards jumped to their feet and started waving their rifles and yelling. I think they were trying to impress the officer. We didn't have the spirit to resist any of them.

When we were untied we stumbled down from the back of the truck, one by one, and stood in a little group on the bitumen. They prodded us with rifles to get us into single file and marched us to one of the covered walkways. A guard with keys opened a gate and in we went, leaving the tourists behind.

When the gate was locked behind us we were marched along the walkway. I kept looking around trying to suss things out, but there wasn't much to see. Every few metres we passed rooms but it was hard to tell what they were used for. Obviously some, the ones with steel bars in small windows set into the doors, were cells, but a lot seemed to be just offices or storerooms. One looked like a lunchroom for the warders; another was a control room, with video monitors and telephones and people sitting at desks looking at screens with lots of green and red flashing lights. We went through another gate, waiting as it was unlocked for us and locked behind us, then we turned left and straggled along to a low fawn-coloured building that was sealed off by yet another gate.

When we had passed through that gate we found ourselves in our new home. This was E Wing, the maximum-security section of the maximum-security prison. In peacetime it was the home of serial killers. Well, maybe that's what we had become. Whether we deserved to be there or not, our lives were now out of our control. Whether we lived or died would be decided by others.

Chapter Twenty-three

At that point I was separated from my friends, and marched to a little concrete room. From the glimpses I'd had of the other cells I'd say they were all identical. Mine was five paces by four and pretty bare. There was a bed, low to the ground and on a solid base, so that nothing could be hidden under it, I guess. There was a toilet and washbasin, both of which worked, as I quickly, and with relief, found out. Only cold water in the washbasin – and it was freezing – but I was grateful to have that much. A desk and chair were the only other furniture and they were fixed to the floor by big steel bolts. All the furniture was gleaming white but the walls were a light pink. The bed was neatly made, as though it had been waiting for me. I checked it out. The sheets were striped flannelette and the bedspread was a cheap white cotton thing with a crisscross holey pattern.

I had the trivial thought that at last I'd be able to sleep in a proper bed again. I couldn't imagine how long it had been since I'd done that.

But there was nothing else in the cell. It was the coldest, barest, starkest, most boring room I'd ever been in. There wasn't even a light switch. The power must have been controlled from outside. There were two lights, both set in the ceiling, both covered by thick glass that I guessed was unbreakable. When I was put in there the lights were on, and the room was almost unbearably bright. Later I found that when the lights were off it was almost unbearably black.

My eyes ranged around, trying to find something to look at, to break the monotony. In a corner of the ceiling, almost invisible in the dazzle of the lights, was a lens, like a thick glass eye. I guessed there was a camera behind it, and remembering how I'd just used the dunny I blushed with embarrassment.

With much rattling of locks and clatter of mechanical parts the door was unlocked, and three guards came in. All were women, one in officers' uniform, the other two in soldiers' gear. The officer had a handgun at her waist in a highly polished leather holster, and her offsiders carried handguns which they held pointed at me. I still couldn't believe how respectfully – well, fearfully – they were treating us.

Although none of them seemed to speak English they made it clear what they wanted. I had to get undressed and they searched my clothes, emptying the pockets, then carefully checking the hems and linings. They were so thorough. When they'd finished they started on me. That was embarrassing and painful, but I put up with it. Not that I had a choice. Then they let me get dressed again. I thought I'd start to try my luck, so I mimed eating, to show that I wanted food, but they didn't react at all. When I was dressed they left, taking the contents of my pockets with them. I realised numbly that I'd now lost everything, even my little bear, Alvin, that Lee had retrieved for me from the wreckage of the Harvey's Heroes campsite. Alvin had survived that, but it looked like he wouldn't survive this.

I lay on the hard bed. It did feel funny to have a bed under me again. I wondered if anyone had ever made a cell aerobics video, and if so, where I could get a copy. Maybe I could make one and become a millionaire, selling it to mass murderers all around the world.

The next thing I knew I was waking up. I'd been asleep? How was that possible? What if I were about to be executed and I'd wasted the last few hours of my life by sleeping? How stupid and tragic was that?

But I'd been woken by sounds from the cell door again. The lights were still on and they were hurting my eyes. But a smell was coming in that had me sitting up in excitement. I realised I was about to be fed. I couldn't believe my luck. One of the female soldiers came in carrying a tray, while the other two stood at the door covering her with their guns. She put the tray on the desk and went out again without looking at me. I hardly noticed her. I was still barely awake but I hobbled across to the desk and sat on the white chair. The cold metal woke me in a hurry. I peered at the plates and cup. There was a bowl of boiled rice and a plate with three small pieces of steamed fish. Another plate held two slices of dry white bread. The only colour contrast came from the cup, which held weak black coffee. It was not an attractive-looking meal, nor a big one, but it was something, and I was grateful enough for it. I took my time, chewing each mouthful dozens of times before swallowing, to make it last, and having sips of coffee in between.

But the coffee was only lukewarm, as was the rice and fish, so it wasn't too good. We'd eaten better meals out in the bush, rough and ready though those meals were.

Still, the fact that they were prepared to feed me was encouraging, suggesting they weren't about to kill me straight away. I ate everything, then – I swear this is true – with a guilty look at the camera, I licked the plate. Yes, Ellie the Fearless was embarrassed to be seen with bad table manners. I think that's when I knew for sure I wasn't a natural born terrorist.

After that there was just nothing to do. I tapped on the walls a few times but got no answer. Every half hour or so a face appeared at the inspection panel in the door and stared at me. I didn't know what to do with myself. The camera made it worse, not knowing whether someone was watching every move. At one stage – probably about midmorning, there was no way of telling – I caught myself actually wishing something would happen. Then I realised that any something that happened was bound to be bad, so I started wishing nothing would happen. I lay on the bed again and stared up at the ceiling.

One of the awful things was the silence in the cell. It must have been well soundproofed. From time to time I'd hear a door slam but that was the only sound that penetrated. I hummed to myself, then started singing under my breath, just to make a little noise. I wondered how long I'd spend in the cell and how long it'd take before I went mad. I'm a person of the mountains and the open paddocks and the big empty sky, that's me, and I knew if I spent too long away from all that I'd die; I don't know what of, I just knew I'd die.

At lunchtime the breakfast tray was taken away and a lunch tray put in its place. The food was much the same: rice and dry bread, but they'd added about half a cupful of curried meat and a small apple with ugly black spots on it.

'Dear God,' I thought, 'how long can I last?' I could feel a terrible dark depression slowly moving into me, not like any depression I'd had before, more like a physical thing, as if some dreadful black fog was drifting into my landscape and wasn't going to go away. It was a disturbing, uncomfortable feeling. I ate my lunch as slowly as I'd eaten my breakfast, thinking about my situation. I decided I had to get myself organised. If I was starting to sink into depression after a few hours, what would I be like after a week or a month or a year? People had told me how strong I was, and now I had to prove it. I knew that more than any other time in my life I was on my own. My survival was up to me. I had nothing and I had no one. What I did have, I told myself, was my mind, my imagination, my memory, my feelings, my spirit. These were important and powerful things. I remembered the poem Robyn had in her bedroom at Wirrawee, the one about the person saying how when she looked back along the beach she saw two sets of footprints, hers and God's, except at the tough times, when there was only one set of footprints. And she says to God, 'How come at the times when I most needed you, you weren't there?' And God answers, 'My child, I was there. Those footprints were mine; I made them when I carried you.'

When I'd first read the poem I'd thought it was nice, but that was all. It was only now, when I needed it, that the poem became important to me. During the time I spent in the cell, that poem became about the most important possession I had.

I decided to divide the time between meals into shifts. I had no way of telling the time, because they'd taken my watch. And in the cell I couldn't tell day from night. So meals were the only measure I had. I decided I'd spend time on physical activities, and time on mental, and time on creative. I started with the physical, because I guess I'm a physical kind of person. My first session of cell aerobics consisted of stretching exercises, followed by a dance of my own invention, which had a lot of stepping backwards and forwards. I had to avoid anything that would aggravate my knee, because it was still tender and swollen. But apart from that I went OK. The worst thing was that the air was not fresh enough. There was so little new air coming in. Normally it didn't matter much, but as soon as I started working out I used it all up. Within sixty seconds I was sweating heavily.

After that I made my brain sweat a bit. I went through some Maths, multiplying fractions in my head – three-eighths by two-thirds equals a quarter, that sort of thing – then went on to Social Ed, mentally listing things like the three main types of erosion, the major causes of erosion, the definitions of terminal moraines, stuff like that. That part was all memory work.

I also set out to remember the words of four different songs. That was quite fun. I chose 'Public Friends', 'Bananas in Pyjamas', 'Sitting on the Dock of the Bay', and 'Reason for it All'. I deliberately chose ones that were a real variety, some from my parents' tapes, some from my CDs. It was amazing how when I worked at it, when I made myself go over the songs four or five times, more and more bits came back into my memory. By the time I'd finished I'd remembered nearly all of them, 'Reason for it All' giving me the most trouble. 'Bananas in Pyjamas' wasn't too hard.

Quite a lot of time had passed, or so it seemed to me. I'd almost stopped being obsessed with thoughts of imprisonment and death, which was good. So I was taken by surprise when I heard the locks on my door being worked open again. I didn't think it could be tea time already, and I was right. When the door opened, two men in uniform were standing there, with two women behind them. They motioned for me to get up from the bed, which I did. They then stood back, inviting me to step out from the cell. I walked into the corridor, beginning to tremble uncontrollably. Was this my death? Had I spent my last afternoon of life trying to think of the words to 'Bananas in Pyjamas'? Was I going to die without the chance to say goodbye to my family, my friends?

My escort fell in around me and we started along the corridor. For the first few steps I was so frightened I could hardly walk, but by the time we reached the first security gate I was in more of a rhythm and moving a bit more easily.

We marched back past the cage, through the gate on my right that we'd come in before. We walked almost the full length of the prison, stopping at a light green building on the left. All the colours in this place seemed to be mild, pastels. This building looked a bit like the new library at Wirrawee. It seemed to have more glass than the other buildings in the compound. There was a guard on the door who ticked a list on a clipboard before letting us in. The four guards and I marched inside. It was more like a doctor's waiting room than a library: a row of chairs and a coffee table. All it needed was a stack of magazines. But none of us sat down. We stood there uncomfortably. I said to the guards: 'What are we waiting for?' I didn't expect them to answer; I was just trying to kid them that I wasn't scared. And they didn't answer. I don't even know if they understood English.

We waited at least half an hour. It was incredibly boring. My greatest hope was that it really was a doctor's waiting room. It was possible that they would give us a medical examination. That would have been normal prison procedure in peacetime, surely. Maybe they would still do it.

But no, I couldn't be that lucky. A door opened along the corridor to my left and the guards prodded me down towards it. All my terror returned in an instant and I wallowed along as though I were a waterlogged boat in a heavy sea. Sick deep in my stomach, I turned at the doorway and stepped across the threshold.

And there he was. Someone I'd never expected to see again. Someone I'd almost forgotten about. Someone I despised so much I felt giddy and faint at the sight of him.

'Ellie, my dear girl,' Major Harvey said. 'Do come in. How nice to see you.'

There was a horrible silence. Although I hated to seem weak I had to put one hand on the frame of the door to hold myself up, to keep from falling over. I started to realise now just how deep was the trouble we were in, just how dangerous was our situation. I felt defeated and hopeless.

Major Harvey was sitting at a big shiny black desk. There was nothing on it but a clock, a ruler, a fountain pen and three piles of paper, arranged with perfect precision. Behind him were two officers. One was the man with the gold braid, whom we'd seen when we arrived; the other was a woman with almost as much gold. They were standing and gazing at me with expressionless faces.

I forced myself to look at Major Harvey's eyes. They were dead and empty. I wondered if there was a person inside, or if he was just a dark devil from Hell itself. At least the soldiers were fighting honestly, under their own flag. This man was a foul shadow of a human being. I knew he would crush me as easily as I would kill a blowie, and I also had an inkling that he would get some kind of perverted pleasure from doing it.

I made myself stand a little taller. He hadn't taken his eyes off me; those black beady eyes that seemed not like eyes at all. It was like his skin had been pierced at those two points in his face and I was getting a glimpse of what lay inside: an empty ugly darkness.

When I did straighten up, I noticed a quick movement around his lips. It was almost a smile, as though he'd expected me to do something very like that. I did not respond. How could I? I was afraid that if I opened my mouth, vomit would come from it; the vomit of fear, the vomit of hatred.

Major Harvey moved his right arm and slid open a drawer in the desk. He brought out a small silver tape recorder and placed it in the middle of the big desk.

'Sit down, Ellie,' he said.

I obeyed, slipping silently into the nearest chair, a trendy grey one made from cane and steel. I gripped its armrests tightly, knowing I was leaving clammy wet sweat on it, but appreciating its coolness and strength. Major Harvey turned the tape recorder on.

'Now, Ellie,' he said, 'I don't think you'll have many surprises for us. We know just about everything. But for the record we do require a full statement, detailing your activities. You can start with your name, address and age, then work backwards from the Cobbler's Bay attack. And, please, don't forget to mention the officer and two other ranks you killed in cold blood when you stole the Holden Jackaroo.'

I sat there staring at him. I didn't know what to do. I couldn't think. I had no idea what was best for me, whether to say nothing, whether to tell him everything, whether to put together a mixture of lies and truth. It was quite likely that he did know most things, especially if he'd already questioned the others. If I got caught telling lies I suspected he'd treat me very badly. I didn't want to make him angry.

So I said nothing, not because I wanted to be a hero, but because I couldn't think of what to say. Then I decided that silence was probably quite a good strategy.

He waited for a minute or so. Then he said: 'You know, Ellie, the first time I met you, you struck me as a particularly rude and pig-headed young lady. It is unfortunate for you that you were raised in a society where standards have been so corrupted that behaviour like yours has been tolerated. But you are a child no longer. You will be treated here as an adult.'

He paused. He seemed to be waiting for me to say something, but I couldn't think of anything. So he continued.

'When a child commits an offence he is punished. But the punishment an adult would receive is modified for the child, who is judged not yet responsible for his actions, not able to grasp the full extent of what he has done.'

He seemed to be quoting from a textbook or a speech or something. I still didn't know where this was heading but I was frightened in a cold sickening way, like no fear I'd felt before. It was like the chill of death was already moving through me, turning my skin white and liquefying my insides.

'We believe in adult punishments for adult acts. You have, for a long time now, acted in a thoroughly irresponsible, destructive way. You have committed appalling crimes. You can, of course, no longer expect to be treated as a child. I'm sure you wouldn't wish to be. We have reintroduced capital punishment to deal with crimes such as murder, terrorism and treason. I've talked to your friends at length today and formed an accurate picture of what you've been up to. I wasn't surprised to learn that you and the Greek boy are the ringleaders of your little group. The only thing I really require from you is a list of these crimes, for our records, and the details of how you committed them, so that we can improve our security. In partic-ular, we are concerned about the acts of terrorism at Cobbler's Bay. In supplying this information it may be that you will make us aware of circumstances that might incline us to consider clemency in your case. We are considering that for one of your companions who has been especially helpful, instead of the extreme punishment that, frankly, is well deserved; in fact has been earned many times over.

'So, Ellie . . .' He leaned back in his chair and crossed his arms behind his head. Up till then I'd thought he was perfectly relaxed, completely in com-mand, but, when he lifted his arms, I saw huge sweat patches in the armpits of his shirt, stretching almost to his waist. It made me feel a fraction better.

'. . . I understand you are something of a writer – the record keeper for your little bunch of hooligans.' He peeled a sheet of paper from the pile on the desk and placed it in front of me. From his pocket he drew a cheap grey biro, with the words STATE GOVERNMENT written in red down its side.

'Stealing pens,' I said. 'That's a criminal offence.'

It was the first thing I'd said since coming into the room, and it was a pretty dumbass comment. Major Harvey just smiled, and shook his head.

'People don't change, Ellie, do they?' he said. 'I don't think you'll ever change. And I feel sorry for you, I really do, because things might have gone easier for you if you had. Well, there's your paper, and here's a pen. As I said, you can start with the mess you caused at Cobbler's Bay. We're particularly anxious to know how you got in there, what explosive you used, and how you got that explosive. We'll leave you alone for an hour. I suggest you write fast. The only chance you have is to write down everything. Everything, you understand?'

He said the last three words with sudden ferocity, taking me by surprise, but I tried not to show it. Instead, I gazed sulkily at the floor as he and the two officers left the room. They shut the door behind them and I heard the key turn.

I sat gazing at the paper. Even if I'd wanted to, I couldn't imagine how to put down so much on paper in just one hour. I'd need months, and hundreds of thousands of words. It seemed pointless anyway. I didn't have the energy to write anything.

Chapter Twenty-four

Major Harvey picked up the piece of paper. 'I see writing on this paper,' he announced.

I didn't say anything; I assumed he was going to make some dumb comment about the blank sheet.

'Yes,' he said, putting it down again. 'I certainly see writing on it. I see your death warrant. That's what it says to me.'

He looked at me, waiting for a reaction. I wasn't going to give him the pleasure of one. I was very confused, uncertain, of what I should do; the only thing I was reasonably sure of was that whatever Major Harvey wanted me to do, I wouldn't.

'A very well-written death warrant,' Major Harvey concluded, milking his little joke for all it was worth.

He sat at the desk again. The woman officer was there too, and she sat down this time, in a chair in a corner of the room. Major Harvey continued to talk to me.

'I'm a very busy man, Ellie,' he said. 'I'm trying to help you but I'm not going to spend day after day persuading you to save your own life. If you're not interested in doing it, I don't see why I should be. You're a very silly, very stubborn girl, and I can tell you now that you'll be shot before the week's out if you don't make the effort to tell us what we need to know.'

I wanted to believe I had a chance, but I couldn't. If they were going to shoot me, a few little details about Cobbler's Bay weren't going to stop them. At the same time there was no point in not telling him.

'It's no big secret,' I said. 'We got into Cobbler's Bay in the back of a broken-down container truck that they towed in. We'd stuffed the container with anfo, and when they loaded the container onto a ship we blew it up.'

'Anfo? What's anfo?'

'You ought to know. You were in the Army, weren't you?'

He flushed a little. 'Just answer the question,' he said stiffly.

'It's ammonium nitrate, fuel oil. You use a detonator and that sets off the anfo, and the whole thing blows sky high.'

'How did you get that material?'

I shrugged. 'You can get stuff like that on any farm.'

'How did you know this? How could you make a bomb of that force?'

'My father used anfo all the time. To blow up tree stumps, stuff like that.'

His head came forward and his small black eyes glittered at me.

'But when I spoke to you and your friends the very first time, on that memorable occasion in the Holloway Valley, I distinctly remember you told me you knew nothing about explosives. "We don't know anything," was the phrase used, I seem to recall.'

I was silent. I sat there blushing, caught out in the

lie, and unable to explain it away. I was trying to protect Kevin of course, but I was off to a bad start. The Major pressed home his attack.

'You spoke of "we" when you described the actual attack. Who are the "we"? How many people attacked Cobbler's Bay?'

'Oh sorry, it was just me. The others helped me get a few things together, that's why I said "we". But I did it on my own.'

He laughed, but with no humour.

'You're not doing a very good job.' He waited a moment without looking at me, then leaned forward again.

'I'll tell you what really happened,' he said. 'Somehow you have managed to link up with trained soldiers. I'd guess, saboteurs of the New Zealand Army who parachuted in. We know they're in this area. You met them and you've been working with them, under their orders, and when you were caught last night you were either on your way to rejoin them, or you were in the middle of a mission that they'd sent you on. Which is it?'

I sat there open-mouthed.

'I know you're trying to protect them,' he said. 'But I warn you for the last time young lady, your life depends on telling me everything. So far you've told me nothing.'

I struggled to get a voice.

'Why . . . What makes you think we weren't on our own?' I finally managed to ask.

He gave a tight little triumphant smile, as though I'd confirmed his theory. I think the way I had asked my question made him think he was right; that he'd busted me.

'Quite simple,' he said. 'You are six school students. I've been working with young people since I left Teachers' College at the age of twenty. I know what they can and cannot do. These things you and your friends claim to have done are simply impossible. When I first met you, and you made various boasts about attacks you'd made on the Wirrawee bridge and so forth, I dismissed them as typical teenage bragging.

'Later, some time after the battle in which I'd assumed you were killed, I found out that the Wirrawee bridge had in fact been destroyed, and at least two girls were witnessed running from the scene. I knew then that I'd underestimated your group, and I realised that you must have had Regular Army support.

'Then there was the explosion in Turner Street – you had some involvement in that, didn't you? That had all the hallmarks of professional terrorists. The attack on Cobbler's Bay. The attack and destruction of a grounded helicopter by a New Zealand Air Force jet: that was just a pleasant coincidence for you, was it? Is that what you seriously expect me to believe? The ambush and slaying of the officer and two soldiers: you think a bunch of kids could catch professionals that way?

'No, Ellie, the truth is that you've become involved in something much bigger than you realise, something that's gone way beyond your control.

'And if you want to still be alive this time next week, you'd better tell me everything and tell me fast. We need to know where to find these people right now. If we don't find them then you'll be dying on their behalf, and I don't think you want that, do you?

235

You're very young, too young to die, if you'll forgive the cliché. These people you've been working for, these people who have in fact exploited you – if only you could see it – they're professional soldiers. They accept dying as an occupational hazard. They know that when they sign up. You don't have to take any responsibility for them.'

It all made a weird kind of sense, that was the terrible frightening thing about it. I could see exactly how he would have arrived at the conclusions he'd reached. In a way he'd paid us a compliment, by being unable to believe we could have achieved what we had. By being such bloody legends we'd got ourselves into an awful mess.

I didn't know where to start. I began by being rational. I tried to explain to him how we'd gone about our attacks. But I was too tired and scared, and the words came out badly. I couldn't remember half the things we'd done or the order in which we'd done them, and within three minutes I was floundering, tying myself up in a fishnet, almost feeling the lines cutting my throat. I switched from rational to begging, at last dropping my pride to the floor and pleading with him for my life. The only thing I didn't do, the only way I kept any self-respect, was not to dob in Homer about Cobbler's Bay or Kevin about the explosives. Perhaps I would have if I'd thought it might make a difference, but I knew it wouldn't. The best story I could finally come up with was to tell him about Chris, and to say that Chris taught me about explosives. But, as Major Harvey said, if that were the true story I would have told him straight away. I had no reason to protect Chris.

There was nothing I could say to that, because it was true.

At one stage, sick of being picked on, I said to him, 'Why don't you ask the others? They'll tell you the same thing.'

That's when he told me that they were in the hands of other interrogators; he'd spoken to all five of them but he'd saved me for his own special attention.

We went on for hours until the Major started to look as exhausted as I was. The woman left at some stage; I was hardly aware of her going. The soldiers who'd escorted me lounged around in the corridor outside, glancing into the office occasionally. In the end I gave up. There seemed nothing I could say that would convince Harvey we'd acted on our own. I sat there in grim silence as he tried and tried again to convince me to tell him everything.

I think he honestly believed his own theory. But I also think he had something to prove. I wondered if he were under pressure himself, maybe to prove to the soldiers that he was loyal to them, and good at his job. I didn't know, and I didn't care a lot. I had enough problems of my own.

The only thing I was grateful for was that it hadn't occurred to him that our attack on Turner Street was aimed right at him. We'd set out deliberately to kill him; that was the main point of it. We'd failed, but in our failure we'd apparently achieved something dramatic, because right at the end of the session he said to me: 'And the attack on Turner Street, that was another coincidence, I suppose, was it?'

'How do you mean?' I asked tiredly. It was the first time I'd bothered to respond to anything he'd said for fifteen minutes.

'How did you know General S – was there?'

I couldn't pick up the name he said; it was not an easy one to pronounce.

'Who?'

'You see, that's yet another reason I know you're lying. Or are you going to tell me your little gang had an intelligence network as well?'

'What?'

'Ellie, it took a very sophisticated intelligence network to know that the General was in Wirrawee that night. Most of our own soldiers didn't even know. But you knew. You and the people who planned that attack. Sooner or later you're going to tell me about that too, how you got that information. It's very important to us. But the most important thing right now is to know where the New Zealand soldiers are. We want them Ellie, can you understand that? And we're going to get them, whether you're alive or not to see it.'

And on that cheerful note I was returned to my cell.

I had a bit of a reaction in there. I was totally exhausted; I had no resistance left. I wanted to crawl under the bed and go into a foetal position. As there was no 'under the bed', all I could do was huddle in a corner. I didn't cry; but I shook a hell of a lot. I wanted to pull myself together because I knew I'd need all the strength I could get but there was no strength there. So I huddled and shook.

They were still feeding me, which was surprising, and when they brought tea in, it motivated me a bit. I didn't get up or even look at them while they were in the cell, but after they'd gone I staggered up, went to the desk and forced myself to eat the meal. I didn't know when I'd get another one. Major Harvey obviously wasn't pleased with me.

Less than an hour later I got taken back to his office. I felt there'd been a very slight change, though. He seemed more resigned, less urgent. Gradually, listening to his threats and insults, I realised what was happening. By then six of us had been through hours of questioning and all six of us must have shown such complete amazement at the New Zealand commando theory that they were starting to doubt it themselves. There was no suggestion that it was going to make any difference in the long run but it did mean that the pressure on me was fractionally lighter. He still ranted and raved but without quite as much confidence. The stumbling block for him was the idea that we could have done so much by ourselves. Because he refused to believe that, he had to look for another explanation and, as they'd caught everyone else in the Stratton–Wirrawee district, he thought it had to be the Kiwis.

We struggled on way into the night, hour after weary hour. At times Major Harvey shouted and screamed, at times he reasoned with a kind of fake patience, at times he became emotional. 'You're an attractive young girl, Ellie,' he said, in a way that made my skin crawl, 'and the last thing I want is to see your life ended at such an early age. But you've got to tell me the truth or I can't help you. I know you're holding out on me. I know young people, you see. I've had a lot to do with them over the years, and I know when they're telling the truth and when they're not. I've developed a sixth sense about that kind of thing. Now, Ellie, please, help me, help yourself, help your friends, by telling me who organised these attacks.'

Thinking that anything was worth a try I started acting repentant.

'I know we did the wrong thing, Major Harvey,' I said, hanging my head. Mr Kassar's drama lessons in body language were quite useful sometimes. 'But we didn't know what was best. We didn't have anyone to tell us, you see.'

He became instantly pompous. It was like adding boiling water to coffee. For someone who claimed to be an expert in young people he didn't seem too smart to me. 'Yes, but Ellie,' he said, 'when I gave you the chance to learn from me, to carry out orders in a proper well-organised military environment, you adopted a sullen and resentful attitude. You can't dispute that.'

'But I didn't know what I was doing then,' I said. I nearly added: It was just a stage I was going through. 'I admit, I was disobedient. But I've learned better now. I won't be like that again, I promise. Just give me a chance and you'll see.'

He looked away, and I sensed with a sad stale sense of despair that there was no hope.

'It's not in my hands,' he said stiffly, and I knew, with my highly advanced expertise in dealing with adults, that for once he was telling the truth. 'Those decisions are made by others. My job is to persuade you to tell us where the terrorists are, and I have been instructed that if you do, there may be some chance for clemency.'

'I can't tell you because they don't exist,' I said wearily, and for the hundredth time. Then I lost my temper.

'What's it matter to you anyway?' I screamed. 'You disgusting filthy heap of shit! What are you helping them for? You're a traitor. At least we tried. At least we did the best we could. I don't care if I do die, I'd

240

rather be dead than end up a complete and utter arsehole like you.' I was standing and screaming, aware that little flecks of spit were flying out of my mouth and hitting his red shocked face. Not that I cared about that. Then the guards were in the room, grabbing me and throwing me onto the floor.

Soon after that I was marched back to my cell. It was dawn, and great grey clouds were being lit by a stormy grey light. I walked along with my head back, my eyes as wide as I could make them, marvelling at the vastness and wildness of it all. I didn't know how many more skies I would see. In my cell, there was no trace of nature at all, so this couple of minutes was very precious, something to be thought about and relived for hours to come. All my life I'd been surrounded by sky and earth and trees and to be cut off from them now, to be cut off so suddenly and completely, was very hard.

The Slaters had a Japanese lady visit them a couple of years back. She was about twenty-three, twenty-four. She told them that until her trip out to Australia she'd never seen the horizon. Twenty-three years old and she'd never seen the horizon! It was a modern-day horror story. I'd realised then how lucky I was.

Chapter Twenty-five

I sat in my cell in a state of expectation, waiting for the next summons to Major Harvey. I was all tensed up, unable to sleep, though I felt unbearably exhausted. Breakfast came and I ate it and then made myself go through the exercises that I'd decided on the day before. But already, less than twenty-four hours after making those resolutions, I found myself struggling to keep them.

All day I waited for the summons and all day it failed to come. Around midafternoon I dozed off at the desk, my head on my arms. When I woke, my head felt heavy and achey, and my left leg had gone numb. I felt worse instead of better.

Tea arrived, brought on the tray by the same group of three women. I was starting to notice the different guards now. The one who carried the tray each time was the shortest of the three. She was a plain-looking dumpy woman with a flat face and sparse black hair. She looked about forty. Her uniform was the least adorned of any of the guards; no stripes, and only one small badge sewn to the left shoulder, so I suppose she was pretty junior in rank.

242

Despite her plain looks she had a kind face. I thought that in her own country she was probably a cleaner or a maid, the same job that she was doing here, except that now she was in uniform. The two women at the door, with guns drawn, were younger and slimmer. They looked like sisters. One seemed nervous, as though she thought I might attack her at any moment. The other, the officer, was more confident, more relaxed. She always watched me with interest, like she was curious about me.

So this time, when the woman put the tray down, I tried making a joke. I was already desperate for human company, for warmth, for friendship. I didn't want to be their enemy. I waved at the tray and said, 'What is it this time, a Big Mac?' The woman carrying the tray looked startled, then gave a little smile and shook her head. 'No, no, no Big Mac,' she said. The officer laughed out loud. The other one just looked even more nervous, as though making a joke was really a kind of attack. They went out again, shutting the door, but I felt encouraged by my first attempt to be friendly, warmed by that moment when we'd laughed together. I ate my tea in a slightly better spirit.

I'd been thinking, of course, of ways of making a dramatic escape. At one stage I'd thought of telling Major Harvey that there really were New Zealand commandos, and I'd take him to them. Then, when I was out in the open air, I'd wait for an opportunity to grab a gun or something, or run away. One of the many problems with that was I could hardly escape from the prison and leave my friends inside.

I told myself it would have been easier if I'd known definitely that I was going to be killed. Then I'd have done anything, even staged a suicide escape attempt, because I'd have had nothing to lose. But while there's life there's hope I guess, and I couldn't bring myself to accept that my execution was such a certainty.

Another escape method would have been to take a hostage. Hold a knife to a soldier's throat and make her lead me to the front gate and let me out. There were a few problems with that too, one of them being the fact that the only weapons they'd given me so far were plastic forks.

After tea I did my exercises again. For one thing, I wanted to wear myself out physically, so I'd have more chance of sleeping when the lights were turned off. So I did more aerobics, flinging my arms out, kicking my legs, chanting songs to myself. This time I just ignored the camera.

When I was pretty puffed I sat on the bed. I realised that what I wanted most was something to read or, failing that, something to write on. I decided to try getting the guards' attention. I was curious to see what would happen and, again, I didn't have much to lose. So I went to the door and banged on it with my fist. The door was so thick and heavy that I couldn't make a loud-enough noise. So I tried shaking it, which didn't work either, as it was too solid, too well fitted. Then I yelled for a bit, first at the camera, then through the door. I wondered if my friends could hear any of this. I hadn't seen or heard a glimpse of them since we'd entered our separate cells. But it didn't seem likely that anyone would hear me as my voice sounded so muffled, even to me. It was frustrating, and a bit scary. I felt so cut off, and wondered what would happen if there were a fire in the prison. It wouldn't be a healthy place.

I yelled for ten minutes. There wasn't much else to do; it helped pass the time. Just as I was about to give up I heard the locks start to rattle. The door swung open and I found myself looking at the two younger women who were always there when my meals were brought. One was standing well back, with a gun trained on me. The second one, the officer, who'd laughed at my Big Mac joke, was right at the door, and she spoke. To my surprise her English was very good.

'Stand against the wall.'

I went back a few paces but she waved me further, till I was touching the furthest wall from the door. Then she came in a couple of steps, though her buddy stayed out in the corridor.

'Now,' she said. 'I teach you correct ways. You want guard, you press button there.' To my surprise she showed me something I'd never noticed: a white button beside a ventilation panel close to the door and up high. I felt sorry for short prisoners. She continued: 'Then you go to back wall, you stand there and wait, OK? You understand?'

I nodded. I understood.

'Some things you not allowed. You not allowed make noise. You not allowed read books. You not allowed make mess in room. You not allowed make names on walls. OK? You understand?'

I nodded again. No making names on walls.

'Can I have a shower?' I asked.

'Sorry, no shower. Maybe tomorrow.'

'Can I see my friends?'

'No, no friends. Maybe tomorrow.'

'Can I get a toothbrush?'

'Toothbrush, yes, OK, I bring.'

'And soap?'

'Yes, yes, toothbrush, toothpaste, soap, towel, all those things, I bring.'

'Can I have some paper, and a pen?'

'What for?'

'Um, I want to, I want to write . . .'

I was trying to think of some good lie that would satisfy her, but I couldn't think of anything, so ended the sentence, rather lamely, with the truth. 'I don't know, I'll go crazy if I don't have something to do.'

There was a silence while she considered my request. It was obviously outside the guidelines. But then she made up her mind. 'OK, pen, paper, OK. That all now?'

'Yes, thank you. Thank you very much.'

It was two hours before the things she'd promised arrived, but it was very exciting to get them. They were brought in by a different guard, one of the ones who'd marched me off to meet Major Harvey. It was like Christmas. I pored over each item in turn. The toothbrush was blue, with twenty-eight clumps of bristles, nine rows of three plus one at the tip. The soap was small and yellow, the size of a matchbox, with a strong, unpleasant smell. The toothpaste was Colgate, in the familiar red, green and white colours, but apart from the word 'Colgate' nothing else on it was in English.

I also scored a thin frayed lemon handtowel with a green stripe running across it at each end, a vinegar-coloured comb, and a cheap plastic disposable cup. So many possessions! I felt rich.

The most important things, though, were the paper and pen. There was just one sheet of paper, lined, very thin, and a cheap blue ballpoint pen that ran dry on almost every downstroke. It was frustrating but it was better than nothing. Suddenly the long empty night that stretched ahead wasn't so long or empty any more. I sat at the desk and in tiny writing, filling the paper as slowly as possible, I wrote a letter to my parents. I knew the chances of their getting it were as good as those of bark in a bushfire, but it was something I wanted to do, so I did it.

Next day there was still no call from Major Harvey. After being in such demand from him it seemed that now I wasn't wanted at all. The morning dragged by, a minute at a time. Breakfast was delivered with a joke from the older lady. As she put down the tray she said, 'No Big Macs today, I sorry,' and we both laughed. There was no sign of the shower I'd been promised though, and when I pressed the button late in the morning and asked for one I was given the brush-off very quickly. It was the same officer who'd brought me the paper and pen, but today she seemed unfriendly, uninterested. With so much time to think, I wondered if maybe I was going to be executed soon, and she was distancing herself from me, like I would have done in her situation.

Lunch came and went, and the afternoon passed even more slowly than the morning. I wrote a poem on the back of the piece of paper and decided I'd start a short story that evening. My writing was so small I could hardly read it myself, but I still had three-quarters of one side left. I did my physical and mental exercises again, but my head felt stuffy and my whole body was slow and lethargic. I wondered even more about my future. To die would be such a terrible, unthinkable, unfair thing. But to be locked up in a cell like this for years and years, maybe decades . . . that would be completely unbearable. I suspected these people weren't like us. I didn't know much about them, but I guessed they'd think little of throwing people into a cell and forgetting them. At least in our system you got a proper trial and you knew what was going to happen to you – usually, anyway. Maybe Major Harvey thought our country had become too slack, but I knew which set-up I preferred.

Nothing else really happened and I got more and more depressed as the evening ground on. I couldn't wait for the lights to go off so I could get some sleep, but when they did and I lay down I didn't seem able to sleep at all. It was a miserable rotten night; I probably only slept for two or three hours and I did quite a lot of silent crying – silent because I didn't want to give the guards the satisfaction of knowing how deep I was sinking.

Despite the warning about 'making names on walls' I used the top of the biro to make some little scratch marks on the base of the bed, to show how many days I'd been there. If I was going to be there for ten years I didn't want to lose count of the days.

If I'd known then that there would be no real change in my routine for the next week I'd have been even more depressed. But seven little scratches had been added in the shiny white paint before anything interesting happened. The only highlights were two showers that I was allowed to have in a little shower room in our maximum-security block; the grudging gift of another sheet of paper halfway through the week; and the middle-aged lady who brought my trays in and out giving me a packet of chewing gum one day and telling me I was a 'brave girl'.

Her kindness moved me very much.

I spent a lot of time thinking about the other five and wondering how they were doing. I was so afraid for them. I could picture Homer, frustrated and angry, walking round and round the tiny cell, banging his head against the wall, quickly going crazy. I thought Fi would be like a heron suddenly locked in a cage, sitting there timidly and in her mind's eye still seeing the sky and the hills and the wild places. Robyn I didn't know about. She seemed to have been cracking up again in the last few weeks. Sometimes, if I hadn't seen evidence of it for a while, I forgot just how angry and depressed she could get.

I thought Lee would be a danger both to himself and the guards. I pictured him getting more resentful by the hour, sitting in the middle of the floor brooding, and then suddenly leaping at a guard's throat in a fit of madness. And Kevin, in my imaginings, would be a mess. I couldn't see how he would occupy his mind for all these weary hours. He relied on other people so much for his interests, not seeming to have ideas of his own. He needed lots of action, things happening around him all the time, or he quickly became bored. These cells weren't made for people like Kevin.

They were the mental pictures I developed as I thought about my friends. But I thought about many other things too, of course. The poem about God carrying the person along the beach. My family and the people of Wirrawee. I started to understand why they had become so depressed and sour, locked for month after month in the Showground.

I thought more than anything about death; my own, how much warning I would get, how I would face it, what it would feel like, and what would happen to me afterwards. I did a lot of thinking but I also became very sullen. I couldn't help it. I so badly needed to breathe fresh air, to see the sky, to do physical things. I even thought about suicide but the irony was that even if I'd wanted to commit it there was no possible way of doing it.

Chapter Twenty-six

When they came for me an hour after breakfast I had no idea what to expect. Desperate for any change to my routine, I followed them eagerly. The shock of fresh air on my face was so strong that I felt like a corpse coming out of a grave. The air was viciously cold – it was a freezing day – but I could have kissed it as it bit at my face.

The route they took me along was what I was used to: straight along the covered walkway to the building where Major Harvey had questioned me for so long. I lingered as long as I could on the walk but the guards had no interest in the bracing air: to them it was just a nasty winter day, I guess. They hurried me into the building and down the corridor to the same office, and there he was again, the same dark face and dark eyes. He seemed more jumpy, more nervous, his eyes not settling on me when he spoke, but looking away all the time, to places around the room. I thought he'd lost weight, too.

'Ah, Ellie,' he said. 'This won't take long. Just a small duty I want you to perform. Take a look at this, please. In fact you can read it to me.'

251

He handed me a sheet of paper with a couple of typed paragraphs on it. I took it and began to read it out loud: 'I am making this statement voluntarily to apologise for my actions in recent months. I have been involved in terrorist activity which has led to a great deal of property damage and caused injury and death to many innocent people. In acting in this irresponsible way I have insulted those who are helping to rebuild my country and who I now realise are creating a new and better society for us all.

'Unfortunately some misguided people in other countries are still engaging in attacks on us. I must ask them to desist. They are causing a great deal of unnecessary suffering. They are committing war crimes in violation of international law. It is time for everyone to work together in our new society for the betterment of all people. I ask for the support of all people in achieving this.'

I threw the paper back on the desk. 'What a load of crap,' I said.

The Major picked it up. He didn't look bothered. 'Now come with me,' he said. We went further down the corridor, and he ushered me into a small room at the end. There was a stool, an umbrella, a couple of lights on stands, and a big television camera operated by a woman wearing headphones. The umbrella was like a big parasol. It was on a stand and seemed to have something to do with the lighting.

'Sit down,' Harvey said.

I hesitated, then obeyed. He handed me the sheet of paper again and I took it.

'Now, just read it again, for the benefit of your New Zealand friends,' he said. 'Look up at the camera from time to time. No funny business, thank you, and no silly facial expressions like some of your immature young friends attempted. It just means we have to start again, and waste more of our time.'

I was ecstatic to hear him mention the others. It was the first news I'd heard of them in more than a week. I'd asked the guards every day but no one would answer. It was obviously a taboo subject. I didn't know if I should read the statement or not, but the others had made it easier for me; sort of taken the decision out of my hands. Of course, Major Harvey could have been tricking me, but I didn't think so. He must have been a great actor if he was. The way he mentioned them came out so naturally.

I still wasn't keen to read it, but I sat there on the hard cane chair thinking about my choices. If I didn't read it, what would happen? I guessed they'd use tougher, rougher treatment on me. I didn't think I could stick that. I was having enough trouble coping with things as they were. I couldn't have borne it if they'd got worse. So if I did read it, what would happen? I'd feel ashamed; that'd be one thing. But forget about me: what damage might it do? Well, none really. It'd be so obvious to everyone that it was a fake. I couldn't imagine that people in New Zealand, or anywhere else, would take one look at this and think, 'Oh well, we'd better stop helping them because they're obviously happy with the new arrangements.'

Major Harvey was getting impatient. I said to him – mainly to make myself feel better about the decision I'd already made – 'What'll happen to me if I don't read it?'

With no emotion at all he answered: 'Don't make things any worse for yourself, Ellie.'

The woman nestled in behind her camera and I heard it whirr into life. Major Harvey switched on the lights. The room instantly became extremely bright and extremely hot. I held the sheet up and read it quickly, without expression. At the end I thought Major Harvey would tell me to do it again – I knew I'd sounded like a robot – and he did stand there silently for a minute after I'd finished. But then he switched off the lights and went to the door and called the guards.

When they came, I followed them back out towards the exit. Major Harvey, who was ahead of me, turned into his office without so much as a back-wards glance, but I couldn't bear to let him go without trying to find out something, anything, about my future. I figured he was the most likely one to know, and I figured I would rather know than not know. So I stopped and asked him.

'Major Harvey, can you tell me what's going to happen to me?'

He was moving around the desk towards his chair but he stopped dead when he heard my voice. There was a long silence, a terrible silence. My heart started pounding fiercely, and I broke out sweating, wishing now that I'd never asked the question. Without look-ing around he said, 'You have to accept the conse-quences of your actions, Ellie.'

It was not only the words; it was the way he'd said them. I knew now. My legs were so weak they wouldn't move. It was like the bones had been taken out of them. A guard nudged me from behind and I staggered forwards. This time I didn't even see the sky. My head was down, my legs were dragging, I felt like I was going to be ill, like I had some serious ill-ness creeping up on me.

But I knew the name of that serious illness. It was called death.

Back in the cell I fell on my bed and lay there. For the first time I didn't show any interest in lunch when the lady brought it. Inside me, I was hoping that she'd notice how upset I was, and that she'd come over to the bed and give me a cuddle and ask what was wrong, and comfort me. Just like my mum. But she didn't. She put the tray down and left the cell. I cried bitterly when I heard the door slam. 'I'm too young,' I kept thinking, 'I'm too young.'

It seemed so unfair that by a fluke I'd escaped being captured when the invasion came and so I'd been forced into a certain course of action, and because of that I was now going to die. Why couldn't I have been captured at the start, like everyone else? Why did I have to be the unlucky one?

I conveniently ignored the fact that one of the soldiers we'd killed didn't seem any older than me.

I lay there for about two hours, I'd guess. If I'd had a way of killing myself I probably would have done it then. The fact that I didn't has taught me something very important about life: that you never know what the next minute might bring. If you kill yourself, it might be seconds before something wonderful happens. What that afternoon brought mightn't seem so wonderful to others, but to me, at that moment, it was.

The door was unlocked and I heard the voice of the officer who'd brought me the toothbrush and paper. She said: 'Exercise now. You come.'

I thought it might be a trick, and that this might be the execution I was now certain was coming, but I got up anyway and went listlessly out into the corridor.

We took the same route as usual: down the corridor enclosed by wire, past the dull green lawns and the tennis courts. But as we came to a gate leading into a small section of the grassed yards I saw a group of people standing together talking. I would have known those people from a kilometre away, let alone from thirty metres. I let out a great gasp of pure joy, then quickly tried to bite it back, in case the guards changed their minds. But I'd made enough noise. The little group broke up, as they turned to see who was screeching at them. I saw with relief that all five of them were there. The guard started unlocking the gate as Fi called out: 'Ellie! Oh Ellie!'

As soon as I got inside they threw themselves on me. It was like a football ruck, like a soccer player had scored a winning goal, like tag team wrestling. For a moment I had to struggle for air. We hugged until we bruised.

It was a wonderful reunion.

And after the hugging came the questions. They flew backwards and forwards so fast that every answer was cut off within a few words.

'Which cell are you in?'

'In that block over . . .'

'Have you seen Major Harvey?'

'Yes, that bastard! He asked . . .'

'What do you think'll happen to us?'

'I don't know. Major Harvey . . .'

'Have you guys been seeing each other every day?'

'Are you OK? Did they beat you up or anything?'

'Be careful what you say. We don't know if they . . .'

'Did you have to do that confession thing?'

'They're so horrible. They make us . . .'

It took a while but eventually I got a sense of what

was going on. Homer and I were the only ones left in E Block. The other four were in a totally different situation. They'd been transferred to a block with a lot of other prisoners, some like us who were 'war criminals' and some who'd been in there for ages, from before the invasion, for crimes committed in peacetime. At meals they ate together in a big room and, at other times, they could talk to prisoners through the doors of their cells. Most amazingly of all, Robyn and Fi shared a cell. I was jealous of them for that and it made me more fearful of what might happen to me. Homer and I had definitely been singled out as the ringleaders.

But I forced away all the dark thoughts, all the fear. I was determined just to enjoy the company of my friends. It was such a relief, such a release, to be with them again. And I didn't know how many more chances like this there'd be.

We talked flat out. I had a funny desperate yearning to play basketball, wanting some activity. The cage we were in was about the size of a basketball court; I suppose that's what made me think of it. In the end I grabbed Homer's shoe and ran to the fence, making him chase me. At once guards up on the wall aimed their shotguns at us. 'Look out,' Fi called. 'Stop. They think you're doing something.' But I ignored her. I was determined not to be too frightened of these thugs. And, although they kept watching us closely as we ran around, they didn't take any action.

After we'd been there about an hour the guards who were supervising through the wire from the corridor unlocked the gate again. They beckoned to me first. I'd been the last to come, now I was the first to go. But as they led me away I saw them signalling to Homer, so I guessed exercise time was over for all of us.

I called out to them all: 'Bye! See you!', but, as I said 'See you', I wondered if I ever would, ever again. The great dark weight of depression and fear was hovering over me once more, but hovering a little higher, and perhaps not quite so heavily.

Chapter Twenty-seven

As it happened I saw the others the next day, and the day after that, and the day after that. Regular afternoon exercise became a part of my routine: the most precious, exciting, anticipated moments in my life. The worst thing was that Homer and I only got an hour each, which apparently went with the deal when you were in maximum security. The others got two hours.

Maybe the guards couldn't afford the manpower: when Homer and I were out there they had three guards assigned to watch us. The others only got one between the four of them. I think Lee felt a bit insulted by that.

For three weeks our lives remained locked into this pattern. Very little out of the ordinary happened. I saw Major Harvey a couple of times from a distance, when we were in the exercise yard, but he took no notice of us. The only exciting things were air raids: there were two during the three weeks and even in my soundproofed cell I could hear the wail of the sirens. I pressed my call button during the first one but got no answer. Later when the guards brought my food, I asked them what the noise was, and they said, 'Planes in sky drop bombs, very bad.' The other five, when I met them next day on the grass, confirmed that there had been air raids.

'All the guards ran off,' Fi said. 'I think they've got a shelter somewhere. Not much help to us though, when we're locked in our cells. Even when there are no guards we can't escape. Makes you wonder why they bother to have them at all.'

Both the raids were at night; we figured it'd be too dangerous for them to come in daylight.

It started raining a lot and for our exercise hour we were put in a gym more and more often. I didn't like it nearly as much. I needed fresh air so badly. We were all looking terrible, but Homer – and me, I suspect – looked the worst. You couldn't exactly call Homer pale, because his skin was naturally dark, but it did get an unhealthy tinge to it, almost green. And he was so thin. Well, so was I. We were skeletal. We looked like Aurora at school when she had anorexia. The others were getting better food and they started smuggling bits out to us but it was difficult: we were watched so carefully.

Yet the passing of time calmed us down a bit. I guess you can't live at full-on intensity for ever. Lying on the bed of my cell in the dark, trembling, waiting for soldiers to come in and shoot me – you just can't keep doing that. There's something in the human spirit that won't let you live that way. Gradually, you start forgetting about your death sentence and thinking about more normal things instead. Not all the time, of course, but enough times to keep you existing. You sleep occasionally, and you don't always dream of death. You get a bit numb.

Well, that's the way it was for me anyway.

The day it changed was a day that changed me for ever. Of course we're changed by everything that happens to us. Of course I'd been changed dramatically by the invasion and everything that had happened since. But that morning, the morning when I finally had to confront what I'd been avoiding for so long, changed me like nothing else had – or ever will again, I guess. They came for me at about eleven o'clock. I remember every detail of the first few minutes. The way the officer flicked her hand to gesture me out into the corridor. The way the door squeaked slightly as it swung heavily open: that little cry from the hinge that I'd never heard before. The faces of the guards: the women and men I'd gotten to know so well by sight but who now, this morning, wouldn't look at me. The long slow walk to a building near the jail entrance, one I hadn't been to yet. The soft throbbing of thunder in the distance. The sweaty palm-print left by the guard as she pushed the door of the building open. I knew when I saw that palmprint that I was walking towards something terrible. From that moment on I hardly remember anything.

They took me into some sort of large room, all lined with light brown panelling. It looked very formal. There were people sitting at a table, about five of them I think, and I think all of them were men. I was in there three or four minutes. No one looked at me. The bloke in the middle read a whole lot of stuff, very fast, in his own language, while a bloke standing behind him translated into English. It was about how I'd destroyed property, committed acts of terrorism, murdered people; how I'd been found guilty of the above charges, and sentenced to death. Sentence to be carried out Monday the 16th, at 7 am. That is all. Do you have anything to say? No? Take her away. Bring in the next prisoner. The next prisoner was Homer, though I didn't know that until he told me himself, in the exercise yard six days later. He'd seen me coming out of the room but I'd walked right past him without noticing him. He said he'd known then, as soon as he'd seen me.

I remember saying only one thing to the guards, and that was to ask them what day it was. They said Friday the 6th, so I knew I had only ten days to go.

It was the same afternoon that the daylight raids started.

I was lying on my bed, knees up to my chest, hands between my legs, rocking myself, trying to think of one thing at a time. But I couldn't. Thoughts were screaming into my head at such speed that it was like a demolition derby in there: the thoughts kept crashing into each other and spinning off into the darkness. I couldn't even slow them down, let alone stop them. I thought my head would burst into flames.

When I heard the dull thundering booms they seemed like the background to the chaos inside me. I hardly noticed them at first. It took a while to realise they were coming from somewhere outside. Just as I realised that, the walls gave a little tremble and a tiny white powder fell from the ceiling. Then I knew: it was an air-raid, an afternoon air raid, and close too if it could rattle the walls in my cell.

I wasn't scared, just fascinated to see what would happen. I got off my bed and stood by the door, waiting and listening. The booms kept going for a few minutes, then suddenly the lights went out. That was scary, but exciting too. I started wondering what would happen if the roof fell in on me. What would my body look like, buried under fifty tonnes of steel and concrete? I was feeling claustrophobic, but still not desperately frightened, more tantalised by the knowledge that something out of the ordinary was happening, and there was no telling what it might lead to.

In fact it led to nothing. The booming noises lasted another ten minutes, then stopped, suddenly and completely. Hours later the lights came back on; two guards came in and inspected my cell, and I was left to guess what might have happened outside.

The next two days there were more raids, one in the morning and one in the late afternoon. Again and again the building shook. Several times I cowered in the corner of the cell. Each time the white dust floated down, till the floor looked like light snow had been falling. By the end of the third raid I found long thin cracks in the wall.

On neither day was I allowed into the exercise yard. I started to fear that I'd never see my friends again, never have a chance to say goodbye. Three more awful days passed, suffocating, excruciating days, when as far as I could tell there were no air raids, though the guards were very jumpy. But on Thursday, just four days before the sentences were to be carried out, I heard them unlocking my door. It was the time when we normally had exercise, and now they took me out as though nothing had happened. I guess someone in authority had decided the air raids were finished. But I was shocked at the damage that had been done while I was locked in my square little white coffin. Every second window in the jail was broken. There was rubbish all over the place – I mean big rubbish, serious rubbish: sheets of galvanised iron, slabs of brickwork, big tree branches. The eastern wall had partially collapsed: about fifty metres of it was more like rubble than a wall. But already they'd put up a huge wire fence to cover the damage. I couldn't see any way of escaping through that.

A couple of minutes later I was in the gym. Conditions were different now. The guards watched us more closely. Homer and I were not allowed any physical contact, with each other or with the other four. We were assigned three different zones in the basketball court and we had to talk to each other from our own zones. I had the keyhole at the southern end.

We each told our news. Homer and I had both been given death sentences, both for Monday. The others got prison terms: thirty years for Lee, twenty-five for Robyn and Kevin, and twenty-two for Fi. I don't know how they'd arrived at the different numbers.

We had a ghastly conversation. No one could think of anything to say. We sat there like we were at a funeral already. Occasionally someone would say something in a hoarse whisper, but usually no one would answer, so the conversations never got far.

It was almost a relief to go back to my cell.

Friday the weather was better and we had an hour outside, but again we weren't allowed near each other. Saturday we were back in the gym. It was another terrible hour. Fi was hysterical the whole time. The rest of us seemed like zombies, barely functioning at all.

Saturday night was the worst time, I think. I'd

written letters to a few people, cramming as much as I could on the few sheets of paper I was allowed, even writing down the sides of the pages. When I asked for more paper I was refused. There seemed nothing else to do. All I could think of was that tomorrow would be my last full day of life. I lay on the bed, trying to find some strength to cope, to get me through the next thirty-five hours. I lay there with my mind running amuck, on the brink of madness. And somehow, gradually, early Sunday morning, I became calm. I can't think of any other word for it. I was thinking about the beach poem again, and I started to feel that I was being looked after, that everything was OK. It was strange: if there was ever a time in my life when I had the right to feel alone this was it. But I lost that sense of loneliness. I felt like there was a force in the room with me, not a person, but I had a sense that there was another world, another dimension, and it would be looking after me. I'm not talking about some place I'd be going to; it wasn't like that. It was like, 'This isn't the only world, this is just one aspect of the whole thing, don't imagine this is all there is.'

That's about all I can say really; I can't give it a name or paint a picture. It existed in a different form to the things we give names to, or try to illustrate. But I do know that I reached some sort of acceptance of what was to happen.

I had been dreading the last exercise hour, the last meeting with my friends. But I was quite settled as I moved slowly along the walkway. It was very overcast and must have been raining heavily during the morning: there was so much water on the ground. Most of the debris from the bombs had been cleaned up. I was hardly aware of the guards; they were the weekend shift, who seemed sloppier, more amateur-ish, than the highly drilled and professional ones I had during the week. But they still had the weapons and they still kept them pointed at me, so it didn't really matter if they weren't so neat and polished. I remembered how I'd thought I would throw myself at their guns rather than die tamely, but I knew now that I would never have the strength to rush at death quite as recklessly as that.

We got to the gym and I was ushered in. The others were already there, standing around waiting for me, looking like actors in a weird play.

The security system in the gym was different from the exercise yard, of course. My team of three guards always stayed, whether we were inside or out. But in the gym one of Homer's squad always stayed as well, to make up the numbers, to compensate for the fact that we couldn't be seen by the sentries on the out-side wall. They spread themselves around the space, one at each wall, and sat there watching us, rifles at the ready. From the moment we'd arrived in the prison they'd never stopped treating us like violent and dangerous people.

I don't know how many other prisoners there were in the place. I'd seen a couple from a distance, and our four in minimum security said there were dozens in their section, but that was all I knew. Lee had found out that the whitegoods factory in Strat-ton, quite close to the jail, was working non-stop producing aircraft parts, and that work parties from the jail were going there nearly every day. So maybe that's why I never saw anyone.

Stratton had been a big industrial centre for a long time. Being near a harbour, being close to the

Marran coalfields, having a big railyard, meant that even when the rest of the country went into recession the factories of Stratton still worked hard.

So, that was why the city had been bombed heavily. And when days and nights of heavy bombing didn't get the results they wanted, they came back.

They came back on that Sunday afternoon.

When the sirens went off, our guards jumped to their feet and started shouting to each other and gesticulating wildly. It was the first time I'd heard the sirens outside my cell, and I couldn't believe how loud they were. For a moment I was frightened, but suddenly I realised that it hardly made any difference if a bomb dropped on me. And I did feel a sudden kick of hope in my chest. I suppose anything outside the normal routine, the routine that was dragging me towards death, was cause for hope.

Then a bomb fell quite close to the prison. There was a tremendous blast, and the whole building shook. A dozen more windows lost their glass: I saw the sheets fall and smash on the floor but I didn't hear them. My ears were numbed by the explosion. The guards didn't hesitate: they raced for the door. One of them yelled something at us, probably 'Stay there,' or 'Get down,' but I couldn't hear him. It mightn't have been in English. But even with the guards gone our situation hadn't improved. There were still bars on the windows and the guards had enough sense to lock the big gym door as they fled for their shelters.

I ran to the door in a mad sprint, and shook it. I knew this was the only chance I'd ever have. But the door was solid. I looked desperately at the windows: if we could somehow get up to them, maybe the bars

267

might have been loosened by the blast. I shouted something at Homer, can't even remember what, but his ears must have been as deafened as mine, because he shook his head to show he couldn't hear. The six of us were racing around crazily, like mice in the bottom of a grain bin when you take the top off and they realise they can't get up the smooth sides.

Then came a blast so huge that it threw me through the air. It was like a giant had blown at us, with a breath so hot and big and dry that it sent me flying, then spinning and rolling when I hit the ground again. Now I was surrounded by noise. It seemed like it would never end. Debris was flying around me and something hit me in the back so hard I was scared it might have snapped my spinal cord. But I clung to one certain fact: that I had to get to my feet. Everything depended on my being able to get to my feet. I stumbled up and looked in shock and astonishment at the sight before me. The prison had been half demolished. The gym looked like it had been demolished fifty years ago. The ground was so covered in rubble I couldn't even tell where the gym had been. I could see Fi, amazingly, only two metres from me, but huddled on the ground, not moving. Kevin was wandering around on my right, looking dazed. Robyn was bending over something, something lying at her feet. I couldn't see Homer or Lee. I ran to Fi and touched her cheek. It was warm and I saw her eyelids move. There was blood oozing out of a great gash on her cheek. I couldn't wait: I squatted, got my arms under her and, with a grunt, lifted her and slung her over my shoulders, praying that I wasn't making her injuries worse.

I took a few staggering steps, trying to get my balance, but couldn't get it properly, so continued to stagger.

I could see what Robyn was doing now: she was pulling weapons from a body on the ground. It was one of the guards who patrolled the top of the outside walls all day. He must have been blown off the wall before he could get to a shelter. Somehow his ammunition and grenades hadn't exploded. I left Robyn and blundered towards the main entrance, where both sets of gates were down and there was a twenty-metre gap in the wall. It seemed to offer the quickest exit. I tried to yell to Kevin but I didn't have the breath for it: he wouldn't have heard anyway. Robyn saw me though, and came after me. She was holding the guard's rifle and I think she had the hand grenades in her shirt, because she was bulging around the stomach. 'Better you than me,' I thought, but I had time to be amused that Robyn, the great pacifist, was now so heavily armed.

Then Lee and Homer came rushing across from my left, jumping over piles of stone and timber. They were both covered with dust and blood but there was no time to ask if they were all right. Lee grabbed Fi and carried her. I still couldn't get my breath to say anything, but I pointed to Kevin, and Homer ran across to get him. My back was hurting like hell, and now my leg was too, but I didn't dare look at it. Lee and Fi were already ahead of me; I saw Fi suddenly come to life and start struggling to get down. Robyn was through the gate. I checked for Homer and saw him leading Kevin by the hand: they were heading in the right direction so I left them to it and followed Robyn.

I ran out into the prison driveway. It was free air I was breathing now, but I wasn't thinking of that. I was just trying to make my mind work, hoping I wouldn't get shot, wondering what I'd find out there.

The driveway was relatively clear but to the right was an enormous crater, only a hundred metres from the prison wall. I seemed to remember that there'd been a little park, quite a few trees, around Stratton Prison, but they were all gone. Not a leaf was left.

At the bottom of the driveway was a blue Mercedes, slewed sideways with the driver's door open as though it had been abandoned in a hurry. In the middle of the driveway was Major Harvey, holding a gun at Robyn's face. Robyn had thrown her rifle on the ground and was standing there with her arms folded across her stomach. I stopped dead, feeling a terrible tightness in my chest. Major Harvey looked across at me. I realised at that moment how much he hated me. 'All right, boys and girls,' he shouted. 'The party's over. Everyone lie down on the ground.' I heard him clearly, so my ears must have come unblocked again. When no one moved he screamed: 'Quickly, or I shoot this one.' I began to kneel. The other four did the same. Only Robyn remained standing. She was a metre from Harvey but he was not watching her, confident now that he had the situation under control. I saw her hand slip inside her shirt. I screamed, but no sound came out. I tried again and this time made a hoarse hacking noise. I knew it was already too late. Major Harvey looked across at me, triumphant. I screamed again and at last said her name. It was the last present I could give her: the knowledge that I knew. She looked across at me and gave a scared little smile as if she didn't know what she had done, or whether she should have done it. Harvey glanced at her and at the last instant realised: he must have seen the pin of the hand grenade. He opened his mouth, dropped his gun and took a step towards her. He

270

reached out a hand, like he was begging. Then they both disappeared. That was all. They disappeared. There was a bang of course but it seemed slight, compared to the bombs; so did the shock wave that hit me an instant later. But they had disappeared, that was the thing. Robyn was there, she was alive, she was real, she was a person and then she disappeared; she had ceased to exist.

Chapter Twenty-eight

After that we had some luck. God knows we deserved it. But it didn't mean much to any of us. We took Harvey's car and drove a couple of k's, but suddenly found ourselves getting shot at from the air, so we abandoned that pretty fast. We were in the middle of the biggest air mission that the Kiwis had launched for the whole of the war, although we didn't know that at the time, of course. They were using planes supplied by the Americans but piloted by New Zealanders and our guys, and they did a lot of damage. There wasn't much left of the Stratton factories by the time they'd finished.

Anyway, where we got lucky was that we saw a plane go down on the highway. There was smoke pouring out of it and the pilot dropped it on the road fast. He braked it so hard that it almost stood on its nose, then he came scrambling out of the cockpit onto the wing and jumped to the ground. We were less than a k away. There were still bombs falling on the other side of town, grey smoke everywhere and terrible toxic fumes that made breathing horrible. We ran towards the pilot – don't know why, just instinct,

I suppose. It was the obvious thing to do. Maybe we thought he was an angel dropped out of the sky to save us. He was, too, in a way. He was running like crazy to get away from the plane, scared it'd blow up. We met in a paddock beside the highway.

'Where'd you come from?' he asked, gasping and puffing and sweating. 'God, this is a madhouse.'

He was red-haired, about twenty-four, tall and skinny, with ginger eyebrows and lots of freckles. But he had nice eyes and he was grinning, like it was all a big party.

Another roll of thunder spread across the sky and there was a flash of fire on the horizon.

'Big hit,' he said.

'How are you getting out of here?' Fi screamed at him.

'Stick around and you'll see. I'll be gone in three minutes.'

'What do you mean?' I asked, grabbing his sleeve.

He pulled a little grey gadget, no bigger than a remote control, out of his pocket. A red light on it was flashing furiously. 'This is my mayday button,' he said. 'It's activated already. They'll be here in a couple of shakes.'

'Take us with you,' Fi screamed. She seemed unable to talk normally; everything was a scream. The pilot was looking at us like we were crazy.

'I can't,' he said.

'We're all injured,' I said.

'I can see that. You look like you've been through hell. But I'm sorry, I can't take you.'

The sound of a helicopter, a giant throbbing noise, penetrated the smoke and the grey. The pilot turned away from us and started looking up, trying to see

273

the aircraft. I could tell he was losing interest in us; worse, he was starting to see us as nuisances, people who were going to try to make things complicated for him.

'Wait,' Homer said. Since we left the prison he hadn't spoken. Tears had been running down his face continuously, just a constant flow from his eyes that he made no attempt to brush or lick away. 'Wait. Did you hear about Cobbler's Bay being blown up, couple of months back? And everything was wrecked?'

'Yeah, yeah, course I did. A mate of mine took photos of it. It was in all the papers.'

'That was us,' Kevin said.

The pilot looked at us again, this time for several long moments. Homer, still crying endlessly, Kevin with snot hanging out of his nose, Fi with her face twisted in a terrible expression of pain and her shirt saturated with blood, Lee his face blackened and bleeding. Behind him a huge helicopter, looking like a pregnant heifer, lowered its belly onto the road. The wind from its rotor blew hard across us. It was tough to stand up, to hear, to see.

'Hurry up,' he said, turning abruptly and running for the chopper.

We followed as best we could, a limping, sobbing group of five. I held Fi, and Homer helped Kevin. Only Lee got there alone. The pilot was already half in the chopper and I could see him gesturing to the people in there. Then he turned to help us in.

If the crew hadn't wanted to take us they didn't show it. As soon as we were in they took off, fast. Even as we were rising they were wrapping blankets around us and laying us on stretchers that were strapped to the floor. I couldn't believe how big the aircraft was, how much room there was inside. I'd never been in a helicopter before. A water bottle was at my lips: for a minute I tried to push it away with my mouth but then I gave in and let them force the stuff into me. Fi and I were side by side, gripping hands so tightly. We stayed that way all across the Tasman, never once letting go. Even now I get terrified if she leaves the room for a few seconds and I don't know where she's gone.

Epilogue

When we'd arrived at Stratton Prison people had crowded around the truck wanting to see us. When we arrived at Wellington, coming in low across the water, through the choppy air to the beautiful hilly city, there was a crowd there, too. I don't know that there was much difference between the two crowds. Both were drawn by curiosity.

We'd been scrubbed up by the time we arrived at Wellington, of course. We'd spent two weeks in an Air Force medical centre at Astin Base, where we'd first landed. We each had a long list of injuries. Mine read: shock, cracked vertebrae, fractured patella, malnutrition, cuts and abrasions, acute anxiety state, head lice . . . I think that was all. I'm still on crutches. Fi was probably the worst, with concussion, shock, a cracked collar bone, a ruptured ear drum, and a long scar on her face that she'll remember every time she looks in a mirror.

The things we'd done did get a lot of publicity. The war had been going badly for a long time and only recently had there been any good news. They were anxious for heroes, I guess. So there were a lot of

276

people at Wellington Airport, and we went to a special press room to talk to reporters and get our photos taken. Every second question from the reporters seemed to start with, 'How did you feel when . . .?' We didn't do very well on those ones.

I don't know what to think about it all. I suppose we did the right thing. Everyone here seems to think we did. The Army Intelligence guy, Lieutenant-Colonel Finley, explained the effect of some of the stuff we'd done, and although none of us said anything at the time, we were pleased about that. The ship we sank was meant to have been the pride of their fleet or something. I guess that was a score.

So, there it is. Sometimes, as we lie around here – we're in a sort of convalescent place outside Wellington – I wish we could wind the clock back a year or two. It all seems so idyllic when I look back. I only remember the good things: the smell of scones in the Aga, the sycamore seeds whirring through the air, the worms writhing in the rich compost, the walks across the paddocks with Dad, and the cups of tea with Mum. I don't remember the dog with its stomach ripped open by a kangaroo, or the possum with blood on its snout that died in front of me after eating rat bait, or the flyblown body of a mouse that I found behind the kitchen dresser. I don't remember Dad yelling at Mum when she drove the car five k's on a flat tyre or Mum yelling at Dad when he criticised some of her friends.

It seems like a lost world that I keep reaching out for.

Meanwhile, our parents and families are still prisoners and we can't do a thing to help them. We just have to wait.

And so we sit around, lie around, or hobble around, in my case. Nothing happens here, nothing at all. We've been living on adrenalin for so long that it's strange when it's suddenly cut off. Other people are doing the fighting now. They're making some progress, too. Colonel Finley thinks the peace talks are getting pretty serious: the more territory the Kiwis recapture the more serious the peace talks get. Maybe one day I'll be able to think about the future again. At the moment all I think about is the past. I don't even notice the present. When I first started writing about what happened to us it was because we all wanted our stories to be known, wanted to be remembered. None of that matters to us now. What I want is for Robyn to be remembered, for what she did to be known. I never stop thinking about her. I used to think heroes were tough and brave. But that last look on Robyn's face: it wasn't tough or brave. It was scared and uncertain.

I learned something very important from Robyn: you have to believe in something. Sounds simple, doesn't it? Well, it's not. It's not for me and it wasn't for Robyn. But she did it, and I'm going to keep looking and keep trying till I do, too.

That's the real trouble with our politicians: they don't believe in anything except their own careers.

You have to believe in something. That's all.